Broken

Also by Travis Thrasher

Ghostwriter
Isolation

Available from FaithWords wherever books are sold

Broken

A NOVEL

TRAVIS
THRASHER

3254

Faith
Words

NEW YORK   BOSTON   NASHVILLE

Copyright © 2010 by Travis Thrasher

FaithWords
Hachette Book Group
237 Park Avenue
New York, NY 10017

www.faithwords.com

Printed in the United States of America

First Edition: May 2010

10 9 8 7 6 5 4 3 2 1

FaithWords is a division of Hachette Book Group, Inc.
The FaithWords name and logo are trademarks of Hachette Book Group, Inc.

Library of Congress Cataloging-in-Publication Data
Thrasher, Travis, 1971–
    Broken / Travis Thrasher.—1st ed.
        p. cm.
    Summary: "The harrowing tale of a woman on the run from a stranger who may not be of this world, and who knows her deepest, darkest secret."—Provided by the publisher.
    ISBN 978-0-446-50555-0
    I. Title.
    PS3570.H6925B76 2010
    813'.54—dc22

2009030658

For anyone who has been there

Broken

So this is how it ends.

Staring at a stranger, blood on your hands, silence coating the house.

Everything has led up to this. This here and now. This empty waste. This utter disappointment. This predictable conclusion.

You taste blood on your tongue from the cut on your lip. Crimson smears the pale satin.

Amazing how your hands remain calm. Unshaking, unwavering, even after what they've done.

Somewhere not far away is a gun that fired two bullets, the second doing its job. Somewhere a voice gently, quietly tells you what needs to happen.

You need to find the gun, Laila.

Those eyes staring at you. You've seen them before, somewhere else, many times before.

You need to clean up and find the gun.

For a moment, the water underneath your hands pours out. So steady, so seamless.

And then it gently caresses.

You wince.

Hard as you try, tears don't come.

You stare at the stranger in the mirror, wondering where childhood disappeared to, wondering where those hopeful eyes wandered off.

Clean up and get in there, then get out.

The faucet flows, and the slight stains of blood that are not yours drip over the ceramic.

For a moment you glance into the bedroom. A room you've never been in before today.

A dead body crumpled on the floor. Seconds counting before the silence ends and more men come.

You look at that stranger and know.

This is where it ends.

This is where it all stops.

Turning off the water, you step out and start your life all over again.

1

If I believed, then I would have to come to this conclusion. God doesn't want me. How could He? People like me don't belong with people like you. If eternity does exist, I've sealed my fate and done it with my hands bathed in your blood.

She hears the fingernails on the door. Scratching to get out. Clawing and scraping at the wood. Then she hears the pounding of fists against the solid oak. Beating in vain.

The handle rattles and jerks, yet the door remains closed.

Behind it she can hear him.

Screaming her name.

"Don't. Don't come in here. Get out. Get out of here, Laila."

It's a desperate and scared voice. And everything she tries to do to open the door doesn't work.

She falls to the ground, her hands wrapped around the knob, the sound of her screaming finally waking her up.

Yet Laila doesn't find herself in her bed having another nightmare.

This time she finds herself standing at the door to her apartment, clasping the handle, trying to get out. The light she eventually turns on wakes her up, revealing a clock on the wall that tells her it's three in the morning.

Six months since New Year's Eve, and the nightmares still come. Seven hundred miles away from Chicago, yet Laila still has horrific visions.

In fact, they're getting worse.

She glances at her short nails and notices that one of them is almost entirely cracked off and bleeding. She turns off the light and goes to the bathroom to find a Band-Aid.

Sleep, she knows, will surely prove to be a little more difficult to find.

The last Saturday of June is hot. Laila is glad to have a day off work, especially since she didn't sleep much after finding herself sleep-walking. Normally she'd be at the pool right around now, but it's so unbearably humid outside that she's reading in her air-conditioned apartment. She's finishing up another Dennis Shore horror novel entitled *Scarecrow* that probably isn't helping the whole nightmare situation. At least it allows her to escape, even if the escape is harrowing in itself.

The phone call surprises her because she rarely gets them. It takes her a few rings to uncurl off the couch and find the phone and say hello.

There is only silence on the other end.

"Hello?" she asks in a louder voice.

"Laila," a man whispers.

She stops moving in order to hear the voice as clearly as possible.

"Laila Torres."

"Who is this?"

"You know who this is."

Though she doesn't recognize the voice, a part of her tells her who it belongs to.

The same part of her that nudges her to look up and see who's coming around the corner. The same part that teases her with images and feelings and emotions at all the worst times.

"I see you."

"Who is this?"

Broken

"I can always see you. And sometimes, if you close your eyes hard enough, you'll see me."

He laughs in a warm, breathy way that sounds like he's quietly coughing. She hangs up the phone, but holds the receiver as if it's a gun—slightly away from her—waiting for it to ring again.

Waiting for it to go off like a bomb.

She waits but doesn't hear anything.

Tucked in the back of the leather journal that rests on a small night-stand are a handful of photos that Laila finds herself examining on a daily basis. For a moment as the sun fades outside her windows and the sounds of the city begin to stir, Laila glances at the black-and-white snapshot of Aunt Maxie.

She can hear Aunt Maxie's Cajun drawl warn her about the phone call she had received hours ago, a call she still can't help thinking about.

"Don't you dare go out, not now, not after that," Aunt Maxie would have surely told her. "You might find a devil roaming the streets."

The small but tough woman from Louisiana used to tell Laila ghost stories when she was young and impressionable. Her favorite was the story about the rougarou, a werewolf that prowled after bad children late at night back in the bayou where she lived. Of course, the story was as fictitious as Maxie being their aunt. She had been hired as a maid by her father when Laila was still just in grade school. Aunt Maxie worked for the Torres family for almost eight years before vanishing with nothing more than a short, cryptic note to Laila.

Laila still often wonders where Aunt Maxie disappeared to.

Maxie was the closest thing Laila had to a mother since her own had passed when she was only four years old. There is no photo of her mother in the few she has kept with her. For some reason she clings to the worn shot of Aunt Maxie taken in the middle of a conversation.

She was probably telling one of her scary stories about a voodoo witch or a spooky spirit.

Of all the things Laila struggled to believe growing up, Aunt Maxie's stories weren't one of them.

The shadows of Greenville at night offer refuge but not necessarily escape. She walks as if she has a destination, passing couples strolling hand in hand, men who stare at her, and women who dismiss her. The eyes of strangers say so much that words are often unnecessary. Laila has grown used to them, used to disdaining and dismissing them, but tonight the stares offer a bittersweet comfort. At least there's somebody else nearby.

Downtown has a character like all the other cities she's lived in. For a moment she recalls the noise of New York, the chill of Chicago. The impressions belong to those of a stranger whispering memories from another life and another world. No matter how far she might go to escape them, the murmurs never stop coming.

The crowd at a local bar she passes suggests life. The music coming from the open doors of a club signifies excitement. She's propositioned a couple of times by amiable country boys who invite her inside. Laila politely thanks them and says no. She's had enough cowboys in one lifetime, thank you very much. She's sure that rednecks are the same whether or not they're from the Lone Star state.

She thinks about Kyle, something she finds herself doing more and more often. It's one thing to have a friend in a coworker at the bank, but she knows anything more is dangerous. She is dangerous, and she knows she doesn't need another man trying to take care of her.

Another man offering hope.

She roams the city trying to outwalk her shadows, but they stay close to her heels. The sights and the smells of life move by like billboards on the highway, out of reach. She knows where she is and accepts it.

Hope is a city she left years ago. In its place, she's found desolation.

The apartment feels dark and silent even with the lights on and open windows letting in noise from the outside. The floor creaks beneath her as she walks across the living room, feeling a chill despite the sweat on her forehead.

The loneliness is still sometimes hard to get used to, especially with the fear that it might be broken by a haunting intruder or a confronting figure from yesterday. This is what Laila lives with. The ghosts of possibility making an outline over every step she takes.

She's in her bathroom brushing her teeth when she sees it. The image startles her and causes her to jam the toothbrush into the side of her gum.

In her bathtub next to the sink lies a blue and red backpack with the white words **TEXANS** stitched on its front.

Laila drops the toothbrush into the sink and rushes back out to her living room. She can taste the acid bite of blood in her mouth.

"Hello?"

The word seems to hover in the stillness.

For a frantic few moments, she examines the rest of her apartment. Nobody is there.

Back in the bathroom, she stares at the backpack. The words on the bag burn in to her.

Houston Texans.

The bag itself would be enough, but the emblem on it laughs at her.

Laila swallows, not wanting to touch the bag, feeling as if it might sear her hands and her soul. She stares at the backpack the way a security person might look at a lone bag in an airport. It's strange just sitting there, waiting for someone or something to pick it up.

She can't force herself to touch it.

Minutes pass as she stands in the bathroom facing the bag, wondering how it got there, wondering why someone left it, wondering what's inside. An urge burns through her telling her it's important. But she holds herself back.

Someone broke into her apartment and put this here.

That alone would be shocking, but after the call this afternoon, Laila can feel her heart beating with worry.

A voice tells her to call the cops, but she knows she can't.

Another voice tells her this is payback. This is just another reminder of what she's running away from. Another sign of what's apparently coming.

Laila is becoming accustomed to strange things. But a backpack, one that looks full, suddenly showing up in her room—a Houston Texans backpack too. It reeks of mockery.

"This can't be from him," she says out loud, hoping someone might hear her speak the words.

Whoever put this in her apartment is playing games with her. Perhaps to taunt. Maybe even to threaten. They know a part of her that is long gone and buried. This might be their way of saying they know everything.

She grabs the backpack and brings it onto her deck, tossing it onto the garden below.

If someone is watching her, they can see she's not scared.

At least that's what Laila hopes they see.

• • •

Lex studies the blonde's face as she passes him. She's oblivious, probably used to this type of gawking from men on a daily basis. Lex looks at the picture he printed off the Web and knows it's her. Something in her eyes gives her away.

He slips the photo into his shirt pocket, stands up, and starts walking. His butt is numb from sitting on the cement wall in the square for the last hour waiting. Waiting and hoping she would be coming this direction just like the guy told her she always did. Sure enough, she stepped over a Manhattan curb, crossed the street, and entered the square on the way to her job, passing right by him.

As he follows her he wonders where this is going to lead him. He knows this is the start, but he fears it will also be the end. He might get nowhere and find the journey he just started is over.

Lex waits for a few minutes, then enters the outside seating area of the wine bar. He's given a menu and glances at a couple enjoying wine and cheese as a nice happy-hour appetizer. When she comes up to his table, the woman has no idea he's here for her.

"How are you doing?" she asks.

"Good, thanks," Lex says, hearing the nervousness in his voice.

She asks him if he's interested in a special Shiraz that just arrived. His mouth waters, and he smiles and shakes his head.

"No, no wine for me, thank you."

The blonde gives him one of those looks people who sit down here but don't order wine surely get. She already starts to glance at other tables, already giving up on him.

"Look, this is going to sound strange, but I need to talk to you about Laila Torres."

The eyes grow cold fast. "I don't know anyone named Laila."

She says this too quickly, yet it doesn't surprise him. She's moving away from the table when he asks her to stop. "Here, just take a look at this."

He produces the photo and shows it to her. When she sees it, tears come to her eyes.

"What do you want?" She looks around to see if anyone is watching her.

"Just a chance to talk."

"Look, I have a job to do, and I really can't talk right now, you know?"

"It's fine," he says. "I just — here's my card with the number of the hotel I'm staying at. I could meet you here after work."

"I don't think so," she says quickly, almost defensively as if she's heard this before a hundred times.

"Then I can meet you anywhere. Anytime. I don't care."

She studies him, then takes the card and puts it in her apron. She walks off without saying a word.

• • •

Laila feels watched. Like a warm whisper in her ear, a nudging finger against her side, an insect crawling over her skin. The feeling makes her want to claw at her flesh to tear it away. But instead she stands still like everybody else as she listens to the strangers around her sing the song about turning someone's darkness into light.

Laila breathes in. Something presses against her, the weight pounding her head. Dizzy and stuck, Laila forces her eyes to remain open. She wants to curl up and drift away. But she knows the darkness only brings layers to the pain. Memories are brighter when the dusk falls.

She glances around the church. She's not like them and never will be. The scars aren't the reason why. It's this life. A couple in front of her holds hands. A teenager sways to the song. An elderly man closes his eyes in what appears to be a prayer. All while she stands feeling watched.

The room is full. Yet it is nothing like the Sunday mornings of her youth stuck in the sweltering heat of that tiny church with people in their church clothes, sitting in the same pew as always, singing from hymnals and shouting an occasional "Amen" or "Hallelujah." Here the dress is casual, the lyrics are printed on two big screens on each side of the podium, and the meeting is set in a temperature-controlled room that doubles as a gymnasium with its basketball rims hoisted up.

She wants to scratch her arms, her neck, her back.

Shelley gives her a smile that Laila returns.

The petite blonde lives a few doors down from her. After a couple of months of coming up with excuses, Laila finally gave in and went with her to church. It's hard to tell the vibrant woman no. But standing and listening to the others singing, Laila wishes she had been honest with Shelley. As honest as she could be.

Broken

Just as she turns her head to glance down an aisle of people in front of her, Laila sees him.

The man turns around. And he smiles the same way he smiled at her right before she shot him.

It's a sickly smile, the kind a ravenous dog might give after ripping out someone's throat, then sucking in air as the blood drips from its mouth.

Laila stops breathing.

She closes her eyes, then opens them again. He's still there. Not smiling but leering, his eyes narrow steel, their color lifeless.

"What is it?" Shelley asks her.

Laila sees something in the man's teeth—something starting to cover them. Blood. Blood covering them like it might smother a fresh wound.

Laila rushes out of the aisle toward the closed back doors and goes into the lobby and still finds it hard to breathe.

She looks out the glass doors and thinks about running through them and not stopping.

She feels the emotion coming to her face. The tears ready and waiting. Yet they remain in holding, in a cell in the darkness of some deep lodge in her soul.

Laila knows she needs to leave the lobby before someone like Shelley finds her.

Before she sees the ghost again.

She rushes to the bathroom downstairs in the section where the classrooms and nurseries are. This isn't a place for her. She doesn't belong here. She breathes in and out and feels dizzy.

She closes her eyes and can see him again.

"That was not real," she says.

She goes into the stall and stares at the ceramic tile on the wall. Laila knows she is being haunted by a demon. That she is being hunted for what she's done. And that there is no way of ever taking it back.

She shakes her head and feels her legs weaken and then falls to the floor into a sweet and rich velvet darkness.

"Don't look at me like that."

"Like what?"

"Like I'm some helpless child."

Shelley laughs and takes a bite of the pizza on the paper plate. "I wouldn't say child. But helpless, well—"

"I told you it was my low blood sugar."

Shelley doesn't seem to believe the lie. She was the one who found Laila on the floor of the bathroom at church. Thankfully it was her and not the spirit or whatever it was that she saw with the glistening blood teeth.

"And that's why you left the service so quickly?"

Laila nods as she sips on the soda and stares at the half-eaten piece of pizza.

"You should eat more than that."

"I know."

"You know—you looked pale when we first got there. I was thinking you were sick to your stomach."

"I wasn't feeling great."

"Sorry," Shelley says.

"What for?"

"I was the one who kept asking to bring you to church. Doing the 'neighborly' thing, you know. Nice first impression, huh?"

"Shelley, listen to me. Don't ever apologize for doing something out of kindness. Ever. Okay?"

"Yeah. Just—how'd you like those bathroom floors?"

Laila laughs. "A bit hard on the head."

"You sure took a tumble."

"I should just take better care of myself."

"Yes. Definitely. Stick around with me and I'll show you how."

Broken

Shelley finishes off her piece of pizza and takes another slice. It makes Laila smile to see such a little thing with such a big appetite.

"You want to hang out here today?"

"Sure," Laila says.

She doesn't want to see what's waiting for her a few doors down in her apartment.

Laila awakes with a cough and the feeling of something snapping inside of her. Something in her stomach, a muscle or tissue.

She opens her eyes to the darkness of her apartment. It is quiet. Even with the window open, it is still. For a second she feels a pain tear at her midsection as though something she ate isn't agreeing with her.

She places a hand on her stomach.

Then she feels it.

Her T-shirt is warm and wet. Her hand moves to her thighs and she can feel something sticky and moist.

She gags and coughs and fights the pain in her belly.

She pulls back the cover and feels her shirt again, her underwear, her legs. They're soaked. Her hands are wet. She wipes them together and then against her shirt as she searches to find the light.

She turns it on expecting to find crimson stains but instead she sees nothing.

Just what she wore to bed. The T-shirt still white. Her legs still pink.

The pain in her stomach is still there, however.

She closes her eyes and wonders what is happening to her. But she can't get rid of the image from six months ago. The blood seeping through his buttoned-down shirt and even onto his pants. There was so much blood. Her hands grabbing at him to see if he was alive and then feeling his chest and feeling nothing and then looking at them all wet and soaked exactly like they just felt.

She stares out a window and wonders if the image will ever go away.

2

I wonder about them. Often. I wonder what it would be like, the sights and the sounds. The sweetness of coming back home. Sometimes I'm reminded. Sometimes the most random, simple thing reminds me of a distant, faraway place that's mythical and magical. I see the beard, the roughness of the hands, the wrinkles under the eyes. I can hear the music in the background. I can see the life I left and the life I imagine I loved and that I could love again. But all of that is the dream, the myth. And all of that evaporates to show the isolation of this island I am on, this place of my own making and choosing, this prison that I will never be able to leave.

James Brennan sits in his car and closes the cell phone. Then opens it again and snaps it in two, throwing the pieces against the glass. He beats his palm against the steering wheel, then against the seat next to him. The stale, hot air suffocates him. But he doesn't turn on the engine. He just sits here, his back and buttocks wet from sweat. He tries to close his eyes hard enough to shut them permanently.

He then reaches in his back pocket to find his wallet. He opens it and looks inside. There are a few bills inside, a few credit cards, not much.

James takes out one of the cards and slowly, deliberately bends it in half. He folds it back and forth until he's able to tear it apart. Then he unrolls the window and lets the two pieces drop on the street.

Broken

There is a glare from the beating sun that causes him to squint.

For a moment, his hands wrap themselves around the wheel again, and he pulls to see if it will move, to see if he can tear it off.

He lets out a loud curse.

Then James leans over and puts his head against the wheel.

And he stays like that for a long time.

• • •

"It's okay, you know?"

Laila glances at the man sitting next to her on the stone wall lining the sidewalk. For the first time since meeting Kyle months ago, she doesn't question what's behind those eyes. They're not like most glances, examining and exploring and wanting. Kyle looks at ease, patient for her response.

"What's okay?" She plays with her half-empty iced coffee bought half an hour ago.

"Okay to say yes," he says.

"I didn't say no."

"Your silence says enough."

She nods at him, then shakes the clear plastic cup in her hands to make some sort of sound. It still seems like yesterday when Kyle offered to buy her a coffee at the end of a particularly horrible day that punctuated her first week at the bank. Laila had been too flustered and tired to say no to her coworker, too guarded to say much during that first afternoon together. It had become a sort of tradition, something they did a couple times a week, something with absolutely no strings attached.

So far Kyle had remained content to let things stay the way they were. Until now.

"It's okay to have dinner," he said.

"What does dinner mean?"

"It can mean a lot of things."

"I know," she says.

"First off, it means food. You do eat, right?"

"Yes."

"I'm just saying—don't give me that look. I just never see you eating at the bank."

"That's because I work."

"You get breaks, you know."

"I eat plenty."

"So prove it."

"I don't have to prove anything to anybody."

Kyle gave her an amused glance, her comment surprising him. "I know that. I just—it's just dinner. It's not a date. We can go up the street. I thought—we both get off work at the same time. And it is dinnertime, you know. Unless you eat at ten or something like that. There's no pressure. It can be spontaneous. It can be Subway."

"It can be another time."

"That's what you said last time."

"I thought you said you weren't asking last time."

"That's because I got a no and my male ego was feeling trampled upon."

She tries to hide the amusement creeping on her face. She doesn't want her resolve to crumble because of his amiability.

For a moment Laila sees this scene without seeing anything else.

Kyle Ewing is a good guy. At twenty-nine years old his boyishly handsome features say he hasn't sold out to the establishment just yet. Wavy brown hair short enough to not get in trouble at the bank but messy enough to say there's something more. Brown eyes that show both resolve and mischief depending on the moment. A lean, athletic frame that says he keeps active, keeps himself out of trouble and bad habits.

But another part of her wipes that all away like an eraser on a chalkboard. A voice deep inside her whispers that behind those eyes probably lurks something dark and twisted. The smile, the glance, the simple question. There is always something more.

Broken

If there isn't and if he really is a good guy deep down, then he shouldn't have anything to do with her.

She knows this and can't even begin to explain it to him.

After another bout of silence, Kyle finally nods and tightens his lips with a smile. She finds it compelling how comfortable he seems to be, how secure yet equally sincere. His look says he's giving in and that he's okay with giving in.

"You working tomorrow?" he asks.

"All day."

"Well, you're lucky then."

"You're working?"

"Nope," Kyle says. "You won't have me to harass you."

"I never said you harass me."

"It's a joke, Laila. They are designed to make people laugh. Or at least smile. See this? This is called a smile. And sometimes they're contagious."

He's charming too. She'll admit that. Not in any sort of fancy way. Just simple, straightforward charm.

"I can see it in your eyes," Kyle continues. "You're wanting to smile."

"I smile all the time."

"Yeah, but not at me."

"Smiling at a man can be a dangerous thing."

"Well, yeah, if you put it that way. You make it sound a bit creepy."

"They can mistake a smile for something else."

"I'm Kyle, not the 'mysterious man' you refer to. And 'they' can do anything. I, on the other hand, think a smile looks very pretty on your face. It just fits, you know?"

"How do you know what fits me and what doesn't?"

Laila regrets the biting tone after the words come out. Kyle gives her a peaceful glance. She knows he wants to say something. Surely he wants to ask something, to probe deeper, but something prevents him.

Maybe it's his Southern politeness. That could be it.

But then again, maybe it's because Kyle knows. He might act younger than his age, but perhaps deep down, in places where nobody usually goes, Kyle knows that there's something there. And he's curious, but knows now is not the right time.

For Laila, there will never be a right time.

"I hope you have a good evening," he says.

"You too."

He stands and starts walking down the sidewalk. Even his walk seems carefree and light. She watches him disappear down the city street and finds it interesting that he doesn't look back. Kyle is the type to turn around and wave and give a flirtatious smile. But he doesn't. And that's another reason for her to find him interesting.

She hasn't found anything interesting in a very long time.

When is it time to let go?

Walking among the racks in the clothing store and looking at the summer sales, Laila feels guilty as something foreign stirs in her.

Hope.

It's been six months since New Year's Eve when she fled with the fragments of her life from Chicago. Six months of silence, of being guarded, of keeping a façade, of waiting.

She wonders if it's time to let go of the reins, perhaps just a bit. She thinks maybe it's time to stop waiting for the door to open and bloodshed and hurt to walk in.

Holding up a blouse, Laila thinks this would look good on her. Maybe she will buy this, and maybe she'll take Kyle up on his offer.

But as quick as the thought enters her mind, Laila stifles it.

It doesn't matter if it's been six months or six years. She doesn't need Kyle just like she doesn't need anybody else. It's too soon. Too soon to let down the wall and settle in.

Laila thinks of the backpack she found during the weekend and feels a dread smother her caffeine buzz.

"Can I help you out?" a lady asks her.

Broken

Laila puts the blouse back and shakes her head, then walks out of the store into the afternoon warmth.

She sees the ghost on the walk home.

At first Laila believes the resemblance is simply coincidental. Not even that. It's more mental. She's been seeing images for some time now. In her dreams—nightmares—whatever they can be called. Sometimes during the day when she closes her eyes, sometimes simply by remembering. Then last weekend at the church. And now after the conversation with Kyle that somehow triggered a memory back to the last few hours of last year, the face still haunts her mind.

So seeing that face shouldn't come as a surprise.

The walk home from the bank is fifteen minutes if she takes her time, less if she's in a hurry. One of the reasons she took the job was because of its proximity to her apartment, which she took because of the price. She knew the owner had lowered the rent simply to have her in his building so he could occasionally maul her with his eyes just like he had the first time they met. Normally she would have found another, not wanting to deal with some creepy landlord, but she had wanted and needed a quick and easy transition without many questions or complications.

The crowd downtown is typical. She finds herself slowing down behind a couple strolling, holding hands, looking perfect in their love. Just as she's about to pass them, she sees the figure across the street.

Standing.

Looking her way.

And that's when for a brief second, she knows.

Just like she knew at church.

She turns away and passes the couple. As she does Laila glances across the street.

He still stands there, arms at his side, just staring. Waiting.

That square face and those desolate eyes. They were lifeless before she shot him. And they're lifeless now.

She can't shake the fact that the face looks the same. That the figure — tall, lean — looks the same.

Then he smiles at her, and she stops.

The strolling couple almost run into her.

"Excuse me, I'm sorry," she says, turning around and seeing the amused faces looking at her.

If it had been New York, those faces would look a lot different. But this is the heart of South Carolina, where a walk down a sidewalk is just that.

Laila turns, knowing the figure will either still be there but look completely different or be gone.

But he's still there, still smiling, still staring.

Laila doesn't move.

The man waves.

He waves gently, deliberately. She can see those eyes even though they're far away from her, can see them probing her with delight.

A man walking a dog — a big dog, the kind that weighs three times what she might — pulls the dog and its drool away from her. The leash gets wrapped up around her leg as the friendly mouth brushes spittle across her thigh.

"Hold on there, Harley! Oh, look, I am so sorry about that."

"It's fine, really."

The man doesn't want to invade her space as Laila delicately tries to step out of the leash.

"Can I get — I'm sorry, he likes people."

"It's okay, really."

"Come on, Harley," the man says as she pets the dog.

She smiles in a polite way, not feeling like talking. For a moment she glances across the street and this time finds the figure gone.

Laila continues walking, wondering if she really saw him. She recalls his smile and his wave and knows she saw someone.

She wonders if this is what purgatory is like. A feeling of fear in every waking moment of the day, feeling that just around the corner a ghoul might jump out and grab her.

The feeling that anything is possible when you take the life of another.

• • •

Lex watches the woman smoke the cigarette in a manner that is as natural and necessary as breathing. The image makes him sad. Her sitting on the couch, legs crossed, wearing a T-shirt and tiny shorts that he thinks might be the clothes she slept in, her mass of high-lighted hair cascading over to one side, her body nervously fidgeting the way a teenager might. She looks younger than she did when she came up to his table at the wine bar. The eyes that stare back at him may have once been beautiful and maybe they still are, but they're hard. They're hard and unflinching.

"What do you want to know?" she asks.

"What happened to her."

"It's been three years. Hell if I know."

"Three years since you spoke with her?"

"No, since she moved out."

"And that was the last time you talked to her?"

"No—let's see—it's been—I don't know—a couple years maybe. I think she called me a few times."

"From where?"

"Last I heard she was in Chicago."

"Doing what?"

"I didn't ask."

"Why'd she call?"

The woman seems distracted by something on the table. She takes a drag and stares at him, disbelief shading the pale face.

"You sure you're not lying?"

"I showed you my license."

"Got anything else?"

He takes a photo out of his coat pocket and hands it to her. "That was taken when I was seven."

"How do I know..."

The woman's face changes in midsentence. She knows. Even though Laila was only ten at the time, the photo leaves no doubt.

"God, Laila's beautiful. I mean look at her. Even then she was so incredibly beautiful."

"What was she doing in Chicago?"

The woman hands back the photo. "She was earning a living."

"How?"

"Does it matter?" She pauses for a moment. "Do you really want to know?"

Lex breathes in and doesn't answer the question. He's torn because he fears the answer, just like he fears where this trip will lead him.

He is afraid, but he knows he has to get these questions answered. Fear has held him back for a long time, but not anymore.

Ever since the unnamed man appeared out of nowhere a couple of weeks ago asking all sorts of questions about Laila, Lex has known he needs to find his big sister.

Silence is no longer an option.

"I need somewhere to go. Somewhere to start looking."

"You might not want to go looking around. You might not like what you find."

"I know that," Lex says. "Has anybody else come looking for her?"

"No."

"Did she tell you where she was living? Where she was working?"

"She didn't tell me anything. It was just high-end. That's all I know. She was making a lot of money. A whole lot more than I make. But of course it was Laila. Of course she was making more money. You know? All I know is that she sounded busy."

"Did she sound happy?"

Broken

The woman laughs. "Happy as in how? I don't even know what that word means anymore, you know?"

"Any names? Anything?"

"No."

He slips the photo back in his pocket.

"You're from Texas?"

Lex nods. He left a couple of days ago, flying into New York with only a name and snapshot. He wonders if Jenna is her real name.

"She never said anything about being from Texas."

"Guess it wouldn't really impress anybody, not around here."

"Why now? Why start looking for her after all this time?"

"Something happened that I need to tell her."

"What? Like a death in the family or something?"

Lex looks away. "Yeah. Something like that."

"I can tell the resemblance now. Should've come out here when she was living with me. You would've had a fun time."

"Yeah, I know I should have. Lots of things I should've done. Hope it's not too late."

"Too late for what?"

"For a lot of things," Lex says again, staring out the window.

He hopes the stranger who interrogated him a couple weeks ago hasn't gotten to Laila first. There was something about that man—something unspoken, something unsettling—that made Lex worry. It wasn't in what he said but how he said it.

Lex knows the man has unfinished business with Laila, just like he does.

3

My father wanted to call me Isabella, but my mother chose my name. Instead we gave it to the Arabian horse that was designated mine when I was only ten. Bella was the closest friend I had growing up.

I knew the grit of dirt and sand well, the vast open land of Texas, the emptiness that could fill fenced-in walls. There's a loneliness in the country, in the wide-eyed skies, in the desert roads. A loneliness that no city sidewalk can ever fill.

I know because I've tried.

And as much as I'd like to write in this journal "I can't go back. I don't want to go back," I hear the winds calling out for me.

Perhaps the sand and the wind and the open skies call for me.

Perhaps that's where I'll end up when my last breath comes and I'm laid into the earth for one last time.

Even behind the counter, in dress clothes that don't stand out and her dark hair pulled in a side ponytail, Laila Torres is stunning. The kind of stunning that makes you stop and wonder if you're really seeing what you're seeing. The kind that makes men do many, many things, but not things like this.

James waits in line, even letting someone go in front of him. He is not here for any other reason except to speak to her.

heckout Receipt

u checked out the following items:

1. **Pete the Cat : Pete at the beach**
   Barcode: 31010006315628
   Due: 1/22/2019
2. **Splat the Cat and the duck with no**
   Barcode: 31010006218400
   Due: 1/22/2019
3. **Splat the cat gets a job!**
   Barcode: 31010006647897
   Due: 1/22/2019
4. **Pete the cat and the cool caterpilla**
   Barcode: 31010006636338
   Due: 1/22/2019
5. **Broken : a novel**
   Barcode: 31010006609962
   Due: 1/22/2019

otal Amount Owed: $1.00

Broken

It took him six months to find her. A few more moments won't matter.

He eventually approaches her and glances into delicious, delicate eyes.

"How are you today?" she asks.

"Fine, thank you. And yourself?"

"I'm doing well. How can I help you?"

"I just want to know what it feels like to kill somebody."

There is a blank look on Laila's face. No color, no emotion, no anything. And James can imagine she's given this look before. That she's gotten used to stepping out of her beautiful, sleek skin to go somewhere else. It's protection. It's her way of coping.

"'Cause see, I don't really know what that's like. It's gotta give you a sense of empowerment, doesn't it?"

For a moment she glances around, but he's not talking loudly enough for anybody else to hear.

There is color and emotion in her face now. White fear. That's what it is, white blazing fear.

"What do you want?"

James nods. She's smart. And she's strong. She's not playing a game. She's getting right to the point. Again, probably out of practice. Lots and lots of practice.

"There's a lot of things I want," he says.

Those hazel eyes don't back down.

This is the first time he understands who he might be dealing with. And he can't help breaking into a smile. He likes her already. Laila's a fighter.

"How can I help you?" she asks again with more attitude.

He gives her a slip of paper with a name, address, and time written on it. He makes sure he speaks very slowly and carefully so she hears every single word he's saying.

"I know where you live and where you work. And if you try to run again, I'll get you before you leave this city. And trust me—I'm not going to end up like my brother."

Her eyes widen, and she stares back in silence.

"Don't disappoint me." James walks out of the bank and into the sunshine of the day.

•   •   •

The silence creeps over her, its hairy fingers caressing her exposed skin trying to find a spot to burrow into. As much as she tries to act normal and nonchalant, a panic is simmering deep inside. She knows she needs to do something and do something fast.

Even though the walk home from work proved uneventful, Laila still felt like she was being watched the entire time. Now, restless in her quiet apartment, she wonders if she's being watched or listened to this very instant.

At least she knows for certain who put the bag in her bathtub.

She's already searched the entire apartment to make sure she is alone, a habit she's becoming accustomed to. She spent a few moments looking at the contents of the refrigerator and the pantry, both paltry and proving to offer nothing worth eating. The call to Shelley produced only an answering machine that Laila doesn't feel like talking into. She finally finds a fashion magazine and attempts to read it, but even that brings with it tiny barbs of the past.

On the sixth page, Laila is halted by the arresting image of an ad. A sad smile covers her face.

She knows the girl's name, a young sixteen-year-old when they first met in New York lifetimes ago. It's a major ad with a major label, a life Laila knows well. She finds herself happy for the girl and hopeful that ten years from now she'll end up in a better place than Laila did.

It's difficult reading magazines like this. They are reminders of a life once lived, of a major dream once fulfilled.

Broken

What happens after dreams come true? That, Laila knows, is the story never told.

She is contemplating throwing the magazine away when the door slams open. She jumps off her couch. For a second she's bewildered because the sound doesn't come from the doorway to the apartment but rather from her bedroom.

Laila looks down the hallway where she had walked just a few minutes ago. She remains silent, waiting. Listening.

A sound rips again through the apartment. She can feel the rattling on the floor.

It sounds like someone is slamming the door against the wall as hard as he can.

She stands.

Another bang rattles the floor. She can not only hear it, but can feel the banging too.

For a moment she goes toward the hallway, then she holds still.

The violent racket continues, as if whoever is doing it is daring her to come back and see.

She didn't imagine James Brennan this afternoon, the man who left the address and time for her to meet him this night.

But Laila is more afraid she'll go back to her room and find nothing.

She is afraid she's imagining this just like so many other things.

She rushes into the kitchen, digs out a small sheet of handwritten names and numbers. Then she grabs her cell phone before leaving her place.

The number she dials isn't just for her protection.

It's for her sanity.

"This isn't a practical joke, is it?"

"No."

Kyle stands and for a moment doesn't know how to greet her. She gives him a friendly hug and then sits down. The Mexican restaurant is packed. The scent of lime and salsa makes her mouth water.

"Thanks for meeting me here."

"You know—when I said maybe another time, I didn't think it would mean the very next night."

"I hope you didn't have any other plans."

"None that I couldn't break." He laughs and rubs his day's worth of stubble. "I didn't know you had my cell number."

"You gave it to me a while ago."

"Ah. I don't think you've ever used it, right?"

"No. Look, Kyle, I really appreciate this."

As she orders a drink, Laila glances around at the strangers sitting at the other tables. She knows she hasn't been followed—as much as she could spot, that is.

Laila wonders if James Brennan decided to forget about the time and location and simply terrorize her in her own home. Yet if that was the case, how did he get into her place without making a single sound?

"Did you come straight from work?" Kyle asks.

"No, I went home. Obviously I didn't have a chance to change."

"You look great. You always look great."

The margarita takes a few moments to kick in. Laila forces a smile, forces herself to eat a few chips and salsa. The music and the people and the motion all around her feel comforting. Unlike their usual conversations over coffee, their discussion feels forced and awkward.

Just like always, Kyle doesn't waste time and shares exactly what he's thinking.

"What changed your mind?"

"Maybe you sold me."

"On what?"

"On you."

Kyle nods, smiles. It's the sort of face and smile that can be told secrets. That can probably keep secrets.

Broken

But hers are not for telling and not for keeping.

"So you've never been here before?"

"No."

"How long have you lived in Greenville?"

"Six months."

"Six months and you've never been here? Seriously?"

"You sound shocked."

"Best Mexican place in town."

"Now I know." Laila takes another sip of the margarita.

"Okay, so do you ever go out at night?"

"Sometimes."

The sound of his laughter is comforting.

"Vague as usual. Do you know that every single time I try to ask you a question about yourself, you're vague? Like where you're from. Your family. There a reason why you never give me a straight answer?"

"There a reason you don't take hints?"

He is quiet, long enough for her to reach over and touch his hand. "I'm sorry. That was rude. I'm just—what is it you want to know?"

"You. That's all. I just want to get to know you. Like people do. You know—where are you from, what do you do for fun, what's your favorite color."

"White."

"What?" Kyle obviously thinks she is kidding.

"My favorite color is white."

He laughs. "Does that even count?"

"Of course it does."

"Not extremely exciting. Your favorite flavor vanilla?"

"You're not supposed to mock my answers."

"That's right, you gave me a straight answer."

"I moved here from Chicago six months ago."

"Right when you got the job."

"I'm not trying to evade your questions."

"Okay. I'll just—I'll just try not to ask so many."

"Sounds good to me."

"We just often spend a lot of time talking about the bank. Or about me."

"I enjoy hearing about you."

"I have no idea why, though I know I certainly don't mind talking about myself."

"Perhaps, but you don't brag," she says. "You talk about the things you see, the questions you have."

"How bad of a teller I am."

"At least you know."

"Just don't tell anybody," Kyle says.

They both laugh.

During the next hour, Laila allows herself to stop worrying. With the help of the noise and a couple of drinks and conversation with Kyle, she actually manages to forget everything for a little while. It feels like someone paddling a canoe in the lake while their town burns to the ground behind them. They're talking about favorite places and dream vacations when Laila becomes more honest than she has been in a while.

"I'd like to go back to New Orleans," Laila says.

"Really? What for?"

"It's such an intriguing city."

"I had some buddies go there for Mardi Gras. Sounds crazy if you ask me."

"Not—not for any of that. It just has this mysterious and melancholy personality attached to it. I went once. Long time ago. And after Katrina, I don't know. It's like I feel like I have to go back."

"Why?"

"I don't know. It's like—it's like a family member being in the hospital. I know that sounds bizarre, but that's how I feel. It's just—since I moved away from Texas, I've never really had a chance to go back. Not that I ever saw myself living in the places I have."

"Like Greenville?"

Broken

"Among other places."

"New Orleans seems just so—so dirty."

"It's a good place to hide from the rest of the world. I thought that once, and I still do. Especially now, since it feels like the world has sorta abandoned it."

Kyle stares at her.

"What?" she asks.

"This is the most real I've seen you be since you started work."

"Amazing what a couple of margaritas will do."

"It's okay to be yourself," Kyle says. "At least with me."

She nods.

"I'm not—I'm not one of them, Laila. I know. It might sound like a line. I'd bet you've probably heard them all. But it's just—I'm not a guy with lines. I'm just this, right here, sitting across from you with salsa spilled on my shirt."

"I wondered if you noticed that."

"You don't have to worry about being yourself around me."

"I wouldn't call it worry."

"Then what is it?"

"It's called safety. It's called learning the hard way."

Her eyes drift away from his and concentrate on a distant piece of art on the wall. It's an acrylic painting that looks as if it's on fire. It's a bold picture of a lake at sunrise, with red and orange and yellow creases in the waves floating toward black underneath a large explosion of white and blue in the sky.

For a moment she's suddenly far away, lost in a painting just like that, in a place she wonders if she'll ever be able to find again.

Laila jerks awake.

It feels like someone just touched her face. Gently, the way a parent might stroke the cheek of a child.

For a moment she pictures Kyle, then remembers him saying good-bye at the entrance to her apartment a few hours ago.

Another image comes to her mind. It's the painting she saw in the restaurant with a slight change. A young couple stands on the shore looking into the heart of a smoldering sky, holding one another as if their very lives depend on it.

Laila erases the thought as she looks for anything in the room, any sort of shape in the shadow.

Her eyelids want to stick together. She forces them apart.

And there, in the doorway—the open doorway which is normally shut—stands a figure. Tall. Slender. Hovering.

Laila doesn't hesitate but recoils out of bed and hits her knee against the wall as she slips into the bathroom adjoining the room. She turns on the light of her closet and rips through a pile of dirty clothes to find the shoe box. She opens it and finds the revolver inside underneath a pair of tennis shoes she hasn't worn since buying them three months ago.

With the light blurring everything after flipping the switch, she aims the gun outward toward the door, then toward her bedroom.

"Who's there?"

She holds the gun and waits for a moment.

She waits to hear anything.

"I said who's there? I've got a gun in my hands in case you're wondering."

Eventually she turns on the light in her bedroom.

The blank, stale room greets her.

She looks at the doorway and sees nothing.

She walks down the hallway to the apartment entry.

Nothing.

She checks the door. It's locked. She continues throughout the rest of the apartment.

Everything is the same as it was when she climbed under the sheets.

She slides open her patio door and can hear the music still playing in the distance. She's on the third floor, and she steps out onto the balcony.

The cool night air makes her calm down.

The gun in her hand makes her feel even better.

Laila stares out onto the street below for a long time, thinking, wondering what to do.

She knows she needs to leave and leave soon. The only question now is how to leave without anybody finding out.

●　　●　　●

"We need you down here, Lex."

His wife sounds tired and concerned over the phone. They haven't even been married for one year, yet Dena talks to him as if they've been together for twenty.

In many ways it feels like they have.

"I know," Lex says in a subdued voice.

"Then when are you comin' back home?"

"When my business is done."

They didn't both agree on this trip he's taking. It was more like Lex telling Dena that he was leaving, that he needed to find his sister, that something was wrong. There are things he can't begin to get into with his wife about Laila. There are things that nobody knows. Not even Laila.

"Where are you?"

"Drivin'."

"It's almost eleven o'clock."

"I can see that." He watches the highway through speckles of rain periodically wiped away.

"Drivin' where?"

"To Chicago."

"What's in Chicago?"

"Stop with the interrogation. I'm not one of your students."

"You're sure actin' like one."

Dena's Texan accent always seems more pronounced when she's angry.

"What do you want?"

"I want you home. I want you to stop this."

"I'll stop when I'm finished."

"When what's finished? How is it going to be finished?"

"Don't yell. You're going to wake her."

"No thanks to you. It took me an hour to get her to bed."

"Just hush now."

"You need to come home, Lex. We need you."

"I know that, and I will be back soon. You're not workin'. You can handle things."

"Neither are you."

"I told work I'd be out for a while."

"You have work here, at home," Dena says. "You have duties."

"Not now. Don't give me the fatherhood guilt. This is already hard enough as is."

"But how do I know if you're—"

"Stop it. Don't. Don't start that, D. I'm too tired. Look—I'll call you when I'm in Chicago tomorrow."

"And then what?"

Lex pauses for a moment, and she hangs up on him before waiting for an answer. There's no answer to be given. Not now, anyway.

He shifts in the seat of the rental car, takes a sip of his energy drink, and turns up the radio over the sound of the drizzle and his own guilt.

4

I often wonder what it would be like if you were still alive.

I wonder how much one life affects another.

An infinity of limitless ways, that's how much.

Every sunrise and every sunset and every full moon and every snowfall and every downpour and every breath remind me.

The motions and music of life remind me that there's one missing.

And in a world so full of refutations and denials, I place the blame solely on myself.

I have to live out every single reminder of what is gone, what will always be gone, and what will never be mine.

James watches Laila walk maybe half a block, then pulls his car next to the curb and rolls down the window.

"Get in."

She glances at him and says nothing.

"I swear to God I don't care about making a scene, little lady. Get in the car."

As far as he can see, there's nobody around.

"I'm not going to hurt you." She continues walking, and he curses. "I'm not even gonna touch you, got it? Just get in."

"What do you want?"

"I was being cordial yesterday at the bank when I thought we could meet over a drink."

"Did you sneak into my apartment last night?"

"Nope."

"You're lying."

A woman strolls by but doesn't bother him. "I watched the outside of your building all night. My butt is imprinted onto this seat, lady. I didn't see anybody strange coming and going. And I sure didn't sneak in. If I had, I would've spent the night in your guest room."

"I don't have a guest room," Laila says in an arrogant, dismissive tone.

"There you go then," he says. "Get in the car."

"No."

"Lady, I swear..."

"I'm getting a cup of coffee, so if you want to follow me down there, we can talk."

James curses, and he lets down on the gas as he finds a place to park. Anything to get out of this car is fine with him.

She doesn't say anything to him in line, and when she orders her drink, she ignores him as she pays. He gets a coffee and finds her at a table in the middle of a room full of people.

"I'm not going to do anything to you."

"Do I look worried?"

This chick has some kinda attitude, he thinks.

"You look like an Oscar-winning actress."

"What do you want?"

He takes a sip, and the burn on his tongue wakes him up. "How did it happen?"

"What do you want?"

"You know—for such a good-looking chick, you sure are feisty. Anybody ever tell you that?"

"I've heard worse."

"Wasn't trying to win a prize," James says.

"What do you want?" Laila's words are slow and deliberate.

"Connor Brennan was my brother."

"I don't know anybody by that name."

"No, you know him. It was the man you left spilling his life out onto the carpet in some swanky suburban mansion."

"You could be anybody as far as I know."

"I'm not here to waste your time or mine. Here."

He gives her his Illinois license. She examines it.

"Never seen someone look so intently at a license," he tells her.

"Older or younger?"

"Connor was three years younger."

The woman stares at him.

"'Was' is the key word there," he says.

"James."

"Yep."

"What do you want from me, James Brennan?"

"Is that really all you have to say to me?"

"What do you want me to say?"

"Tell me something. Anything about that night."

He studies the freckles on her nose as she bites down on her lower lip.

"How did it happen? I need to know that."

"You're a long way from Chicago, Mr. Brennan."

"So are you."

"This is my home now."

"That was fast."

"Did you come here just for me?"

He nods. "Yes. Aren't you lucky?"

"I need to get to work."

"Maybe."

"If you're going to threaten me, why don't you go ahead and do it. I'm not in the mood for any games. Your brother got what was coming to him. And so will you if you continue this."

He laughs. "You're a real piece of work."

"You don't even know."

His eyes move all over her. "I can imagine."

"Leave me alone."

"Or what? What are you going to do, Laila Torres?"

Something in her eyes catches.

He knows he got to her.

"That's right. I know your last name. Sure took some doing, but I know. That's why I'm here in June and not February. Anybody can be tracked down these days. Unless you're Osama bin Laden, anybody—and I mean anybody—can be tracked down."

"My last name is no big secret."

"I'd bet a hundred dollars your license doesn't say Torres. Then again, I don't have a hundred bucks to bet with. But you most certainly do."

James smiles as she stands. "You can leave now, but we'll continue this conversation."

"We're not continuing anything."

"What are you going to do, Laila? Who are you going to tell? Who can you go to to help you out? I dare you to go to the police. Go ahead."

James examines every inch of her as she moves away. Then he takes the napkin on the table and starts to rip it in even, clean strips, dropping them into the coffee cup.

He's going to enjoy every second of this.

• • •

This is what it feels like to be a murderer.

No different than the day before. No different except for waiting for someone to come and get you, waiting every morning and afternoon and night, waiting for the inevitable.

For six months she has carried this guilt carefully wrapped in a black cloth and bundled in her backpack over her shoulder. For six months Laila has forced herself to move on. Not feeling any different than she did before it happened, yet knowing that she will never be the same.

But just as the waiting feeling was beginning to subside, this man shows up and every fear that she's been carrying with her finally gets unpacked and laid out on the side of the road.

For four hours as she's dealt with customers and counted money and deposited checks and slips, Laila has been debating about leaving work, getting the three or four valuables she has in her apartment, and taking off.

She knows how to do this.

She's a seasoned veteran at leaving everything behind.

The question isn't whether she can do it. The question is how far she can get without being followed.

Every time she passes by a grinning Kyle, she wonders if she can tell him.

She wonders what he would say if she did.

"You okay?"

"Sure."

"You don't mind me walking home with you?"

"It's not a long walk."

"The way you're walking it is."

"Yeah, I guess so."

She surveys the sidewalk and the street she is on carefully, yet she doesn't see anybody she recognizes. No hiding faces or parked cars or eyes peering out of the shadows. No trace of James Brennan anywhere.

Her nerves almost make her forget Kyle is walking right next to her.

"Laila, what's gone on the last couple of days?"

"What do you mean?"

"Some type of cloud moved over you and stayed. Something— I can't really explain exactly—it just seems like something's wrong. And yet you also don't mind me being around. It just makes me think—well, that's crazy."

"What's crazy?"

"It makes me think you're—that you're scared of something."

She stops and looks at him without moving or blinking. "I'm not scared of anything."

"I know. And that's what—I believe that, Laila. I don't know you that well, but I know you well enough to know you're not scared of anything. Remember that jock harassing you when you first started work? That's what showed me that, man, you better watch out for this girl."

"He was just some idiotic muscle head. I've dealt with my share of them."

"You know—you say that, and I believe it. But looking at you—it just doesn't add up."

Laila rolls her eyes and keeps walking.

"What? What'd I say?"

"Maybe you should stop looking then."

"I didn't mean anything—Laila, come on. Stop a minute."

"What?"

"You wanna know something? You want to know one of the reasons I look forward to this dead-end job every day I wake up? It's because maybe, just maybe, I'll be able to hang out and have coffee with you. Do you realize that?"

She sighs, shaking her head. "Kyle—"

"No, just—look—I don't claim to know you. But I've spent enough time with you to know that something's up. So what's going on? Tell me. I know it's not me because I haven't done anything. God knows I do things and I've done plenty in my life, but I haven't done anything this time."

"It's not you."

"Then what is it? Did something happen at dinner last night—did I say anything wrong?"

"Of course not."

"I'm missing something. Just fill in the blanks for me."

"I can't," Laila says. "Not now."

Broken

"How long does it take to really get through those walls of yours?"

Laila scans the sidewalk. This city is so clean, so picturesque, so much so that she sometimes wonders what she's doing here.

For a moment she thinks of the sidewalks of Manhattan or the city streets of Chicago. Then she thinks of another city, a place of refuge and secrets, a dark place she knows she belongs.

"Nobody's getting through," she tells Kyle. "Because there's nothing to find once you're in."

• • •

Lex follows the stocky, hairy legs in plaid shorts and black socks ascending a third flight of narrow stairs. When they reach the top and enter the apartment, he's surprised the studio is so expansive and bright, with sunlight coming in from every possible direction except the floor.

Breathing in, Lex is more winded than the landlord it took him half a day to find. He spent much of the time in a library searching for Laila's name online. He found one mention of an address somewhere after an hour and a half of Googling. Half a dozen calls later, he was talking to the short and round man next to him.

"You're not the first person that's come around looking for her," the man says with a slight Eastern European accent.

The man's name is Robert Farnick, and he agreed to come out and show the apartment after a couple of calls.

"Who else did?" Lex asks, walking across the vacant floor and hearing the creaks in the wood.

"I don't know. Some guy—dark-haired, cocky guy. Not very friendly."

"What'd he want?"

"Same thing as you. Looking for her. What happened to her?"

"That's what I'm trying to find out."

"What'd you say your name was?"

"Lex Torres."

"Brother, huh?"

Lex nods as he looks around the empty loft. He can imagine Laila in this space, living out the dream of a young girl making it in the big city, seemingly living out another person's life. He can picture art on the walls, framed shots of her from the New York days, modern furniture, everything neat and orderly just like the way her room used to be back in Brady when she never seemed to spend much time there.

Perhaps she didn't spend a lot of time here either.

"She left everything behind?"

"Even clothes. Crazy thing too. Called her cell number and discovered it was out of service. I eventually decided to sell most of the stuff. Haven't been able to find a taker for this loft. Times are tough, you know."

"Any personal things that you still have?"

"Personal like what?"

Lex glances at the man's necklace that's almost hidden underneath a jungle of hair. "Like anything."

"I don't know. Maybe."

"Mind if I take a look through them?"

"I don't know."

Robert Farnick appears to know a lot and wears a face as if he knows it too.

"Look, man. I haven't seen my sister in years, and I'm really worried. You got any siblings?"

Farnick doesn't answer him but instead examines him to see if he's lying. Lex stares back. He's tired and isn't in the mood for games or negotiation.

"I'll see if I have anything."

"Can you just — can I look around here a little?"

"Nothing's here. But fine by me. Looking for an apartment?"

Lex wants to say he's going to look for a bar of soap and some deodorant to try and get rid of the foul body odor Farnick is carrying around with him, but then shakes his head. The guy is just trying to make a living and obviously couldn't give a rip about a missing woman. Farnick wanders away and slams the door shut, leaving a haunting echo in this hollowed-out shell of an apartment.

Lex walks over imaginary footsteps, trying to find any semblance of Laila, seeing nothing but emptiness.

He is afraid there's nowhere else to go.

5

I never knew what I wanted to do with my life when I was younger. Each day was all that mattered, living in the moment. I never thought about life after school, life after Texas, life after everything. I would open my eyes and see the day before me and take it in. They say that's a good way to live, but I'm not so sure. I'm not so sure about a lot of things.

Sometimes I wonder if I'll ever be able to live those days down.

What good is living in the moment when the past always inevitably overshadows it?

Sometimes I tell myself I need to find a good shrink, someone different than the ones in New York and Chicago that needed more help than they could prescribe. Sometimes I tell myself I need to find someone, anyone, that will accept and love me for who I am. But I can't imagine — I can't begin to imagine the layers I'd have to go through to get to the core.

And then — yes, when I hear those words "accept" and "love" and "who I am," I think that what I need is the faith of my father. But every time I think about praying, think about going to church, think about any of that, I go back to the mess I left behind.

My problem is not wondering why God could allow bad things to happen. My problem is believing that God can do wondrous things. Yes, the Garden of Eden might have been real, and Moses parting the Red Sea and all the prophets *of the Old Testament doing their miracles and yes, even Jesus coming and dying on the cross next to a couple of criminals and surrounded by masses who mocked him. That might all be real, but to me right now, it seems like a fairy tale. Just like in all the stories of old, the stories from youth, when things worked out happily ever after. Those stories sell because people are looking for happily ever afters, and that includes people going to see a shrink or people living their whole lives in their own bubbles of a family, or people sitting down in church and getting saved.*

What are they saved from? That's what I want to know.

If James lives to be one hundred years old and never hears another country song, he knows he won't have missed a single second. Between his recent trip to Texas and now having spent several days in Greenville, James finds himself tired of the twang rooted in every accent heard and every guitar plucked. He wants his old life back, before the new year rang in with blood and caused everything to go to hell.

He sits at the bar and glances at his watch. A couple of stools down sits Willie Nelson, or at least a man who James thinks looks exactly like him. When he hears his cell phone, James knows who it is without even checking.

"I just need a little more time," he says.

"A little more time for what? You planning on robbing a bank or something?"

"Give me a few weeks."

"I've given you a few months, James."

"Give me one more."

"I don't want to give you another day."

"I'm going to handle everything. I just can't make it all happen overnight."

"Then when is it going to happen?" The man on the other line curses.

"Give me a week. One more week."

"Do you know what a week means? Do you?"

James takes a sip of his bourbon and hears the sound of country music in the background, and he feels his eyes water from the bite. The barrage of insults continues on the line.

"Seven days. By next Monday," James tells him.

"That's eight days."

"Sundays don't count."

"What?" the man says. "You going to church or something? We're not allowed a day of rest. Not for what we do."

"Then give me eight days. Eight days, all right?"

"You really are something."

"I'll get it to you."

"Your word means nothing, and it hasn't in a very long time. And if your brother was still alive, he'd say the same thing. And I hate saying that, because I know how much it hurts, James. But it's true, and you know it."

"Yeah."

"Next Monday. And that's it. That's all the time you have. So if you're a praying man, you better get on your knees and start praying you find something fast. Because hell will come knocking on your door if you don't."

James places the cell phone on the bar, and he stares at it as if it might talk or explode. He takes another sip and glances at his watch again.

He is tired of this.

"Nobody should owe anybody anything," he says.

Just a little longer.

The drink burns and bites as it goes down.

Just a little longer.

•　　•　　•

The voice wakes her up.

Laila sits up and looks around. This time she doesn't see any-body.

But she hears it again.

"Who's there?"

But nobody can be there. She's hearing things that she's making up. The ghosts of madness are seeping in. This is what guilt does. This is what running away can do.

The voice says it again, a whisper that somehow floats all around her.

"No."

She shakes it off because it's not real, because the word is imag-ined just like the voice and just like all of this. She refuses to acknowl-edge the word because it's a lie and it's hateful and cruel.

"No." Maybe the louder she says it the more awake she will be.

For a moment she stops breathing in and out, listening, waiting, wondering.

The voice doesn't come again.

The word uttered is no longer there.

Her head makes its way back to the pillow, where she waits and listens for a very long time.

Laila is walking and sweating from the midday sun when she hears a refreshing and hypnotic sound. She rushes toward it.

It's just over a small hill of grass.

She arrives at the crest, and then she sees it. The small creek twisting its way down the mountainside.

Skipping down it, splashing, is a small figure.

"Hello?" she calls out.

But it seems like the sound of the water is getting louder.

"Hello. Hey you."

She walks over to the boy who has his back to her. The rushing sound is piercing now, as if she's standing at the edge of the falls. The boy doesn't hear her and she taps his shoulder and then he turns and she sees him.

The face reveals empty holes that should be eyes.

Laila stumbles and falls as the black pits stare at her, burning her from within.

She starts to shout, but she can't over the sound of the rushing water that's suddenly all around her.

She's drowning and coughing and sucking in water and she cries out but nothing can save her and all she can see when she closes her eyes are the eyes of death mocking and taunting and blaming her.

Choking on her tongue, gasping in too much air, Laila wakes up and keels over.

Her body is burning from sweat. When she finally realizes what was happening, Laila tries not to look at the clock.

She doesn't want to know how many hours are left in this night.

By midmorning Laila is bored and restless. She calls Shelley to see if her friend is up.

"Have you recovered from going to church?" Shelley eventually asks.

"You're not going to ask me to come again, are you?"

Shelley laughs. "You make it sound like it's going to the dentist."

"You make it sound like I need to go."

"Well, I'm still hoping you might go and not pass out. You doing okay?"

"I didn't sleep much last night."

"Any reason why?"

"No," Laila lies. She pours a glass of orange juice as she balances the phone between her shoulder and ear.

Broken

"What are you doing?"

"I need something to drink. I swallowed some of my toothpaste this morning while I was brushing my teeth, and I can't get rid of the burn."

"I could take you out for breakfast if you're that desperate."

"Amusing. So do you have any stories from last night? Any crazy Shelley stories to brighten my day?"

"You could just come down the hallway you know."

"I need to put some pants on. I don't want Crazy Larry seeing me."

"Well, okay, fine. I do have some stories. Actually I have big news."

Laila listens as she goes into the sparse living room and sits on the plush love seat, the only piece of furniture in the room. She can close her eyes and imagine herself back in Chicago, or back in New York, or back somewhere else. The open space makes her feel comfortable. She has a laptop on her kitchen counter. Occasionally she will listen to songs off that. She doesn't have a television or an Internet connection.

It's nice to be mostly unplugged from the rest of the world.

But as Shelley talks about the guy she met last night, Laila knows she's not completely disconnected from the real world.

She still has to earn a living. Or at least feign like she's earning a living. She still has time in the day to kill.

The job at the bank allows her to do both.

But sooner or later she knows she has to do more.

She knows she has to have a bigger plan than just today.

Today seems like a big task to fulfill, so she loses herself in Shelley's story and her hot tea and her drab, quiet apartment.

•   •   •

Lex knows it's her handwriting. Even after so many years he still knows her and would still recognize that writing. It just feels like her. Like the Laila he once knew. The phone number and the name and the star sign.

He stares at it and shakes his head.

"Come on, Lex, just get it over with."

He's been staring at it ever since pulling it out of a box the landlord named Farnick gave him to look through.

The note was surely a mistake, something she would have tossed or taken but that she didn't find when leaving. If she left on her own. That was one of the many questions. Where did she go, and why did she leave so quickly?

Obviously someone took some stuff and left, whether it was Laila or someone doing it for Laila.

"Rodney."

The note was a bookmark in a novel he found. *Sorrow* by Dennis Shore.

In his dreams last night, however short they might have been, Lex imagined meeting this Rodney one-on-one. Rodney told him that Laila was dead, that she had been dead for a long time. And right before Lex woke up, he found himself driving back home, driving back to where this had all started, ready to face everything. Ready to face it alone.

"So who exactly are you, Rodney?"

It's been so long not knowing where Laila disappeared to, so many years of silence. Lex wonders what dark alley he's heading toward and fears what breaking the silence will reveal.

He dials the numbers and waits, resting on the edge of the bed in the hotel room where he'd had the nightmare.

On the third ring, he gets a voice mail.

For a moment he's going to say something, but then he hangs up.

He shakes his head and tosses the phone on his bed. He needs to get some fresh air.

The high-pitched chords of the song on his cell phone begin to play, making him grab for the phone again. The number he just dialed appears in the display.

"Hello?"

"Who's this?" a voice barks out.

Broken

"Lex."

Part of him knows he needs to hang up, that he needs to hang up the cell right now.

"Lex who?"

"I'm a friend of Laila's."

Silence.

"Is this Rodney?"

"Where'd you get this number?"

"From Laila."

"What do you want?"

"It's about her."

Again, silence.

"Look—I don't want to bother you in any way—"

"Yet you called me and didn't even leave a message."

"I want to talk in person."

"Why's that?"

"Because I have some information."

"Who says I need information?"

"It's something Laila wanted me to give you."

"Really?"

Lex's head spins. He's making this up as he goes, hoping it doesn't sound as lame as it seems.

"Where are you calling from?" the man asks.

He tells Rodney he's staying at the Hilton by O'Hare airport.

"Stay there."

"Until when?" Lex asks.

"Until I call you back."

"And when—"

But just like the nightmare, the voice is gone, leaving him in this room in complete silence.

Leaving him with a hundred more questions.

6

At the core, every man desires the same thing. This drug, this drive, this consuming longing always comes down to the same thing: control. Control over others, control over life, control over everything. So many are scared that life is completely out of control, so they fight it and they battle it and they usually lose the battle and they need some type of control.

Their eyes always reveal it. The longing. The fear. The caged-in ferocity. The hope.

I've heard every possible thing that could be said. Everything. And eventually every word means nothing. Every sensation and feeling means nothing. Eventually the waking sun seems dull, the setting sun seems stale. And you go through life completely devoid of emotions and you give over control.

But nobody has control.

Because in a moment, that can be taken away. With a simple act, a life can be taken away.

They used to come to me wanting control, wanting to feel empowered, but the moments were always fleeting. They might have left thinking they were fulfilled, but they weren't. They never could be.

Nobody ever is nor ever will be.

The lie remains. Day after day after day.

Broken

J ames knocks for the third time.

"I know you're in there — let me in."

He glances down the hallway, then pounds on the door. There are perhaps a dozen or so apartments lining this narrow corridor.

"I'll kick this thing in if I have to."

His palm is aching, but James still bangs away. The bolt turns, and the door opens.

Laila stands there, stern and tall. "What?"

"You gonna let me in?"

She appears to think for a moment but then opens the door all the way. He goes inside and closes the door.

He glances around and curses. "Six months and it still looks like you just moved in."

She is still standing by the door, as if she's deciding whether to run out or kick him out.

"I told you I'm not going to hurt you."

"What do you want?"

"You know what I want? I want my brother back, that's what I want."

Her glance doesn't waver.

"Connor Brennan, ring a bell? Connor? Blondish-reddish hair, doesn't really look like me but you might be able to see the resemblance. He was my little brother. And he was shot on New Year's Eve and died sometime before the new year came. Before I could find him."

A long strand of hair falls across her tempting eyes and face. She glares at him.

"Tell me something. Was it before or after Connor got what he came for?"

She curses back at him, and he chuckles, knowing the comment stung. James looks at the folding table, a couple of folding chairs.

There is a stack of mail on the table. In one corner there is a duffle bag that looks packed.

"Going somewhere?"

"That's my workout gear."

"Really?"

"Go ahead and look."

"Good to see you're still taking care of that body of yours. Would be a shame for that to go to waste."

He steps into the mostly empty family room. "So lifeless in here, you know that?"

Laila is still by the door.

"Why don't you come in here for a moment?"

He studies her as she walks. She's wearing jeans and a baggy Chicago Bears sweatshirt. Something in her steps, the way she moves her arms, the sweatshirt she has on — something about all that gives it away.

"You have a gun on you?"

She stops and freezes and then looks at his hands.

"I'm not going to do anything to you," he says as he sits on the love seat. "Comfy."

"So why are you here? Why do you keep showing up?"

"I'm waiting for some type of acknowledgment. Some type of apology."

"I don't know what you're talking about," she says.

"You don't? You've more or less acknowledged it anyway."

"I want you to leave."

"That I'm not going to do," he says. "You can come in the room. I'm not going to bite. Not now."

She stands against the wall.

"I want to know why."

"That's all you want? An explanation? Reasons?"

"No, that's not all I want. Think of what I might want. There are two things I can think of."

Broken

She keeps her guard, continuing to watch his hands, his eyes, his movements.

"The most obvious—well, I'm not like my brother. My brother had his issues. His—what do you want to call them? His appetite? His preferences? No, I'm a lot more practical. It's a whole different world out there today."

"Practical meaning what?"

"Meaning cash. Meaning money."

"How much do you want?"

He smiles. "Oh, what, you going to just go and write me a check?"

"How much?"

"A lot more than what you could give me. Today that is."

For a moment he sits on the edge of the couch. "You have no idea, do you?"

"What?"

"Who you're dealing with?"

"That sounds like a bad line."

"Bad line or not, you have no clue. No idea. You think you got away with it, don't you? But I'm going to tell you something right here and right now and you better remember it, okay? I want you to remember it for however long of a life you still have left. Whatever life that might be. I'm never, ever, ever going to let you go. I'm going to make you see Connor's face for the rest of your life, you got that? And no amount of anything can ever repay what's been lost. I'm willing to deal with the hand I've been dealt, but you gotta play too, lady. You got that?"

"I can give you everything I have, but it's not much."

He laughs. "There are other ways of getting money. I'm not stupid."

"How?"

"Are you going to keep lying to me? Playing this game?"

"What do you want me to do?"

"Brady, Texas. Ring a bell?"

Her face doesn't change. He curses out loud. "You'd be a good poker player, you know? I know. I know your family. I know everything."

"So what?"

"You're a very rich little girl."

"Not anymore."

"You can be again."

"No," she says.

"Your family—well, all I can say is there's been some interesting developments down there."

She hovers back and forth, anxious, but remains quiet.

"You don't have to believe me. But I know. Lex. Ava. Rafael. Or should I say Mr. Torres. I know them all. Funny—never would've guessed a Mexican could do so well for himself, you know? But then again, you and your siblings aren't a hundred percent, are you?"

"You can go to hell."

"Yeah, maybe, but you can join me there. Right with my brother."

Laila appears nervous. He knows he's getting to her. Just the very mention of the names.

"You really haven't been in touch with them, have you?"

"And I don't plan to either."

"Yeah, I think you're going to."

Laila pulls at the side of her sweatshirt and twists, then pulls out a .38 and holds it firmly as if she's practiced quite a bit.

"Ah, there's the gun. Is that the same one?"

"Get out."

"Get out or what? What are you going to do?"

"Get out."

"I'm not playing around here."

"And you think I am?"

He smiles. "That's the same gun you used on my brother, isn't it?"

"I'll use it again."

"Ah, there we have it. An admission."

She curses.

"That's right. Sure. Go ahead. Why don't you go two for two?"

"You need to leave right now."

She moves a little closer toward him, and as she does he jumps off the couch and swats the gun out of her hand. It's so easy, too easy in fact. Then he grabs her by her throat and launches her into the wall with a gasping thud.

"Listen to me, you skinny little whore. If I wasn't in a bind, I would have killed you three days ago when I first spotted you, you got that? Unfortunately for me, but very, very fortunate for you, I need cash. And a lot of it. Otherwise I would just keep—squeezing—and I wouldn't—stop until your pretty blue face popped."

He lets her go. Laila crumbles to the floor, coughing, gagging.

He takes her mass of hair and jerks her head to look up at him.

"You listen to me. You have until tomorrow afternoon to have a nice little family reunion via the phone. I don't care how you do it, just do it. Your life—and your family's life—depends on this. I don't want anybody else involved. I just want money."

"How much?"

"Start with a hundred grand. That'll be worth my time having to chase you all the way to this hick city."

She rubs her throat, shaking her head. "It isn't going to happen."

"Yeah, it sure as hell will. You don't have any other options. What are you going to do? Go to the police? The only reason I haven't done that is because I don't need them prying into my family business. But that doesn't mean I won't. Nor does it mean I won't decide to take another trip to the Lone Star state. You don't want me doing that, Laila. Not again. Because there'll be only one reason I'm going there, and you won't like it."

With that warning, he leaves.

But not before picking up the weapon from the carpeted floor.

•   •   •

"What are you talking about? Are you serious?"

"Do you?" Laila asks Kyle again over the cordless phone.

"No. Why would I own a gun?"

"A lot of people do."

"Do I look like one of those 'people?'"

She hears him laugh but doesn't laugh back. She doesn't say anything as she gently massages her throat that still throbs with pain.

"Look, my cousin does. He owns about fifty. He probably wouldn't even know if I took one from him."

"Can you borrow one?"

"If you tell me what's going on. Are you in trouble?"

"Yes."

"Like—right now?"

"I'm just—I'm just worried, and I don't—I can't involve the police."

"You need me to come over?"

"No. Not now. Just—I'd feel better if I had something here. Just in case."

"Just in case what?" Kyle asks.

"In case someone breaks in."

"What? Laila, what is happening? Why would someone be breaking into your place?"

"I can explain but not now, not over the phone. Just—it would really help me. Or at least give me peace of mind."

"Look, if you need a place to stay, you're welcome to stay at mine. My roommate wouldn't care. And I could sleep on the couch. It would be no big deal."

"That's kind. Thank you. No. I just wondered if you could help me out."

"By getting you a gun?"

"Yes."

"I'm assuming you're talking about a handgun, right?"

"No, I need a shotgun. Of course."

"Look, let me put in a call. Just—you sure you're okay?"

"Yes."

Broken

"You promise?"

"Yes."

"Let me see what I can do. I'll give you a call back. Are you talking like—would you want me to try and get it tonight?"

"As soon as possible, if you can."

Kyle doesn't say anything for a moment.

"I know it's a lot to ask."

"It's not that. It's just—it's a gun."

"I know," she says.

"Okay. I'll try."

Laila puts her phone on the table and then glances at the clock. It's a little after eight. She rubs her neck and winces, then lets out a deep sigh.

She goes into her bedroom and pulls out the suitcase that's already half full. She unzips it and begins to cram in items. There's very little she needs to bring. Everything of value is already in the duffle bag, the one James had spotted, the one she had filled earlier in the day.

Even slight mementos and reminders of her time in Greenville will stay behind. There's no reason to take them.

The question that rolls around is where she will go.

And she thinks of the phone again, thinks about calling her family. But she can't and won't.

That door closed a long time ago.

She's already dead to them.

The phone rings, and she picks it up.

"Okay—I'm heading over to my cousin's. Do you need me to stop by before I go?"

Laila shakes as she hides the tears and controls her voice. "Thank you."

Kyle is a good man. She knew she could rely on him, and regardless of his motives, he's helping her out.

"I can swing by if you want."

"No. Just—if you wouldn't mind, could you bring it over right away?"

"Of course."

"And stay. Just for a while?"

"As long as you want me to."

Laila stares at the suitcase and finds herself lost, thinking of nothing and feeling tired and feeling everything. Then she fades out of her trance as she sees a small edge of something white lying underneath a T-shirt.

She picks it up.

It's an old picture of Isabella. It's a black-and-white square photo, a kind that she hasn't seen in years. Isabella is standing proudly showing off her white coat.

"She's actually gray," Laila says, mimicking her father's accent. He would teach her things about horses. Nevertheless, Isabella was a tall and striking horse that looked white and shimmering and something out of a fantasy.

Laila never brought any photos of Isabella with her when she left Texas.

The image twitches at something deep inside of her.

For a moment she feels more pain than when James Brennan was over and almost squeezed the life out of her.

She takes the photo and puts it back in her suitcase, not sure where it came from and too tired to try and figure it out.

•   •   •

Lex twists his head, and something in his neck snaps. He howls in pain and tries to remember what side the phone is on. Then he realizes the ring filling the room isn't his cell phone. He reaches for the receiver in the dark.

"Yeah?"

"Lex?"

"Yeah."

"Come on down to the lobby."

"Who is this?"

There's nobody on the end to answer the question.

Broken

He finds a light and turns it on, stretching as he stands up and searches for his jeans. The fancy alarm says that it's 3:16 a.m.

"This is probably very stupid," he says as he tries to comb back his mass of hair with his hand.

The only person in the lobby is a man wearing a sports coat and pants with a casual shirt underneath. He isn't particularly large or threatening, but he doesn't give any sort of greeting either.

"Are you Rodney?"

"Come with me."

"Whoa, hold on. Where're you going to take me?"

"To a car waiting outside. He wants to meet you."

Ignoring his instincts, Lex climbs in the open town-car door. This is his only chance to find Laila. Another man waits inside, examining him with a tired, dismissive glance.

The car starts to drive off with the first man behind the wheel.

For a moment nobody says a word. The man in the seat next to him is stocky, maybe in his late forties, mostly bald, with a long face and narrow eyes.

"This is all very mysterious," Lex says, looking around the town car.

"What do you want from me?"

"Are you Rodney?"

"You said you had something for me. Something from Laila."

"How do you know her?"

The man shakes his head and lets out a chuckle. Then his jaw tightens as he grabs the back of Lex's hair and slams his head into the seat in front of him.

For a moment everything goes white and Lex remembers getting hit square in the face with a baseball when he was in high school. This feels about the same.

He also feels something leak out of his nose.

"You said you had something for me."

"I just said that—look, she's my sister. Laila is my sister, and I'm looking for her."

The man has a big hand, and that hand finds his face. He grips his forehead and twists like one might do to an orange when juicing it. Lex coils back and tries to push the man off him.

When he's finally let go, Lex rubs his forehead and tries to gain his vision back.

"You're looking for Laila?"

"Yeah."

"You look like her."

"Yeah, I know."

"If you didn't I seriously might throw you in the lake somewhere."

"She's my older sister."

"Didn't know she had any family."

"I didn't mean anything calling. I don't have any leads, and I'm just concerned."

"Are you, Lex? That's interesting because so are we."

They are on some highway somewhere, driving with few cars around, the world passing by in a blur.

"And you haven't spoken with her recently, have you?"

"Not at all. Not for years. That's why I called you."

"You don't look like a liar, Lex."

"Why would I lie?"

"Most people lie," the crack of his mouth says, his eyes like the windows of a tank. "Everybody lies, in fact. But you better not be lying."

"I'm not."

"Why are you looking for her?"

"Because I think—because I know—she's in trouble."

"Really?" The man laughs. "And why would that be?"

"Because people are looking for her."

"I bet they are. So you decided to join the crowd, did you?"

Lex nods.

"Here's a bit of advice. I would leave your sister alone. I would go back to whatever home you have and leave things be. She'll be found. But not by you."

Broken

"What do you want with her?"

"What do I want? Nothing. Nothing at all. Just two or three years of my life back. But that's all. Nothing else."

The air blowing out of the vent above him is cold and causes Lex to shiver. He is still groggy from the blow to the head.

"You're not a part of this, so my advice to you is to leave. Leave Chicago today. This is not your problem, and Laila is not yours. You seem like a good kid so stay that way. You have family, Lex?"

He nods.

"Then go back home to them. I don't ever want to see your face again. I don't ever want to get another call from you. And hear me when I say this. If, in some miraculous bit of blind, stupid luck, you do find your sister, you tell her to come back home to Rodney. Because if she doesn't I will not only hunt her down, but I'll add you to the mix. You got it?"

"Yeah."

"That's good. Hey, Dan. We're all done here."

The car slows down as it pulls off to the side of the freeway. "Get out."

"Here?" Lex opens the door and hears a blast of sound coming from a passing semi.

"You've wasted enough of my time and energy for one night. That's all it's going to be too. You forget about that skank of a sister, and you go back home."

Lex watches the car drive off, and then he stares off in the distance, the Chicago skyline beautiful and bright.

He stares at the heavens above it and wonders if this was all a mistake.

"Lord, please help me. Help me find her."

Then he starts walking, continuing to pray, continuing to try and beg God to let him find Laila.

Especially now.

7

There was a time, as brief as a blink, when I thought things were going to work out. When I thought the busyness had brought me to this place in my life, this place of meaning. I began to believe that I could let go and live. But that all crumbled before me, and I realized how foolish I was to believe in the first place.

Hope is a dangerous thing. Because when it is pulled from underneath your feet, you find you have a long way to fall.

The drop is always painful.

So many things break even though you have to get back up on your feet and try walking again. Even if you have no idea where to go.

The young man, probably in his mid or late twenties, gets out of his car and tries to make his way around to open her door, but Laila is already out.

They walk into her apartment complex, a newer building with gates at the front. Nothing hard to get into, especially with all the people going through. James already knows the traffic patterns coming and going well. He's been here spying on the place long enough to have them memorized.

He turns up the radio and stares at the darkened street in front of him.

Broken

This is the third time he's seen the two of them together.

It's a habit he doesn't like. More than that, it's a habit that's making him nervous.

He thinks of making a call when a hand tugs at him through his open window.

"Hey—you awake?"

James curses and looks through his open window. It's a cop.

"Wide awake," he says.

"Then you better move that car of yours. I don't see a handicapped sticker."

"Well yeah. I'm waiting for somebody."

"Saw you here an hour ago."

He studies the pudgy face and the lazy eyes and then forces himself to smile. "Guess they aren't going to come."

"I'm not in the mood to write a ticket tonight."

"You're a kind man."

James starts the car as he wonders what it would sound like to break the fat man's neck. There are few things in this life he hates more than a guy who gets a badge and a gun and thinks he's king of the world. Where he comes from they aren't anything except someone to pay off.

"You have a good night then," the policeman says with a slow drawl that James would like to smother.

"You too. See you around."

He wonders if the cop can hear the sarcasm on his words. Doesn't matter.

He drives around the block and finds an empty spot to park his car. Then he gets out, making sure the handgun he took from Laila is safely tucked underneath the passenger's seat. If his car was searched, they would find more than that in the trunk, but James knows there's no reason for the rental car to get searched.

James walks toward the front of the apartment building, then sits on a bench to wait for Laila's new friend.

He wants to make sure he gets a good look at the face he's about to bloody up.

• • •

Even before they had made the trip out to see his cousin and pick up the handgun, Kyle had brought a bottle of red wine to help Laila relax. At the sight of it, she had rolled her eyes and almost said something, but Kyle quickly made it clear he had no bad intentions and that he would leave whenever she wanted him to.

That was a couple of hours and several glasses ago. The bottle is finished and has settled in well with the two of them. It sits on her table in the family room right next to the handgun they borrowed.

Perhaps having those items make it easy for Laila to talk. She can't remember a time when she has simply opened up and talked about anything and everything. A little personal and a little forgettable but all a little too enjoyable.

"Where'd you grow up?"

Laila is tucked under a blanket sitting on her love seat, Kyle sitting next to it on the floor with one arm leaning on the couch.

"A small town in Texas that you've never heard of."

"Try me."

"Brady."

"You're right. Never heard of it."

"It's the dead center of Texas. That's the way you'd find it."

"I don't think I would have guessed that, though you do have the spunk of a Texan."

"I get it from my mother. So I was told."

"You don't know for sure?"

"She died when I was four."

"Sorry."

"Yeah. Never knew her. I grew up knowing stories. She was German, my father is Mexican. How they ever got together beats me."

"You don't know?"

Broken

"No. My father's many things, but not a romantic. He doesn't like dwelling in the past. My mother is more of a historical footnote than a heartfelt memory. My father can show emotion but certainly not talk about it."

"What made you move away?"

"Brady or New York? Hmm. Which city have you heard of?"

"So that's what did it?"

"It's a long story, and I'd need a lot more wine and time."

"I can oblige."

"I'm sure you can. I'm fine with all we had. Tell me about yourself. I like listening rather than talking."

"Not much to tell. I'm not originally from Greenville."

"I can tell. You don't have a strong accent."

"I grew up in Cincinnati, Ohio. Moved down here for school. Then stayed."

Laila shifts as she asks him which college.

"Gamecocks."

"Sorry?"

"Don't follow football, do you? Not even a little?" He sees her shake her head. "University of South Carolina."

"Oh."

"Did you go anywhere?"

"No."

For a moment the no is open-ended. There is more to come. But then it hovers in the air like a golf ball, finally coming back down on the fairway and landing all by itself.

"You know. My questions are just to get to know you. To find out a little more about you."

"Why?" she asks.

"Because . . . well, among other things, many other things, I think you're fascinating."

"I'm really not."

"Anybody who asks for a gun late on a Sunday night is interesting."

"Or psychotic."

"I guess if you had wanted to kill me, you would've already done so."

She forces a smile and takes a sip from her glass.

"What type of trouble are you in?"

"It doesn't matter."

"It matters enough to get a gun," Kyle says, his face so fresh and seemingly innocent.

"But it shouldn't matter you one bit."

"Is there anything I can do?"

She smiles, finishes the wine, then laughs. "You know, we used to have coyotes on our land back in Brady. We had a lot of property, and sometimes these nasty coyotes would come and get into things. Kill our animals. I remember when I was young and scared, I asked my father what he was going to do one night. It was late and he had a rifle and he was going out. He had that look on his face, that look that said he was up to something. And that's what he said to me."

"What?"

"'It shouldn't matter you one bit.' I think the better saying is it shouldn't bother me one bit, but I always liked the way he said that. Imagine this big gruff Mexican with a deep accent saying, 'It shouldn't matter you one bit.'"

"It matters to me, Laila."

"I know. Thank you. Thank you for doing this."

"For sipping wine with probably the most beautiful woman I've seen in my life?"

She tightens her lips, glancing away.

"I'm sorry. It's true. I just had to say that. Not that you haven't heard that before."

"Thank you. Thank you for everything."

"That sounds like something you've said a thousand times before."

"Maybe." Laila pauses. "But I've never said it to someone like you."

"My cousin sure liked you."

"Yes, he did."

Broken

They both laugh.

"Sorry he was a bit—well, you know."

"That's okay. He was harmless."

"Yeah. But he's got a one-track mind."

"I'm used to one-track minds."

"Yeah, I bet."

"Sometimes it seems like the world has a one-track mind, you know?"

Kyle nods.

"Do you like it around here?" she asks, changing the subject.

"Where? Greenville or the South?"

"Both, I guess."

"I love Greenville. Never thought I'd still be at the bank, but I guess in today's economy, any job is a good job. Especially at a bank, you know? Believe it or not I always wanted to be a photographer."

"Why aren't you?"

"Oh, I don't know. Back in college it was a hobby, but I was never really serious about it. You blink and ten years pass, you know?"

She nods.

"I still do it from time to time. Not sure how I could have made much money from it. That's what it usually boils down to. A dream is just that. You realize you have to be like the rest of the world and earn a living."

"Dreams are overrated."

"Think so?" Kyle asks.

"I know so."

"See. The fascination continues."

She shakes her head. "I'll write you a book, okay? Then you'll realize I'm not particularly fascinating. You'll realize the sad truth. Ordinary, boring, not at all fascinating."

"But do you really look at life like that? Seriously?"

"I've seen ten thousand dreams destroyed. Or so it seems, at least."

"Sounds like a country song."

Laila smiles. "Could be one. It'd sure be a sad one."

"Here's the way I look at life. My brother was killed when he was ten years old. Some freak accident riding his bike — one of those you'd never believe unless it actually happened to your family. It changed everything. For me, for my family. But I'll tell you something crazy. It's made me appreciate life, even now, almost twenty years later."

"I'm sorry."

Kyle appears to think for a moment. "And I have no idea why I just told you that. None. Except — well, you mentioned the sad bit. Do you know that some days I feel Keith looking over me? Looking out for me?"

"Maybe he is."

"You believe in heaven?"

"Not anymore."

"I believe everything happens for a reason, that Keith watches over me. And so — I say that because this — this right now. I don't think this is random. There's a reason we're here."

"Yes. It's because I needed a gun and you were someone that appeared trustworthy."

"Yeah, but, sure — I get that."

"That's all. Everything is completely random."

"Do you really believe that?"

"Did my mother's death have deep profound meaning? No. It just happened. I've seen some people who have lived charmed lives. People said that about me — how lucky I was. How I had a charmed life. I don't know if anybody really has a charmed life, to be honest. But I think some people are protected more than others. And it comes down to fate and chance. It comes down to complete and random luck."

"That's a pessimistic view, I'd say."

"You have a right to say whatever you want. I say it's realistic. I say it's true. It's the only truth I know."

"Do you believe in miracles?"

"No. But I bet you sure do."

Kyle smiles and looks away and scratches his arm, appearing nervous.

"Go ahead, tell me one," she says.

"No. Maybe some other time."

"I believe that crazy things happen every day to everybody. But I just don't believe there's a puppet master behind them."

"Man, I just—I don't know what I'd do if I didn't believe. That's the scary thing. Thinking that all this—this crazy, big fat world is just drifting through time and space completely on its own. That would make everything feel so—I don't know. So fragile. So breakable."

"But that's what we all are. We're all delicate, fragile souls. Every single one of us."

For a moment he's about to say something more, but Laila sits up, stretches, then glances at a nearby clock. "I better get to bed."

"Look, I didn't mean to be so deep. So personal."

"It's okay. I went there too. It wasn't just you. This was nice. Sitting here, talking."

"I told you I don't bite."

"No teeth marks yet." She checks her arms. "But wait until I wake up tomorrow."

Laila thinks about what she just said. "I mean—I didn't mean—"

He laughs and says, "I know. It's fine."

"It's late."

Kyle stands and takes her glass, bringing both to the kitchen and washing them out. Then he stares at her for a moment.

"You sure you're going to be okay?"

"I'll be fine."

"I don't need to go. That couch looks very comfortable."

"Thank you, but no. I'm fine."

"You have my cell, right? And home number?"

She nods. "Want to give me your blood type too?"

"You better not need anybody's blood type, okay?"

"I won't."

As Kyle stands at the door, looking so cute and awkward and speechless, Laila leans over and gives him a kiss on his cheek.

"Good night."

She locks the door and stands there in silence, wondering what's outside waiting for her.

Wondering if they'll come lurking when her bodyguard is gone.

•   •   •

Lex dumps the bag on the hotel bed. Scraps of his sister's life stare back at him. He looks at them again, wondering if there's something he missed, wondering where to go from here. His head still hurts from being rammed into the leather headrest. He is just thankful he was close enough to a gas station to call a cab back to his hotel. He knows he needs to leave.

His family needs him back home.

Yet a lost member of that family needs his help too.

None of these things help him. A tank top. An empty journal. A ticket stub to *Wicked* from a couple of years ago. Random little bits of nothing.

He goes through the journal once again and finds the same thing he found twice before. Empty, blank pages.

Even the couple of bills don't help. Too bad there's not a cell phone bill. That way he could get some more names and numbers.

"Yeah, that's probably all you need, Lexi."

He smiles saying that name. That's the name Laila always used to call him. The more he told her he hated it, the more she called him by it.

He picks up the three photos that were in the journal.

One is a shot of her, except only the top of her hair and one of her eyes is shown in the corner of the photo. He can tell she is laughing, however. She's got that look about her. She still looks the same. Beautiful, exotic, haunting. Strange to think in those terms because she's his sister, but she is nevertheless. He can't tell where this shot was taken, but it looks like she was trying to avoid the picture and managed to just slightly get in the shot. The next is a photo of a man—maybe in his thirties, good-looking, wearing a tie and a coat. Something about the glance makes Lex think this man is in love with the person taking the picture. And something about the glance makes Lex believe it was Laila behind the lens, snapping it. There is no name on the back of the photo, no date, nothing.

The third picture is of a boat, probably in Lake Michigan. It looks like the photo was taken on a pier looking out.

"*Precious,*" he reads from the side of the boat.

He thinks of the *Lord of the Rings* saga and of Gollum fondling the ring and whispering that word in his very unique way.

The pictures are interesting but again don't give him anything to go on. The man in the picture and the boat (probably both related) are somehow meaningful enough for Laila to have kept. So why didn't she take them with her?

It's early Monday morning, and soon the sun will be rising. He will need to call home.

He's unsure what he will say.

8

I was baptized in fourth grade. It was after my father's big conversion, his big On-the-Road-to-Damascus saga that changed our lives. Changing it enough to make us move and have him go in search of the Almighty somewhere in Texas. Believe me, if the Almighty exists, He sure isn't hanging out in Texas.

It's funny. So many people I came to know in New York and Chicago would probably look at me in complete bewilderment after saying a phrase like that: on the road to Damascus. Papa took us to so many churches that I grew to know the stories well. I can still recite them. But knowing the stories doesn't get you far at all. It just reminds you of what you're supposedly missing, or how deluded some loved ones are.

I always wondered after our family got baptized in that little church whether I was a different person. But inside, deep down, I still had all these questions. "Okay, God, if You're there why did You take our mom?" And, "Okay, God, if You're there, why would You continue to allow things to happen again and again and again?" Soon I stopped saying "okay, God," and I finally began to simply say "okay," and I moved on.

I guess that baptism was supposed to mean something, but if you don't have the faith and the belief, then it's nothing more than warm bathwater being poured over your head and that's that.

Broken

By the seventh or eighth blow, it's no longer any fun. There's no more information to get because the guy doesn't have any to give. He's pathetic. He's wailing with his nose gushing and spit slobbering all over his shirt and chest and hands, and he's just a complete mess. James has seen many men resort to becoming blubbering mushes after the pain sets into something worse. A fear of more. A fear that perhaps this is it.

"Just shut up for a minute already," James tells him.

He hands the young guy a towel. His name is Kyle Ewing. He works with Laila and has been trying to get her to go out with him for some time, and it's only been a few days since she said yes. She's in trouble, and she wanted company. That's it. That's all Kyle said and by now James believes him. The guy is confused and bewildered and blabbers nothing at all, and James tells him he's not going to kill him.

"Please, look, I don't know what else to say, and I didn't do anything wrong—"

"I know, I know, just shut it for a second." James curses. "Laila owes me something, and this is a nice little way to remind her. I just want you to remember something—you have nothing to do with any of this, you got that?"

The beauty of the country is that a nice twenty-minute drive can bring complete and utter seclusion. Enough to where a man can get a kid held by gunpoint on his knees at the edge of a dirt road, and then he can pummel that kid into telling him whatever.

"I'm going to take you back to our little friend's apartment, and I want you to send her a very specific message, you got that?"

The guy nods, blood staining the towel he wipes his face with.

"I don't want to hurt anybody," James says. "I don't like hurting people."

The guy just looks at him. No clever lines, no bravery, no nothing.

James likes that. It's easier when they don't decide to try and be brave.

His cell phone rings, and James picks it up.

"Right on course. Now leave me alone."

• • •

The soccer ball looks ordinary, scuffed, still solid enough to be used for a game.

But as Laila looks at it, a wave of terror fills her.

It was right next to her on the bed when she awoke a few moments ago.

More than anything, the terror she feels comes from confusion. She doesn't get it and wonders whether she's supposed to. If the ball is supposed to be a message, a threat, she doesn't understand what he's trying to communicate. Was he that lacking in creativity and simply wanted to show that he had slipped inside her apartment last night?

The thought of James standing at her bedside watching her in the darkness makes her skin prickle.

Laila continues to wonder if someone is still there. She searched every place in her apartment that somebody might be hiding, but still she has doubts.

She hates having any kind of doubt.

And the ball isn't about to provide any answers.

Even though there's nothing scary about it, she can't help shivering as she touches it. She wants to make sure it's real.

Her buzzer sounds, causing her to jump slightly. Laila goes to the monitor.

"Hello?" she calls in.

But the buzzer just keeps going off.

She walks out on her deck and looks over the railing. She calls out to see who is there.

"It's me. Let me in."

She sees Kyle.

She doesn't ring him in. Instead she bolts down the stairs and opens the door and rushes to see it up close. She curses and asks him what happened.

"Just let me in, okay."

"Who did this?"

"I think you know who did this. Let's get off the street."

"Are you hurt?"

"Yeah, I'm hurt. But I'm not gonna die or anything. Let's just get in."

Inside, after cleaning up in the bathroom, Kyle leans against the kitchen counter and says it again. "We need to call the cops."

"No." Laila has been in action mode, helping Kyle wash his face and stop the bleeding and also giving him one of her T-shirts while she's soaking his bloodstained shirt in the sink.

"Laila, just listen to me for a minute."

"I'm listening."

"Then stop running around."

She pauses and breathes in and doesn't want to tell him the truth.

All of this will hit her eventually if she slows down long enough to think about it.

"Listen—if he did this to me—someone he doesn't even know—what in the world is he going to do to you?"

"Nothing."

"Who is he, Laila? And why did he do it?"

"Let me see if I can find you another T-shirt. That one looks too tight on you."

"Stop—please."

She turns and looks at him. She can see it all over his face, and she hates herself because she's the reason the fear is there.

"I'm sorry that you had to get involved."

"Involved in what?" Kyle asks, the swath of paper towels filled with ice pressed against his temple.

"I can't tell you."

"Not even after this?"

"Kyle—just—you have to leave me be. Okay?"

"Leave you to what?"

She sighs.

"Leave you to what?"

"This will all be over very soon."

"And what's that mean?"

She doesn't answer.

"He told me this is just a little 'taste' of what's to come if you don't help him out. Where's your family?"

"I told you—they're in Texas."

"If I were you, I'd call them."

"You're not me, and you don't understand. And I'm sorry to have involved you in any way, I really am. I just—I can't say anything more."

"I almost got killed out there," he says.

"That was not my fault. I didn't do it."

"You can at least tell me why."

She curses. "I'm not going to tell you, so you can stop asking. And all this will be out of your hair in just a short while, and then you can do whatever you want."

"I'm just trying to help."

"Well look where that got you."

He goes to say something but then pauses. She can tell his left eye is swelling. For a moment she feels protective, and all she wants to do is hug him and tell him it's going to be okay. But that would be a lie.

"Did he say anything else?" Laila asks.

"No."

She stands there looking at Kyle. Light seeps in from the window and makes lines over the floor. A bird on her deck is singing away.

It's just another day.

She looks at his bruised face.

"I'm not responsible for you," she says.

"I never said you were."

"Okay."

"But give me a little more responsibility. Let me help you, Laila. Please. I don't want anything—I don't want this—to happen to you."

"It already did and it's already done and there's nothing you can do. There's nothing anybody can do."

"We can get help."

"Help isn't going to come, and believe me—just please, believe me. And get it out of your head. You and I both know that if I wasn't some chick you wouldn't be so obliging and helpful."

He shakes his head. "That's unfair."

"It's true, and you know it. So you need to take that big, kind heart of yours and spend it on some other girl who surely deserves it. Okay?"

Kyle puts the ice in the kitchen sink, and he cleans his hands again. He glances at her, waits to see if she's going to say anything, then he opens the door and leaves.

•   •   •

"You need something to drink, honey?"

It's been a while since somebody called Lex that. "Just a Coke."

"That really all you want?" the waitress asks him.

"That's all I better have."

"What about something to eat?"

"I'm still debatin'. Let me keep the menu."

Lex notes the Budweiser logo on the wall and thinks about how long it's been. That's what Dena's scared of most. Not that he's gone and missing household chores but that he's going to do something stupid just like the ten thousand times before and leave Dena alone. The thought of a cold one is nice. It'd be nice to just have one and relax. But he's never known what it's like to have just one and probably never will.

He rubs his eyes and sips on his Coke and wonders about lunch when his phone rings. He quickly opens the cell phone. "Dena, where you been? I've tried calling you half a dozen times."

"Lex?"

For a moment he can't say anything, and he turns because it's as if the voice is just behind him, taunting him. Haunting him.

"Lex, is that you?"

"Laila?"

"It's really you."

"My God, Laila, where are you?"

"I'm in trouble."

Lex marvels at how prayers can be answered. Rather than finding her, she's found him.

"Let me come get you," he tells her.

"No. I just—how are things back home? I'm worried."

"Where are you right now?"

"That doesn't matter."

"Yeah, it matters a lot. You need to come home."

"How's Papa?"

"Laila—it's been four years, right?"

"Tell me."

"It's complicated. It's been—a lot has happened that you need to know about and I can't just—I'm not going to just tell you on the phone."

"I need to know." Her voice is vulnerable, and he can almost hear the ache throughout it.

"I'm lookin' for you—you know that?"

"What do you mean?"

"I'm in Chicago. Or I was. Laila, what have you been up to? What sort of men you been hangin' around?"

"What kind of question is that?"

"I got another hundred where that one came from."

"Lex, how is my father?"

Lex doesn't say anything for a moment. He can't help the emotions building inside. All this silence, and then suddenly out of the blue he gets this.

He forces himself to calm down. "Look, just tell me where you are, and I can make sure that ... hey, you still there?"

He calls out her name but doesn't hear anything.

The line is dead.

He curses and looks at the caller ID.

The number is unfamiliar.

He calls back, but the phone just rings and rings.

After a few minutes, he calls information and asks what area code 864 is. Then he finishes up his drink and leaves a few dollars on the table.

With the cell phone in his hand, he leaves the restaurant and knows where he needs to go.

He at least knows where she's at. For now.

All he has to do is buy a map and figure out where Greenville, South Carolina is.

As he climbs into the car and starts it, another thought enters his mind.

Maybe Laila wants him to know where she is. Without having to tell him.

Maybe this is her cry for help.

9

My sister was the firstborn I could never live up to. And my brother was the rebel I could never outdo. I was stuck in the middle zone—the dead zone as I called it—where I couldn't do any better or any worse. I couldn't do anything, not in my father's eyes.

Perhaps I was misguided like most kids growing up. I never doubted that my father loved me. But he also didn't know what to do with me. Ava had her place in this life. She was smart and strong and knew where she wanted to go even when she was ten. Lex had his place too ("behind bars" as Papa said many times). But I was the odd one out, the piece that didn't quite fit the puzzle, the one that my mother would have had a handle on if she had stayed alive.

My father never remarried. Talk of remarriage or even dating again became almost as taboo as talking about my mother. I hated the silence. I hated living with elephants in the room, day after day. I hated going on with this shadow over my soul that could never go away. The sun was always there, but I could never see it for the troubling, damning shadows.

When I won that first contest, I was heading into eighth grade. What did I know of the rest of the world? All I knew was there was more out there and I wanted to find it, that I wanted to get away from the dust and the dirt of Texas and find my place.

I always believed my place was never stuck in Brady,

Broken

Texas. That it wasn't stuck between Ava and Lex. That it wasn't stuck in the middle of nowhere doing something simple and easy.

I wanted to see the big world.

I guess I eventually grew disappointed at how small and simple the world really is.

The front of the car scrapes against the curb, and the front door opens. James doesn't care that it's parked sideways across three spaces in front of the motel. Nobody's here anyway. He takes out the key card, swipes it a couple of times, and enters the room. For a moment the chaos makes him think it's a dead body folded into the sheets of the bed. Then the half-naked figure moves, and a bruised and bloodied face stares at him.

"You're supposed to be gone," James says.

Her mouth opens and tears into a scream.

"Shut up," he tells her, but instead she stands up on the bed and lunges toward him. Before he can get her off him, she bites him on the arm.

Cursing, James pivots his arm and pounds her in the head with his elbow. Her mouth stretches open, spitting blood over the bed. She begins to howl as she notices the blood. He then sees her back, the cuts in them, the gashes.

"Stupid broad."

He goes into the bathroom and turns on the light. Several damp towels are on the floor. The bath is wet with blood. The toilet is clogged with something.

"What are you still doing here?" James asks. "I thought I told you to get out of here. But you didn't listen, huh? And this is what you get."

Her eyes are rolling back, and he knows this is bad.

James looks for clothes and finds some jeans. It takes him a few minutes to get them on her. She is skinny from drugs, and her dull blonde hair color is showing its truth in the roots. He can't see her face for all the blood.

He finds a T-shirt that must belong to her and he slips it on her. The logo across it says "Yum-Yum Donuts."

"Let's get going." He tries to get her to stand.

"Sickos. Perverts. Nothin' but a bunch of perverts."

"Would you stop it and just stand?"

"You did this to me."

"Oh yeah? Really? You want me to finish it? Huh? Get up. Now."

She has her eyes closed and can't stand on her own. She's lost a lot of blood. She's already pale, but she's turning a bit grayish and deathly.

For a moment he thinks of the final days living with his mother, of her increasing dementia and how every day was something he needed to clean up after. The memory jars him into action.

James hoists her over his shoulder, brings her out, and props her up against the car. He opens the door and drops her down in the passenger seat and doesn't care that her head falls forward against the dash. He looks around, but doesn't see any trace of life. He goes back in the motel and finds everything there is to find. With two suitcases and the duffle bag filled, he drives off.

He starts to dial a number and then stops and shuts his phone.

"Where's the nearest hospital?"

What comes out of her mouth in response can't be English.

"Tell me again. Point. Which way?"

The woman grabs his arm, but she's too weak to do anything.

"Look, lady, I'm going to save your life here, so just tell me where you can get a little medical attention. You lost a lot of blood and are still losing it."

She mumbles something.

"Is that really the way you talk? Speak English. Come on."

She says something else. He vaguely can make out what she's

saying underneath a drawl that sounds like a combination of trailer trash and redneck.

After ten minutes of her pointing and yelling and hitting him, he finally makes it to some hospital.

"Get out."

She curses at him and slaps his face, and he grabs her bone-like forearm and pulls her close to him.

"You do that again and so help me I'll keep driving, then I'll drop you off the end of a very long and very high cliff. Get out."

He opens the door and watches her stumble out of the car. The back of her T-shirt is bloody. He finds her purse and tosses it out, then he closes the door and keeps driving.

Just as he's about to stop and find out where he is, the phone rings.

Things would be so much easier if he wasn't such a nice guy.

•   •   •

Laila is not really sure where she's going. She's left one state behind, and she's close to leaving another. But after driving for more than an hour and getting off at three different exits first for gas, another to use the restroom, and the third just to confirm that nobody is following her — it still doesn't mean she won't be followed. James found her down in Greenville and revealed he was Connor's brother. A part of her still doesn't believe it, yet she knows anything is possible. All she wants is to be left alone and to leave everyone behind.

The sun is starting to set, and she knows she better find a place to stay for the night. The thought of driving all night worries her. She did that before and almost wrecked her car twice falling asleep. She told herself she would never do that again. But some things in life are hard to avoid.

She's well into Tennessee, past Knoxville and not sure which direction she wants to go. She just needs to get away. She doesn't want to go back north. That's all she knows.

Laila examines the list of lodging preferences at each exit. At this point it doesn't matter. Nobody is going to know whether she gets off on exit 112 or 122.

A sign saying Apple Ridge Farm Bed and Breakfast looks fine. It's probably a house run by a retired couple trying to earn some extra bucks.

For a moment, after parking the car and stretching and getting her backpack, Laila wonders if anybody is here. The sky is a deep orange glow. She knocks on the front door of a two-story log cabin. There's no doorbell. She tries a couple of times, standing there on a wide porch with faded, splintering wood. Then she starts to walk away.

The sound of the door opening makes her turn.

"Sorry, honey. You coulda just come on in. The door's unlocked."

"I wasn't sure if anybody was home."

"My, aren't you a lovely one?" The gray-haired woman barely comes to Laila's shoulders. "Lookin' for a room?"

"If you have one."

"We have two suites. Haven't been too busy. Not in these times anyway. You haven't stayed with us before, have you?"

"No. But it looks lovely."

"Come on in, and we'll make you feel at home."

Laila smiles, smelling baked apples as she enters. She can't help looking behind her for a moment, at the driveway where her car is parked. Then she shuts the door and lets out a deep sigh.

The bed is comfortable, but she can't sleep. The windows don't have blinds, and they let in the harsh light of the moon. The cold, blue glow streaks across the wooden floor. She's in one of the two bedrooms in the suite upstairs. It has a name she's already forgotten and includes a private bathroom and sitting area in the loft. Laila stares at the wall and sees the outline of a framed portrait of the farm.

It's warm, but she doesn't want to open the windows. She locked the door even though she would hear someone coming up the old, creaky stairs. Laila knows she shouldn't feel frightened, yet another part of her tells her that fear is what's keeping her alive and has been ever since killing Connor Brennan six months ago.

The couple's last name is Simon, and they fit their B & B. Sometimes back in the city she would wonder if there really were people out there in the "heartland" who had a truly simplistic life. Where each day was just like the last. Where they weren't wired and plugged in. Where they prayed before each meal and went to church and had Bible verses hanging up on the walls. Where they didn't know the latest brand of clothing or cologne or club to hang out in. Where family meant everything and even a distant stranger off the street could be made to feel at home at their table.

The Simons were pleasant enough to share a piece of pie and coffee with her and to have conversation but not pry. The little lady seemed to know that's one thing you didn't do with guests. They could both probably tell that Laila was tired and in no mood to talk. She had gone upstairs early even though she wasn't ready to sleep.

The creak in the floor startles her. She sighs, knowing it's just the house stretching.

Laila thinks of the past day, of the past week, of the man who just showed up. She thinks of Kyle and of all the things she could have said to him and maybe should have said to him, especially before leaving. There wasn't any apologetic e-mail left behind. No heartfelt note. No simple card.

She left and it was that simple and easy.

As Laila finally closes her eyes with her mind still doing somersaults, she feels the hand.

It's warm and strong and soft and it touches her leg.

She's under the covers yet feels the touch on her bare calf.

Laila jerks up, bends her knees, and rips off the light covers. She stares at the edge of the bed. The mattress is bathed in cold blue.

Her heart pounds away.

She takes her hand and slides it against the sheet to see if there is anything there. An animal. Maybe a cat or a dog. But even as she does so, she knows it wasn't an animal that touched her. She knows the feeling of a hand on her leg. Touching it, nudging it almost like someone might do when waking someone.

She carefully steps on the floor. The bed is an older type with the bedspring several inches off the floor, wheels on each side, and a dark opening underneath.

For a moment she hesitates. Then Laila gets on her knees, and she looks under the bed.

She can't see or hear anything.

She stands up and turns on the light and examines the room for a few minutes. Then she sees a slight image of herself in one of the windows. The T-shirt and the shorts and the outline.

There is a closet in the corner of this mostly white room, which she opens. It smells musty and is mostly empty, with an extra pillow and some extra sheets and an ironing board.

The door whines as it closes. She sits on the bed and examines the bottom where her feet had been lying.

She stretches out her legs and looks at them. She had forgotten how pale she is. Normally around this time of year she is dark from being in the sun by the beach or the pool.

She rubs her ankle and knows.

What she felt was real, as crazy as it might sound.

It felt as real as her hand does now.

In her dream Laila parks outside the big mansion hidden behind trees and a stone gate. She pulls up to the sweeping driveway with floodlights blinding the cold night and feels the wind against her face. Her coat doesn't keep her warm. Neither does the tiny skirt and low top she's wearing underneath. She goes to the door and rings the doorbell and waits for a long time.

Then it opens, and she sees him.

She sees that face. She sees the sneer. She sees the eyes that already start undressing her even as she stands outside in her long overcoat in the howling wind.

Broken

"You're the first to arrive," he says as he lets her in.

She can hear his breathing behind her as he takes off her coat.

Laila can smell the liquor on his breath as he curses in astonishment at what he's seeing.

She can feel the scratch of his beard as his eager mouth finds her neck.

And she suddenly knows what he's thinking when she hears him say these words.

"There'll be more coming in a little while. Wait till they get a look at you."

She really isn't there, she really never was there, she really can't be, can she?

And then something snaps and something whispers inside of her and it's the first time she's heard a voice this distinct.

You need to get out of here, Laila.

She needs to get out as soon as possible. Because this is going to end badly, and there is no hope outside of this house unless she leaves now.

"Go to sleep."

Laila jerks awake again and sits up and looks around the room.

"Who's there?" she asks.

But it doesn't respond.

Her head against the pillow, her eyes wide open, she thinks of the boat named *Precious* and of riding on Lake Michigan and she remembers how Tyler used to hold her hand.

She lies awake and thinks of this for a very long time.

•   •   •

Lex is sleeping in his car, his head leaning on his palm, when the grating at the door stirs him. His eyes open, but his mind is slow to follow. The lights of the rest stop in front of him glow but don't reveal anybody around. He glances out the window at nothing but empty parking spaces.

The sound comes again. It's like someone or something is brushing up against the car.

Then he hears the handle fumbling up and down. Someone is trying to get in his car.

He checks that the locks are secure.

Scanning all sides of his car, he doesn't see anybody.

The handle keeps banging away, the intruder wanting in.

He starts his car and then slowly rolls down his window. He probably shouldn't, but he wants to know who is doing this.

He peers over his window but doesn't see anybody.

"Who's there?"

Then he hears footsteps scampering away. Light, steady, fast.

Lex opens the door and steps out but can barely feel his legs from sitting so long.

He doesn't see anybody as he moves around the car.

Nobody.

Not a sound or a sight.

Then something comes from behind him. Something high and light.

A creepy little laugh.

He turns around but doesn't see anybody. It's warm outside, and the back of his shirt is damp with sweat. It's late — maybe close to midnight.

"Hello?"

He hears cicadas droning away in the nearby woods, an occasional semi on the freeway he's alongside. The Kentucky night is humid, the sky clear.

He thinks of another night more than a decade ago. Another hot summer night when he found himself in a car waiting.

"Not now," he tells himself.

He gets in the car and quickly pulls away. Time to keep looking.

Even if he doesn't really know what he'll do once he finds her.

10

Sometimes, in my dreams, you are there. In a desert, flat and dry and endless, I see your shape. A figure walking toward me. Walking toward me with water. And I'm so scared and I shake and yet you come up to me and hold my hand and tell me it's going to be okay. And I stop shaking and I look into your eyes but they look just like mine. It terrifies me.

Because the eyes start to bleed.

And then I see that they're empty holes.

Y ou had a young lady spend the night here last night."

"Why yes."

"Any idea where she might have went?"

"No."

James looks down at the bob of a hairdo and the smile caked in wrinkles. The woman tries to look out past him to the parking lot, but he moves to prevent her.

"Can I have a look where she stayed last night?"

"Is something wrong?"

He looks at the woman. He examines the eyes. Then he releases a smile and extends his hands.

"No, nothing wrong. It's just—Laila is a dear friend. And we're planning a getaway. I want it to be a surprise. But I have a feeling she's trying to plan a surprise on me."

"How romantic."

"Yes. Well, she's really the romantic one. I'm just trying to keep up with her."

"She didn't mention anything about that this morning at breakfast."

"Did she mention anything—anything that might be helpful?"

"No. Just that she was passing by." The woman stops and smiles. "And to tell anybody that might come looking for her that they can just forget about her. That she's long gone."

James realizes the old woman is a far better actor than he is. He no longer carries the forced smile on his face. "Let me see her room."

"Well, I still have to—"

"I want to see it now."

"Okay," she says. "Follow me."

There is nothing in the room that's been left behind. Nothing of interest. Even though James knows he's not going to lose her, he still wants to know where she's headed.

The more information he knows, the better it will be when he reaches her.

"You have a phone in here?" he eventually asks.

"No."

"Do you remember—did she use your phone at all?"

"Why would she do that?"

"Just answer the question."

"No."

"What about a cell phone. Did you see one on her? Did you see her use one?"

"She had very little on her."

He sighs and curses and looks around the room.

"Why are you looking for her?" the old woman asks.

"Did she take her car when she left?"

"She sure didn't leave it here. Hey—what do you want with her?"

James just ignores her and heads back downstairs.

Broken

When he gets in the car, he dials the phone.

"That was useless. Utterly useless like this whole trip."

But he listens to the instructions and says yeah a few times and it all sounds so easy. Just like everything. Everything was supposed to be so easy, but Laila didn't take the bait when she was supposed to.

"I'm done chasing and playing games," he says in the phone. "When I catch up to her, I'm through with all this. This was supposed to be easy. She was supposed to be easy. If I find her, I'm going to make it easy again."

•   •   •

Laila has been driving since the morning. She passed the exits for Nashville half an hour ago and finally decides she's driven far enough to stop. More than anything, she wants to get out of the car and rest. She's driving west, but beyond that doesn't have any idea where she's going.

She finds a fast-food restaurant and barely eats a chicken sandwich. She sits outside and warms herself in the sun. It feels good against her bare arms and legs. Her feet are bare, and she reminds herself that she needs to purchase something besides sandals, which aren't the best to drive or walk around in. This makes her think of other things she needs, but then she glances at the car and knows it holds everything she owns. They could bury her with all her possessions. And maybe that's the way life should be.

The Honda CR-V still has the new-car smell inside it. She purchased it in Greenville just a month ago, just as she was thinking her life was moving ahead. Perhaps not moving. But she was standing up on her own two legs and finally ready to start moving. All before the past showed up on her doorstep.

She glances at the car.

"Alabaster Silver Metallic," she says.

It can't be called just silver. Of course not. Now paint colors for cars had three-word definitions. But silver is silver.

She thinks of what's in the car. The only things she really cares about are the photos she's carried with her since leaving Brady, their meaning continuing to grow as the years go by. In New York she had several thousand shots that she left in an instant. Many of them her, many of them her with the beautiful people, with celebrities and friends. She had photo albums and framed shots and magazine covers and pictures shot by the big-name photographers. But none of those meant anything. Not like the dozen or so she still had—some of them folded, some of them blurry, some of them really bad outtakes. The other shots were all part of the fallacy and the façade. But these pictures were real.

For a moment Laila thinks of the pictures she left behind in Chicago. Those were left for a different reason. Different but the same.

The pictures she still has are all that matter. They are a piece of life reminding her of her humanity.

And along with those pictures, she has the handgun Kyle's cousin loaned to her. It's hers now. One day she'll send Kyle some money for it.

She scans the parking lot and sees a family going into the Wendy's. The father and mother hold the hands of the two-year-old girl. Laila watches this and knows there is some meaningful and melancholy thought attached to this image somewhere deep inside her, but she has managed to keep it down in the hidden well far underneath the grime and the gunk in the seeping waters of yesterday. There is no emotion swelling inside of her. She knows what the picture is and what it could mean. To her it's just a picture of another life and another existence. The same way that family might look at a fashion magazine and see an image that is real but which is a pure fantasy, a delusion, a fairy tale.

The fantasy and fairy tale do exist. But they come with a price.

She glances at her watch and isn't sure why. It's not the time that bothers her. It's the nagging feeling that if she stays still for too long, someone will catch up to her. So she gets back in the SUV encased in Alabaster Silver Metallic paint and starts it up.

Broken

It's just a moment.

A second in the span of twenty-seven years.

Back on the road, she switches to the left lane and rolls to a stop at a red light. As she waits to drive down the street a hundred yards or so and turn onto the exit to the interstate, she glances at the car next to her.

And sees him.

The face of death. With blood still on it. The same lifeless, soulless eyes staring at her. The gashes still there from her nails. His teeth smiling. His hand waving.

Laila turns around and then looks again at the car next to her. It's him. It's the pale figure of Connor resting behind a wheel waving and leering at her.

She jams her foot on the gas and heads out without looking.

A car horn blares next to her as a vehicle veers out of the intersection to avoid her.

She continues ahead and looks in her mirror to see the car.

But she can't see it.

On the interstate, driving ninety miles an hour, she tries to slow down her breathing. She puts a hand on her chest and can feel the beating.

She shakes her head and tries to wave this off.

She didn't just see that.

She imagined it just like the other things she's imagined.

Yet she continues to look in her mirror at the cars she passes and at the seat behind her.

Just in case.

•　　•　　•

"Is this Kyle Ewing?"

"Yeah."

"Kyle, my name is Lex Torres. I'm Laila's brother."

There is silence, and Lex asks if he's still there.

"What's this about?"

"I got some information from the bank that said you recently saw Laila."

"Who told you that?"

"I'm just looking for my sister. She called me yesterday and sounded like she was in trouble."

"I don't know anything about that."

"Is there a chance we could just talk?"

"No."

"That was quick."

"Why do you want to talk?"

"I just want to see if you know anything about where she might be."

"I don't have a clue."

"Is she in trouble?"

"How do I know this is really her brother?"

"If we meet, I can prove it to you."

"I bet you can."

"No, look, I'm serious," Lex says.

"I just — I don't know anything about her, okay? She works at the bank. That's all I know. And she was supposed to come in to work today, and she didn't. Did you try her apartment?"

"Yes. Nobody's there."

"Well, then you can wait for her. I'm sure she'll be coming back anytime."

Lex listens to the silence that follows and clicks off his cell.

Getting to this point was really easy, a lot easier than Lex thought it would be. He tracked the number she had called him from to her apartment, where he spoke to the manager. The guy let him into her apartment, but they didn't find much. It looked like she had taken off with the few things she brought here. Besides discovering that she worked at the bank, Lex didn't gain any more insight on where Laila might be or why she was in Greenville in the first place.

The people at the bank had offered no other clues except for a

Broken

name—Kyle Ewing. Now, waiting in darkness in Laila's apartment, Lex tries to picture his sister here. There's an empty smell to this place, as if there were no meals cooked here, no visitors let in, no pets running around, no life lived. The manager said she had paid in advance for a year, yet it doesn't look like this place has been occupied for even a month.

"What are you running from?" he asks as he stares at the blank walls in the blank bedroom.

There are some clothes still here. Outfits that don't seem to fit her, or more like common outfits that don't seem natural on someone so uncommon, but he guesses they're for work. The other things are even less revealing than what he found in Chicago. Some books from the library, none of which have any significance: a little booklet on Greenville, a couple books on New Orleans, a few novels. He doesn't find any fashion magazines or other signs from that life.

The alarm clock looks like it might have been bought at a Wal-Mart for ten bucks. The same goes for the iron on the creaky wood floor.

The phone in the apartment rings, and he picks it up. He listens for a moment and doesn't hear a voice. Rather he hears a grinding drone. It seems to get louder as he listens, so he clicks off the line. There is no caller ID on the phone.

Lex checks his cell, then walks out of the bedroom, needing to get out of this place for a moment.

As he walks he hears something behind him.

It sounds like laughter.

The same laughter he heard back at the rest stop.

His skin feels electric, and he can almost feel something vibrating in the air.

Lex turns around and calls out to see if anybody is there, then goes back into the bedroom and turns on the light.

"Hello?"

The sound is gone. He wonders if he heard someone in an

apartment next door. But he hadn't heard a thing sitting in silence just a few minutes ago.

On a whim he checks the bathroom. And when he turns on the light, he jerks back.

There's something written on the mirror facing him in bloodred. It's a message in lipstick. One that wasn't here when he first got here.

Follow Kyle

That's all it says.

He looks around the bathroom, but no one is there. He touches the lipstick, and it smears on the mirror. He's not imagining this.

For a moment he wonders if he had missed that, but he knows he didn't.

"Hello?"

It's stupid, really, saying this to the nothingness in this place. But he doesn't know what else to do, and talking and hearing his own voice strangely helps.

He searches the apartment again to see if anybody is there.

The longer he looks, the more tense he feels. Lex suddenly grows cold, feels bumps rise on his arms, and knows he needs to get out of here. There's nothing here anyway except echoes of emptiness.

He closes the bathroom door and ignores the message's advice.

He's not thinking of who wrote it.

Part of him doesn't want to know.

11

When you lose hope, you let yourself go. You fall. And whatever warm, numbing, freeing place you land, you let be.

Hope.

Hope is a dangerous thing in these times.

It's an illusion. A painted picture framed and mounted and hidden under glass and protected by armed security. It's not for people like me.

Hope is a promise that can't be fulfilled.

Hope is a pipe dream.

Hope is a person I killed, who will haunt my days and drain my nights.

Hope is pathetic, because it is not and will not and never will be.

How's the progress of your little quest?"

"It's only Tuesday, and I told you—"

"I don't care what you did or didn't tell me, James. Why do I get the feeling things aren't working out the way they should be?"

"I don't know. You tell me."

"You know what I'm thinking?"

"I'm sure you're gonna tell me."

"I'm thinking you might need a little help. I'm thinking you might need a little motivation."

James curses. "I've got enough motivation to last me a lifetime."

"Then how come you let her go?"

James shifts his head and scans the parking lots of the gas station.

"You watching me?"

"Everybody is watching everybody, James."

"I told you I needed another week."

"Time is ticking away."

"Yeah, and I'm wasting it talking to you."

"I don't have much confidence in you."

"You wanna come down and do it yourself, fine."

"No. This isn't fine. You've left me in a mess, and the last thing I want to do is micromanage here. I'm tired of this."

"And you think I'm not?"

"That is not the point. However you might feel or whatever you might think is not the point. That's what you're missing. You came to me, remember? You came to me because you were in trouble, right? Because you needed help. And did I not help you out?"

"I never said you didn't."

"But that means you don't have a say anymore. It means you are the one that owes me. And I was reasonable with you. The people I deal with aren't reasonable, James. And just because your mother and my mother are sisters doesn't give you the right to disrespect me."

"I'm not disrespecting anybody."

"You're not going to run off on me, are you?"

"I wouldn't do that," he says.

"I used to think that. But nowadays a businessman doesn't know what to think."

"Get over yourself, Danny."

"I'm being serious."

"Since when were you a 'businessman'? You're not Donald Trump."

The man on the other end launches into a nasty tirade. James can picture the taut veins in Danny's neck as he curses. The guy is younger than him but has the audacity to act like this.

Broken

"Do I still have a week?"

"Less," Danny says.

"Good. I'll get you your money."

"I want you to report every day. Every morning and every afternoon and every evening."

"I'm busy, okay?"

"And I'm busy too, keeping you alive. And you've got only a little more time or you're gonna join your brother in hell, James."

•   •   •

Laila takes an exit an hour south of Memphis already into Mississippi and pulls off at the first hotel she finds. She knows she needs to stop and breathe and figure out where she's going. This looks like as good a place as any to do so.

She's been here before. Many times before.

The room on the third floor with the two double beds resembles any other hotel.

Laila locks the door, then sits on the edge of the bed facing the window. Outside she can see the tops of trees just beyond the parking lot and the hovering sun fading behind them.

She could be in any state. It doesn't matter.

They all feel the same.

She stretches out and feels the rough surface of the hotel comforter against her face as she closes her eyes.

She kisses him, but something in the way he kisses makes her pull back. She glances at him but only sees a stranger's eyes. They bore into her.

"What?"

But he keeps kissing her as if he's trying to devour her. Everything is more rushed, rough, and she starts to shake.

"Ben, what's with you?"

Something on his face is off. Something on it scares her.

"Say something," she tells him.

"I love you."

She closes her eyes and kisses him and feels a little better, and then she hears the knock.

His expression changes.

She sees it and suddenly she knows.

Something bad is about to happen.

Nobody should be knocking at the door.

Nobody knows the two of them are here in this motel room.

He is wired and tense. And he glances and smirks, and she knows.

Ben is not surprised at the knock on the door.

"What are you doing?" she asks.

But Ben just smiles, and she suddenly realizes she doesn't know this boy and that she's never really known him and that she's alone here and can't do a thing.

She sees the phone but can't make it there in time.

She turned off her cell.

He drove the car to this place.

Nobody knows she's here.

"Hey, man," a voice says.

Two figures walk into the room.

And when she sees their faces and sees Ben's face, she knows.

She wants to scream but nobody is going to hear.

She swallows, but her mouth is numb and her throat is dry and her lips itch like they've kissed the devil himself.

She closes her eyes but knows she can't leave.

When Laila wakes up, it's dark. The blinds are still open, and she looks outside. She sees a couple of restaurants and a gas station along with the passing lights of vehicles on the interstate. She can see her faint reflection in the glass and shuts the blinds to get rid of it.

"You need to get a grip and figure out what's going on."

Broken

Laila touches the phone on the desk, lets her hand stay on the receiver, then lets it go.

On the edge of the bed, she thinks through her options. Something keeps gnawing at her, and she doesn't have to think hard on it. She knows where she wants to go. She will leave tomorrow and keep driving until she gets there.

She glances at the phone again. She stares at it as if waiting for it to speak, as if it's going to spring up and coil around her neck and strangle her.

•   •   •

There is something in the apartment with him. Not someone, but something. Something that reminds him of his teenage days and nights, of the things he sometimes saw, the manifestations in the heart of the depths of the desert. He thinks of Aunt Maxie and of the voodoo magic she often talked about with such fondness.

"Get away from me, Satan," Lex says again.

He knows that he is safe from harm, that nothing can happen to him outside of God's control. But that doesn't mean he is safe from fear.

And even perhaps from pain.

The sounds started at midnight. The first came in the form of a bouncing ball, a basketball, pounding on the floor of the kitchen. Lex woke up and jumped out of the bed and went in to turn on the light, only to find nothing. This happened again with the sound of laughter. And then with the sound of fireworks going off.

Each time he went outside the room to see if someone was there. With the last, Lex could smell and taste the scent the firecrackers left behind.

Yet he still found nothing. No visible proof of anything in Laila's apartment.

He kneels at the edge of his bed with his head propped against it, and he does all he knows to do. He has been deep in prayer this entire trip, but now more than ever.

As he prays, the handle on the door turns.

"God, help me. Deliver me from this darkness, Lord."

The door swings open and slams against the wall. Lex looks at the entryway but doesn't see anything.

He hears the sound of spraying and then smells the fumes.

"What..."

Lex goes to the doorway and walks into the bare room outside the bedroom. The scent of fresh paint burns at his nose.

He turns.

In various colors and sizes, a message is painted across the blank wall.

"Follow him," it says, over and over and over again.

Lex walks up to the wall and touches it. Red paint rubs off on his finger.

He smells it.

It's real.

He shakes his head and walks back into the bedroom. It's almost one in the morning.

He gets his bag and decides to get out of this apartment.

He knows there are other things out there that are not of this world. And even though he is no longer a slave of them, it doesn't mean he doesn't have the sense to avoid them when they're running rampant.

12

Words have a freeing power to them. Almost as if they can take the blame and the guilt and the pain when written down. I write these words in this journal for no one but myself. For no eyes to see. I think that I ultimately write them for you. And to you.

It helps a little. But I know they can't atone. I know they can't amend. I know they will never ever make up for my mistakes.

I write because sometimes they bubble up inside and boil over and the only thing I can do—that I can possibly do—is write them down.

How I long to know what it would be like to take these confessions and bundle them up and leave them at someone's door.

What do you mean it's not working?"

"I swiped it twice and put in the numbers, and it still doesn't work."

James looks at the pimply kid and wants to yank that look off his teenage face.

"Try again."

The boy tries again in a way that looks like he's sleepwalking. Then he shakes his head slowly and gives the card back to him.

"You got any cash? It's just four bucks."

He's going to say something but then doesn't. James grits his teeth, then walks outside the gas station and spits on the ground.

It's the middle of the night, and he's starving. And he doesn't even have enough money to get some crackers and a soda.

Sitting on the curb, James curses. He needs a drink. Or maybe he needs a little more. Just a little taste. It's been a couple of years and that was why he got into this mess in the first place, but now with his head hurting and the voices whipping back up in a hurricane, he knows a little taste would calm him and help him think more clearly.

With a sigh, he opens his phone and makes a call.

He doesn't want to, but he has to.

"We have to go to plan B," he says.

"What exactly is plan B?"

James curses again. "Do I need to think of everything here?"

"What should we do then?"

James sighs and moves his boot over the gravel in the parking lot. He thinks for a moment, then tells him what they're going to do.

He speaks slowly and carefully.

This wasn't going to be part of the plan, but right now he doesn't have a choice.

Nothing's been part of the plan for a very, very long time.

"Will it work?" he asks James.

"Just trust me, okay? Two more days of this, then I'm done. Two more and that's it."

James hangs up the phone and listens to the cars passing on the interstate nearby. He thinks of the words he just said and realizes he's been saying that for the last two years. And really he's been saying that for the last two decades.

"I'll never be done."

No matter what he does and what he says and what he plans, he knows the same devil chasing him will be there, right beside him, right there to warm his cheek with that nice little grin.

Broken

• • •

The tongue licks her forehead, and that's when Laila awakes in a scream.

She blinks her eyes but remains still.

Then she hears it.

The laugh.

A hellish, deep laugh from right next to her.

And as she goes to move, something holds her back. An arm bears down on her chest.

She smells something foul. Something unlike she's ever smelled before. And in the darkness she can make out a figure sitting on her bed. She starts to scream again, but a hand like sandpaper cups her mouth and forces her wail to wilt away.

"Shut your mouth," the voice breathes on her.

Laila tries to reach out, but her arm just touches the darkness. For a moment she wonders if she's dreaming this, but she's feeling light-headed from the hand restricting her from breathing. She lies still and mumbles okay over and over, and he releases his grip.

"You can't run away from me," he says.

Even in the darkness she knows it's him. It's Connor. The same voice and the same stench and the same everything.

"What do you want?"

"I don't want anything. Not anymore. You took it all away, you piece of trash."

His outline in the darkness just sits there. A hand finds its way over her skin and wanders.

Laila shivers.

"You don't get it, do you?" he says.

"What?"

"I'm not here for anything. Except to hurt you."

He laughs and clutches her, and she tries to pull his hand away but can't.

He reaches up to squeeze the bones in her face.

"There are things I want to do — that I want to do so badly but I can't. That doesn't mean I'm done with you."

She shivers. "Please..."

"Please what? Please don't hurt you?"

The grip tightens and compresses, and she howls in pain. Her skull feels like it's bending.

"Don't kill you? Why would I want to do that? Why, Laila? Maybe because that's what you did to me? Leaving me shot and bleeding to death in a house that wasn't even my own? Leaving me for the others to find so weak and pathetic and sick and twisted. You little — piece — of — garbage."

He presses down, and then he finally lets go of her. His shadow changes, and she sees him slightly bent over, his hands tightening.

The ghost moves back toward her.

"You owe me and you owe my family and there is only one way to get rid of me."

"How? What? What do you want?"

"You know and don't tell me you're too stupid to figure it out."

His lips touch her cheek, her neck, her chest. Then he whispers back in her ear.

"Don't make me keep coming back because who knows what I'll do next. I have ideas. Oh, do I have ideas and...oh, what I can do with them."

With that he puts something against her face that feels like a cloth, and she gags and cries out again but then suddenly feels everything leak out and away toward black.

The smell of chlorine wrings her nose. She feels blurry and smothered as she adjusts her body and sits up to find herself looking at a blank stone wall that stands above a pool. The lights bear down, and she looks out the window and sees that night is still around, and then she looks back down at the pool. Something smoky spreads out from the middle of the water.

Groggy, she stands and feels nauseous. Her throat tightens, and she dry heaves a few times, getting control and walking over to the pool.

She looks around and can't see anyone.

In the center of the pool something black and wet floats. Like a round mass. And all around it seeps blood.

For a moment she thinks she sees someone's face. But that's her imagination. She sees the wavy flakes of hair on the surface of the water.

It's an animal in the pool.

It looks like a big dog. Too small to be anything bigger than a dog.

The blood looks fresh, like it was just cut and is still bleeding.

Her eyelids are heavy, and her legs weak. She glances around the pool again, swaying a bit and seeing the clear water a little too close.

Then she hears the voice. Calling out to her.

She shakes her head and looks where it came from.

A figure is at a doorway. Standing. Waving.

She rubs her eyes and walks toward the doorway. The door is propped open with something. She begins swaying toward it and leans toward the water and almost falls in. Then she feels the tug of something guiding her along, pulling her away from the liquid swishing next to her.

Laila reaches the doorway and sees the item holding the door open.

It's a heavy toy dump truck with big wheels.

She touches it to see if it's real and can feel the grooves in its side.

Laila walks down the hallway and ends up finding a sofa and sits there, still groggy and drained. She drifts off for a moment, awakened only by a woman's voice.

"Can I help you, ma'am?" she asks.

Laila stands. "I locked myself out of my room." She gives the woman her information in order to get a key.

A clock on the wall says it's three thirty.

"Did anybody just come from the pool?"

The woman looks at her to see if she's drunk.

"Anybody?"

The woman only shakes her head.

Laila takes the key without thanking her and heads toward the elevator.

She presses the button and feels her stomach drop slightly as she moves upward.

•   •   •

"How's everything?"

"You know how everything is."

"Did she sleep much?"

"No. I was up all night."

"Sorry." Lex shifts in the seat of his car. He can smell the coffee in the holder.

"If you were sorry you'd come home."

"I can't, Dee."

"You told me. You promised me. You said you wouldn't take off again."

"This is different."

"Have you been drinking?"

"Why do you keep asking that?"

"Because you keep drinking."

"Not a drop."

"Promise?"

"I promise," Lex says.

"Promise on her."

"One promise should be enough."

"Not for you."

"There's stuff you don't understand," he says.

"Then help me understand."

"I will, but not like this."

"Then when?"

"When I find her."

Broken

"You're not going to find her, Lex. When will you get it into that skull of yours that Laila's gone? That she might as well be dead."

He curses at her, and then he pauses, apologizing.

"No need for that kinda language."

"Then don't go on like that."

"She's missing because she wants to be," Dena says.

"I'm going to find her."

"Probably shacking up with the devil himself."

"Stop it."

"That girl doesn't deserve to be found. What're you gonna do? Bring her home? Save her soul?"

"I can try."

"She needs to stay away. She's no good."

"So was I."

"God shined His face down on you."

"Yeah, I know," Lex says. "And I'm hoping He's got some more mercy to spare. That's why I'm here. That's why I'm going to find her."

"Heartache is all you're gonna find. Heartache and death."

13

When they raped me, it was really just two of them, the third just watching. I think Ben was scared. More scared than I was. In his mind he'd probably imagined something different. But when he heard my screams and saw my face, he couldn't do anything but watch with his mouth wide open. He couldn't do anything yet he couldn't look away. That taught me a lot. If only he could've done something. If only he could've tried and stopped them. But he looked and didn't stop looking, and I'll remember that look until the day I die.

Sleep stays away, so Laila eventually takes a shower and gets ready to leave around midmorning on the overcast day. She pays cash for the room and goes to the parking lot. She knows now where she's going to go, even if she has no idea what she's going to do when she arrives. But it doesn't matter now because Laila finds the tires slashed. Not one but all four of them on the Honda. Slashed and shredded. She glances around, but there's nobody nearby.

Somebody is surely watching. She knows this.

She waves her hand high and then tosses her bag back into the vehicle. She keeps walking across the small entrance road to the hotel to the fast-food restaurant. She's hungry and doesn't care who's watching or who slashed her tires. Perhaps the same person who slashed her tires slashed the throat or stomach of the animal in the swimming pool. Or perhaps that was all in her head just like the figure of Connor sitting on her bed and touching her.

Still able to order breakfast, Laila finds herself hungrier than she thought. She sits near a window periodically looking outside. An elderly couple sit across from her in what appears to be a morning ritual of biscuits and coffee and reading the morning paper. She watches them for a long time and finds herself smiling at them. In some ways the couple acts like little kids with their innocent, sweet conversation and their obliviousness to the rest of the restaurant.

The large coffee wakes her up but doesn't get rid of her headache. She sips it and tries to rework her plan.

She may be derailed for the moment, but it doesn't change where she's going.

She looks up at the sky and remembers another overcast day and a conversation.

A decade has passed and still she remembers like it was yesterday.

"I need your help."

Lex stares at her. "My help for what?"

"To know what to do."

"I don't know."

"Just tell me."

"Tell you what, Lai?" her brother says. "I don't have anything to tell you."

"What do you think?"

"I don't know. I honestly don't know."

"That doesn't help."

"I'm here, aren't I?"

"Yeah."

"Maybe I shouldn't go."

"Maybe."

"Tell me," Laila says.

"Tell you what?"

"Should we go back home?"

"I don't know, Laila. I don't. I don't know what to say."

"What about Ava?"

"She doesn't know."

"Nothing?"

"No. I told you."

"Maybe we should go home."

"If you want to."

"I don't know. I really don't."

"Laila—it'll be okay. Don't cry."

"I'm not crying."

"Okay."

A little while later she watches them hoist the CR-V onto the flatbed truck and then drive away. They tell her it will be a few hours, but it's already lunchtime. She doesn't want to stay at this hotel but has gotten a room just in case. The wind blows and storm clouds gather above her. There's a blue and yellow kite gliding above. She looks around to see who is holding it, but she can't see anybody.

For a few minutes she watches the kite. It dips and then takes a nosedive and lands in the field beyond her and the road.

She doesn't see anybody retrieve it.

Laila goes back into the hotel and knows it's time to make a call.

• • •

For the last twenty minutes, Lex has watched as Kyle loads up his small car with a suitcase and a couple of duffle bags. He's inside the apartment now, and Lex is still waiting, ready to follow if necessary. His gas tank is full, and he's had enough sleep and coffee to make him wide awake even if his back is sore from sleeping in the car.

He knows what he heard and what he saw in the apartment, and he knows he needs to follow the man. It's the only chance he might have to find Laila.

Kyle eventually gets into his Toyota and drives off. Lex follows him and nearly misses getting on I-85 when Kyle does. He sees that they're heading south toward Atlanta.

Maybe Kyle knows something he doesn't. Greenville was a lost cause, and the only nugget of hope he has is this guy suddenly getting away.

If this proves to be nothing, then he'll go back to Texas and his family. At least he'll be able to tell himself he tried, and if he sees Laila again one day, he'll be able to tell her the truth that he finally decided to go find her and reach out even though it might be too late.

14

What is real beauty?

The question is a cliché used a hundred or a thousand times before in commercials and ads and slogans and billboards. But the question is still one I've asked again and again.

Studying the photos, glancing at the ads, looking at the images.

I remember one of my teachers in seventh or eighth grade sitting me down for a nice chat. She was probably early thirties, but to me she was old. I'd been goofing off and being rebellious, and she pulled me aside and told me to stop the nonsense. And then she told me something that has stayed with me ever since.

"Your beauty is going to get you a lot of things in this life, Laila, but don't let it define you. Don't let it change who you are on the inside."

Sometimes, after winning the model competition and heading off to New York City and being in ad after ad and being touted as this kind of girl or that kind of girl, I'd think about that teacher's words. I don't even remember her name, but I remember her words. I would recall them when the doors would open and when the smiles would come and when time after time after time, I would get my way.

I didn't take her advice.

Broken

Sometimes I forgot there was somebody inside to even concentrate on.

I was given so much and had the great opportunity to travel and see the world all because of the genes I was born with. It had nothing to do with my personality or my mind or my drive. It was the color of my eyes and the texture of my hair and the shape of my legs and the curl of my smile.

Over the years, I used every bit of those looks I could.

And over the years, I grew to detest them.

What is real beauty? I don't know. I don't know because I've seen so much ugliness I've forgotten where to even look. I'm oblivious to the beautiful things in this world. They're overshadowed by my dark deeds and my dark soul and all the darkness that follows me.

The beauty is broken with far too many pieces to pick back up.

James calls again but doesn't get anybody. He looks at his watch, then gets out of the car.

"Enough with this," he says.

He walks through the sliding glass doors of the hotel and past the lobby and the desk to the elevators. He goes to the third floor, then he finds her room.

He looks at his cell and then ignores it as his other hand finds the plastic key card. He swipes it and opens the door. It opens easily without catching on a bolt. James walks inside and closes the door.

Laila jumps out of bed and screams. He moves toward her and slaps her in the head hard enough to send her to the ground. He steps on her back and holds her down and tells her to be quiet. She's wearing jeans and a short-sleeved top. Dark hair spills out onto the floor and her back.

He lifts his foot and then backs up.

"Get up."

Laila gets on her knees and turns around, giving him a look that doesn't conceal anything.

"What are you gonna do?" he asks her. "Get up and sit in that chair."

She winces as she stands, and then she sits in the chair. For a few moments he examines the room.

"You're not very good at following orders."

"How did you find me?"

He smiles at her as he examines her purse. Nothing in there worth finding.

"You know how easy it is to track people these days? Things like GPS. They're simple and easy. You don't need to be James Bond to put one on somebody's car. We could track you all the way to Alaska."

James stares at her as she remains silent. "You're looking very pale, you know that?"

She curses at him.

"Just saying the obvious, lady."

James checks his cell phone again. Nothing. Then he holds it up to her face.

"See this thing? See this cell? You're going to make a call, and you're going to make it right now. And if you don't, the person on the other end of this phone is going to die. You understand me?"

Those eyes don't move off him.

"You're going to call your father and tell him that you're coming home to see him. That you're in a lot of trouble and that you need a lot of money. I know your family is loaded, and after all the time it took to find you, it was certainly well worth the wait. You're going to say that you're coming home and that you need a quarter of a million dollars and you need it by tomorrow. You got that? You tell him this and tell him that if this doesn't happen, you're going to die."

"Who says he's going to care?"

James laughs. "Oh, he'll care. I know he'll care."

Broken

"I haven't spoken with my father in years. How do I know if he's even alive?"

He slips out the photos in his back pocket and flings them at her. They show a shot of her father at his house, another with her father and a man, another with her brother.

"A little older and less hair, perhaps. More gray hair. More of a belly maybe. But that's your father, and that was taken maybe a month ago at his estate. Pretty difficult even getting these, let me say."

Something in Laila changes, and he sees this. Good. He's getting through to her, and perhaps he should have done this when he first saw her.

"Ready to talk to your father?"

She shakes her head. He goes over and hovers inches away from her face.

"Listen to me. You're going to call him, then you're going to get in a car with me and we're driving back home. You've created enough grief for my family, and I want what I deserve. You got that?"

"What'd you say to him?"

"Nothing."

"How do I know that?"

"You don't. But I said nothing. What would you care anyway?"

"He won't give you money."

"Yes he will. That I do know."

"How?"

James laughs. "I just know."

He recalls the conversation he had with her brother. A simple and straightforward conversation, but one that told him enough.

One that told him too much. One that gave him this idea. This idea that went nowhere.

He opens the cell phone and finds the number and then presses talk. He hands the phone to Laila. She grips it in her hand and then drops it. James gets it, listens, and then gives it back to her. She clings onto the cell phone and brings it to her ear.

"Hello?" she asks.

Her hands and her lips shake as her eyes and her face move somewhere else, far out of this room to somewhere far away.

"Papa?"

James puts his ear up to the phone and can hear the voice on the other end.

"Papa, it's me, Laila. Yes. It's me. I'm—yes, I'm here. It's really me."

Laila coughs and holds the phone down and cradles it for a moment, then brings it back up to her mouth.

"Papa, I'm in trouble, and you need to listen to me now. Please listen. I'm coming home, and I need you to give me some money. I will explain everything when I'm there, and I will let you know why but right now all you need to know is that I'm coming home."

James nods and stares at her as she looks up at him. He motions her with his hand.

"I need 250,000 dollars. I know that's a lot, but I'll explain why. Okay? I just—I'm so sorry. Papa, I'm so sorry for everything and for this, but I can't help it."

Laila swallows, fear filling her face. "Yes. Yes, I'm okay. I'm okay. It's just—I need you to do this for me, and do it by tomorrow—"

James takes the cell phone and shuts it off. Then he puts it back in his pocket.

"See? See how easy that was? Now we're going to take a little drive to Brady, Texas. And you're going to be a good girl and stay with me or else 'Papa' goes bye-bye. You got that?"

He sees a bag on the ground and asks if that's all she has. She nods. He tells her to get her things and to put her shoes on.

` •   •   •

They are about ready to leave when the devil arrives.

Laila has her duffle bag in her hand and the purse over her shoulder, and in between her and the door stands James. When the door opens, both of them look to see who's there.

Broken

"Hello, Laila. James."

Connor smiles, and then James turns from Laila to Connor.

"Going somewhere?" Connor says.

And then he looks at Laila and widens his eyes and sticks out his tongue.

"Connor, man, what are you doing—"

She knows this time he's real. James can see him, and he's real.

For a moment Laila looks at the door and at the figure, and then she sees James turning to face her and she sees the two twin beds and the television and the framed piece of art and suddenly she's fifteen again.

She reaches in the duffle bag, slips her hand under some clothes and finds the gun. She aims it at James and fires. He falls clutching at his arm just as Connor drops to the floor and crawls out through the doorway. She fires again and then again. Then she goes to James and puts the gun against his forehead.

"Give me your keys."

"You stupid little tramp, you shot me in the arm, you ignorant—"

She bashes the butt of the gun against his mouth, splitting open his lip and squirting blood over her hand. "Give me your keys."

He finds them in his pocket and gives them to her. His cell phone drops on the floor, and she takes it as well.

She neglects to tell him that the "conversation" she just had with her father was only one-sided since she had pressed the mute button.

"What's your car look like?"

"I'm going to kill you."

She sticks the barrel of the gun in his mouth. "I'll do the same thing I did to your brother."

He mumbles something, and she takes the handgun out of his mouth.

"A black Hyundai Sonata. It's a rental."

"You're not getting it back."

121

He moves toward her but she backs up, still aiming the gun at his head.

"Connor isn't dead," he says, laughing at her.

She looks toward the doorway.

"Yeah, he's out there, and he's going to hurt you for what you've done."

"He's going to have to find me first."

She takes the pistol and whips it against his face. She can feel and hear something in his face crack. He crumbles to the ground with a cough as she steps over him and heads to the hallway.

She's not afraid of what's out there, now that she's holding this gun.

Now that she knows the man she's dealing with is alive and not a ghost.

•   •   •

Lex rushes out of the gas station and doesn't see Kyle's car. He runs around to the back but still doesn't see anybody. He shakes his hands in disgust and then goes over to his car. For a few minutes sitting inside the car, he stares out the window trying to figure out what to do. This exit is about ninety minutes west of Atlanta, heading toward Birmingham, though Lex can't be sure where Kyle was headed.

He rubs his eyes and then jerks when he hears the knock on his window.

He rolls down the window.

"Why are you following me?" Kyle asks.

"What are you talking—"

"Just shut up and tell me why. Are you the guy who called me the other day?"

"Yeah."

"What do you want?"

"I want to find my sister."

Kyle stares at him for a minute. His expression changes under the bruises and cuts on his face.

"I can show you my license."

"You don't need to. Not anymore. I thought you looked like her. When I saw you go into the station."

"Are you driving to her? Do you know where she is?"

"What do you want with her?"

"What do *you* want with her?" Lex asks.

"Did she call you?"

"I haven't seen her in eight years. And haven't talked to her in the last few years. But just like that she called me, out of the blue. Just the other day."

"She called me today."

"And?"

"Look, I don't know you —"

"It's Lex."

"I don't know you, Lex."

Lex puts out his hand, and they shake. "I need her to come home."

"Why?"

"It's personal."

"Yeah, well, this is personal too."

"I think she's in trouble," Lex says.

"I know she's in trouble."

"Why?"

"See my face?" Kyle looks around the station, then back at Lex. "You hungry?"

"Am I hungry?"

"Yeah."

"Not really."

"Well I am. And I was going to scoot out of here when I saw you walking into the store looking for me."

"Why didn't you?"

"Because I just knew. You two are related. I knew when I saw you. Plus, if you really were some bad guy, you wouldn't be so obvious trailing me. You'd sure fail as a spy. Or a thug."

"I'd fail at a lot of things," Lex says.

"Follow me over to that McDonald's and we can talk, okay?"

Lex nods, sighing, shifting the clutch as he feels his heart continue to pound away.

"You have her eyes."

"I've heard that before. Even though I haven't seen them in quite a long time."

Kyle is halfway through his burger. "You not hungry?"

"Not really. I'm still getting over the thought that I almost lost you."

"How'd you know I was going to find her?"

"I just knew."

"You just knew, huh? Just like that?"

"Yeah."

Kyle's eyes probe him. "Where are you from?"

"Cedar Park, Texas. It's not far from Austin. I work at a country club."

"That close to where you grew up?"

"Not far."

"And you've been tracking down Laila because of a family thing?"

"Something like that."

"Why'd she leave?"

"She didn't tell you?"

Kyle sums up their relationship at the bank and tells him about the last week, starting when she suddenly decided to have dinner with him and explaining how they borrowed his cousin's gun and ending with him getting beaten up by a stranger.

"He worked over your face pretty well."

"Yeah, I know. The bank told me to go home. My manager said his branch wasn't a fight club. Pretty funny. I gotta give him that."

"Who was the guy beating you up?"

"I don't know. Said that Laila owed him something."

"Why didn't she call the police?"

Kyle shakes his head. "I don't know."

Broken

"Why didn't you?"

"I don't know. I mean—I helped give her a gun. You want to know something crazy? In twenty-nine years of living, I've never really thought much of what I wanted to do or where I wanted to go. But it's like—this will sound crazy—but one night changed it all."

"One night with her?"

"Yeah, but not like that. Not that kinda night. Just—just being with her. I mean—I just seemed to come alive. It was like someone opening up my lid and letting me start to come out. I've known the same types of people all my life with the same personalities and families and lives, and then she came along."

"Laila has always had that effect on men."

"Maybe. But it's not just a physical thing."

"You really believe that?"

Kyle nods.

"Looks always comes into the equation with Laila. You can't take it out."

"I don't know," Kyle says. "I just—I woke up today wondering what happened to her and wishing I could help, and then she calls."

"What'd she say?"

"It was as if—as if she was worried that her phone was bugged. It wasn't even her phone she was calling from. She told me she was in a lot of trouble and didn't know where to turn or who to go to and that's why she called me. She said she could trust me. Out of everybody else she could trust me."

"Must've been some night."

"She worked with me for several months, remember. We're friends."

"Laila's never been the most trusting soul. But she has reasons not to be."

"Why?"

"She just has her reasons," Lex says. "Where did she say she was planning on going?"

"She told me there was a place that she had once mentioned, a

125

place she said she always could see running away to, a place that time had seemingly forgotten about. She warned me not to say it out loud. Like I said—she thought the line was bugged. She said that if I wanted to help—that she wanted me to help—she told me to go there and that she'd find me."

"And just like that, you left?"

"Yeah." Kyle laughs and lets out a sigh. He takes a sip of his drink. "Maybe one of the craziest things I've ever done in my life. But you know—sometimes you gotta do things like that. Things like they do in the movies. Where you wake up and just go."

"So where are you going? Obviously it's somewhere down south."

Kyle finishes his food without saying anything.

"You can trust me, you know."

"I know you're her brother, that I know. But how do I know you're not following her for the same reason those guys are? How do I know you're not with them?"

"Why would I be?"

"You said yourself you haven't seen her for eight years. Not much of a relationship there."

"I'd never hurt Laila."

"You don't look like you would. But buddy, I'm telling you what, when I got the tar beat out of me, I told myself I needed to be a lot more careful."

"Yet you have no problem sitting here with me?"

"I said I need to be more careful. But it looks like I can trust you. I just wish you'd tell me a little more of why you need to find her."

"That's my business."

"And this is my business."

"Then why didn't you leave me behind?"

Kyle thinks for a minute, looking around the restaurant again and then back at Lex. "Because. Because if she's in a lot of trouble, I might need some help."

15

I never told anybody. Because I blamed myself. Typical ignorance when it comes to being violated and attacked and shamed, but that's what happened.

He wasn't some random stranger. Ben was someone I'd taunted and harassed and toyed around with who was older and wiser. A guy in college who I knew. A bad boy. And he showed his true colors when he finally said yes. And when he finally called my bluff.

I had been with boys before, but nothing like that. And it was the first time I really, truly began to understand the depths of evil. How a normal, nice, rebellious but cool junior in college could turn into the face of the devil.

After it was all done and his friends left, he almost convinced me that it was something I wanted. He never did blindly beat me. But everything that happened happened against my will. They knew it, but once they were in that room there was no going back. There was no stopping the outcome. And Ben still told me afterward that he loved me. And I actually believed him and felt like I could forgive his act because he truly loved me for who I was.

I was fifteen at the time and so stupid.

So many years later I still wonder if I'm that same silly, stupid girl.

Damn that's a lot of blood."

"Find me another towel."

"I got every single one in our room."

"Then go to another one."

"Easy, killer."

James looks at his brother and then takes the towel off his arm and glances at the wound. He's sitting on the toilet bare-chested with the white tile underneath him spotted with droplets. Nearby sits a pile of red-stained linens. The faucet is running, and he keeps twisting the towel dry and rinsing it in warm water and then putting it on the wound. His lip has finally stopped bleeding, but the gash in it almost feels as bad as the bullet wound.

Connor, meanwhile, is not doing much of anything to help him.

"Should I ask the front desk?"

"Yeah let's just try to be more obvious. I'm sure someone called the cops after hearing those gunshots."

"There's nobody here. It's the middle of the day."

James puts pressure on his left arm and winces. "I need to get something for this. And we need to get out of here."

"You want me to call a hospital?"

"Sometimes I just don't get how stupid you are," James says.

"You're bleeding more than I did."

"It grazed my arm. It's fine. I just need to stop it and clean it up."

"You know how to do it?"

"Yeah, Ma taught me when I was eight."

"Just asking."

"You're just stupid."

Connor leaves for a few minutes, and James ties the towel around his arm and uses his teeth to secure it. He stands and glances at himself in the mirror.

"You're stupid, boy, you know that?"

Broken

When Connor comes back, he takes off the bloody towel and reapplies the clean one to his arm.

"This isn't going to last long. I need something to clean it out with."

"That chick sure doesn't have second thoughts about shooting someone, does she?"

"Obviously not."

James stands and tries to get his stuff together.

"Didn't you say there was no way she'd use a gun again on someone?"

"Yeah, maybe I said that," James says.

"You were wrong."

James curses.

"I'm just saying you're wrong."

"Maybe I shouldn't have saved your sorry ass. Maybe I should have left you to die in some rich guy's house."

"Maybe you should've. Seems like that would've been a better plan than this one."

He curses again and gets everything that belongs from the room they've been sharing and urges Connor to do the same.

"What are we going to do?"

"We're following her."

"You know she has our car."

"Yeah, I got that much."

"How are we going to follow her? Hitchhike?"

"You are stupid."

"I'm just saying. Not much we can do, is there?"

"If you didn't waste the only money we had, we'd be fine."

"That was my money."

"You owe me," James says.

"Really? That's funny because you owe everybody."

James brushes his hand through his hair and looks in the bathroom and then picks up his bag.

"Where are you going?" Connor asks.

"I need to find a Walgreens or some kind of pharmacy."

"And how are you going to get money?"

"You're going to get it for me."

"How's that?"

"You got a gun. Be creative."

"Be creative? That's helpful."

James stops and walks back toward Connor. "I could still whip your tail with one arm."

"What?"

"Why'd you come back to her room?"

"It was time."

"I tell you when it's time, and it wasn't time."

"Yeah it was. Your plan was going nowhere."

"Yeah it was."

"Yeah. South."

"Find us some money fast. But don't be stupid."

"Stupid is letting that whore shoot you," Connor says.

"Look who's talking."

"I didn't know she had a gun. You should've known this time."

"Yeah, there's lots of things I should've known."

"How are we going to find her?"

"I'm going to ask where the nearest pharmacy is and then you're going to meet me there with some money," James says.

"And what if I don't?"

"Then don't meet me. Period. You find your own way of getting back home."

"I'm not the one Danny is looking for. Danny thinks I'm dead."

James just nods and walks out and heads toward the elevator.

Then, just as he's about to get in, he realizes his arm is bloody and he can't ask anybody anything.

He goes back into the room.

"You have to ask for me."

"What are you going to do?"

Broken

James holds out his hand. "Give me the gun. I have to do everything myself, don't I?"

"I keep waiting for you to do something, but it never happens."

"Well, it's happening now. I told you we're on to plan B. And she knows you're alive now."

Connor shrugs. "I don't think she cared whether I was alive or dead. That girl doesn't have a soul. It don't matter to her one way or the other."

"Yeah, but her family matters, and I saw it firsthand. She called her father. We just gotta find her again and deliver her back home."

"What do we do once we get there?"

"First things first," James says, shoving the gun in his pants and taking off again.

•   •   •

Laila drives for three straight hours before needing to pull over and get gas. She takes an exit and then pulls to the side of the road somewhere a couple hours outside of New Orleans. She gets outside, walks onto the grass, kneels down, and throws up.

She leans over the ground with both hands flat and she feels tears in her eyes from vomiting and she wipes them away.

Laila looks at the sky. She's left the gray behind, and now it's clear blue.

"You like this?"

She can see straight up without clouds blocking her view.

Straight up into heaven.

"Is this Your idea of punishment? Your idea of judgment?"

She swallows and then spits out the bitter taste in her mouth. She stands up.

"I'll do it for You. Why wait? Why not just get it over and done with? It's going to happen soon, right? So why not? Why not just do what I should've done a long time ago. I'll save You the problem, okay?"

She ignores one passing car in an otherwise empty exit. In the distance there is a gas station. She opens the side door and looks in the bag where she put the revolver. The revolver that she got from Kyle. The same one she just used on James.

This will be quick and painless. Does it matter that she will die on the side of a one-lane exit somewhere in Louisiana? Death doesn't need to come dressed up. Death simply comes, and Laila thinks of this and knows this. She thinks of Rexy in New York, and she knows this. Death can come in all shapes and packages and with all the bells and whistles, but still in the end when death comes, it comes. And it's over. And she knows all it will take is swallowing that revolver so the barrel scrapes the back of her throat and then pushing the trigger and getting this mess done and over with.

As she looks through the bag, she doesn't think of all the things they say you think of. Her father and her brother and her sister and the mother she lost and the few friends she made and him. She doesn't think of any of them.

But something does come to mind, and when it does, it gives her reassurance that this is the right thing to do.

It's right, and it's time.

Ghosts or not, it's time.

Demons or not, it's time.

She finds the gun and takes it out and puts it in her mouth and presses the trigger.

She hears the snap go off. Not the loud booming sound she heard in the hotel room but the snap.

Laila is still there, almost gagging on the pistol, her eyes still looking up at the sky.

She mumbles a curse and then presses the trigger again. The same light crack goes off. Again. And again.

She takes the handgun out of her mouth and stares at it.

She looks in her hand and for a moment doesn't believe what she's seeing.

Broken

Laila turns it over, then swings her hand to feel its weight.

Laila presses the trigger again.

The snap goes off.

It's a toy gun. Made of metal and plastic. In the shape and color of her gun, but different.

"What is this?"

She pushes the trigger a dozen times, and it does the same thing. There are no bullets because this isn't real. It's a gun that a kid would play with.

Laila tears back through the bag she placed the original gun in and can't find it. She takes out everything, then looks through her car. The more she looks the more frustrated she gets.

She tries to think how those guys could have done this, but she knows they didn't.

Laila shot James and then walked out of the hotel and took the car and started driving south.

She didn't stop once.

And now the gun she used to stop James—not to just stop James but to hurt and wound him—is a toy gun that won't go off.

"No. No. No way."

She says this because it can't be. The gun. This exit. This failed attempt. This life.

She tries again, putting the gun to her temple and firing.

But the crack sounds hollow and light and mocking.

She hurls the gun out into a field and slams the door shut and heads to the gas station.

·   ·   ·   '

"How come I never heard of you?"

The big man puts the handgun back in the briefcase and snaps it up. He stares at Ron Winfield, a skinny guy in a denim shirt who owns the garage they're in front of and the dump of a house right next to it. "I'm not supposed to be heard of."

"What kind of name is Amos?" Winfield asks.

"The name my mother and father gave me."

"You like some kinda prophet or something?"

"I can see your future."

"Really? And what's it look like?"

"Grim."

Winfield laughs at him, but Amos doesn't laugh back.

This rat hole of a house and neighborhood is fifteen minutes south of Chicago. Amos already has everything packed, and this is his last trip before heading north.

"Hand me that," Amos orders.

"You know how to use that?"

"If the question is whether I know how to hit what I'm aiming at, the answer is yes."

Amos holds the Brügger and Thomet MP9 submachine gun in one hand. He extends the shoulder stock, then sees in another open briefcase a red-dot sight, a tactical light, and a silencer along with several spare magazines.

"How many extra magazines do you have?"

"Starting a war?"

"Danny told me you could help out."

"I'm helping."

"You're talking."

"Eight—I think. Let me see." Winfield looks in the duffle bag. "Yeah, that's eight."

Amos puts the handgun in its case.

"So you got a Kimber 1911 .45 brand spankin' new. A Walther PPK with seven-shot magazine. An MP9. A Smith and Wesson 500 Mag."

"And the Para Warthog too," Amos says.

Winfield curses. "What are you planning?"

"To take them off your hands. You want to count the cash?"

"No, I trust you. Why do you need all this firepower?"

Broken

"Why do you ask so many questions?"

"Just making conversation."

Amos looks up from the trunk and stares at the man for a moment. "What?"

"Do you realize that after the fourth or fifth time a man doesn't answer your questions, he's not going to? Ever?"

"You told me your name."

"Danny told you my name, and I just filled in the blank when you asked a stupid question about it."

"You always this ornery?"

Amos smiles. "I'm not the least bit ornery. I take my job very seriously, and when I'm looking over materials I just purchased, I don't want to waste my time with frivolous conversation."

"Frivolous, huh?"

"How would you categorize it?"

"Just friendly talk," Winfield says.

"Save the commentary for someone else."

Amos shuts the trunk and wipes his forehead.

"Want something to drink?" he asks the big man.

"Only if it's to go," Amos says.

"Long trip ahead?"

"Do you see what's in the trunk?"

"I saw."

"It'll be a long trip for somebody."

16

Someone once very dear to me told me that I would never change and that he didn't want to even try to change me. And that was when I realized perhaps I couldn't change, perhaps I was destined to forever be this person those closest around me claimed I was. Even the love of my life defined me in this way. The darkest star. That's what Tyler called me. And then I realized I might never change, that perhaps I didn't want to change.

There were things I did that I deliberately chose. My life. My lifestyle. My comfort. My bubble. I chose this road even though I didn't choose who I encountered on it. I chose to continue down it and leave others behind.

Can someone go so far down the road that she makes it impossible to ever come back?

Can someone keep driving, keep running, keep heading toward the sunset and never expect to reach an end?

"I don't want you to be someone else for me." Tyler meant it, but I didn't know exactly what it meant.

He said he loved me despite my baggage and my past and my sins. He said he loved me for who I was deep inside.

Yet I left him. The same way I always leave. The same way I always run and forget.

But like I find with each morning sunrise and each blank page of a day ahead, forgetting is hard to do.

Forgetting is impossible.

Broken

And sometimes the voices whisper and the demons haunt and I find I don't know what's real and what's imagined and what's gone and forgotten.

James watches the man jostling his keys before opening the trunk and placing the suitcase inside. It looks like he's by himself, a man in his forties on a business trip. James scans the parking lot, then walks over to him.

"Stop there for a minute."

The guy turns around and stares at him. Then he sees the gun in his hand.

"Give me your wallet."

The man has thick hair that's starting to gray. He stands solid but doesn't move.

"Look, man, don't make this tragic. Give me your wallet and then give me your keys. Right now."

"I don't have much."

"You have something, and that's more than I have."

The man stares back at the hotel, and something on his face changes. James sees Connor coming.

"He's with me. And you don't want to mess with him. So give me your wallet now because I'm not asking again."

With the addition of Connor, and a glance at his bloody arm, the man's hesitation evaporates. He pulls his wallet from his back pocket and gives it to James along with the keys.

"Start walking that way."

"Toward the highway?"

"Yeah."

"What for?"

"Because I said so. Come on. Start moving."

By the time the man reaches the side street toward the interstate, he is in a full jog.

"Get in the car."

Connor looks at the small vehicle. "What are we going to do with this?"

"We're getting out of here, that's what we're going to do."

"And go where?"

"We're going to get cleaned up and regroup."

"I'm heading back home."

James stares over the top of the car and points at him. "You're sticking with me, and you're doing every single thing I tell you to do."

"Cops will be looking for us you know."

"And since when has that stopped you before? Huh? What do you think they're doing after the stunt you pulled in South Carolina? Beating and raping some streetwalker you met back there doesn't count?"

"She's not talking."

"Yeah well, she's lucky to be alive after you left her for dead in that motel room. You're sick, you know that?"

"I'm not the one holding a gun and a wallet that belongs to some man sprinting like he's in the Olympics right about now."

"I'd beat you senseless if you had any sense in you. And then I'd take all your possessions, but God knows you don't have any."

"I have you."

"Yeah you do, and one of these days you're going to realize how lucky you are."

•   •   •

She has been here before. And time has not been kind to either of them.

This section of the French Quarter is quieter, with fewer tourists. They had found it together, and it had been perfect. A hotel occupying three 1830 town houses with thirty-three rooms. They had gotten a room with a balcony and had stayed in the city for a week.

As Laila walks in the remodeled lobby, she wonders what she's doing here and if this indeed is a sanctuary. She wonders if the memories will serve to heal or to imprison.

It doesn't look very busy. She is greeted by a gentle woman who could be her grandmother who talks about the grounds and the surrounding neighborhood. Laila books what is called a superior room on the third floor and says she will be staying for a few days. She pays in cash and has to leave a copy of her license because she doesn't leave a credit card on file.

Laila walks up the spiraling staircase and down a hall decorated with antiques to her room. Unlocks the door with a real key and then locks it behind her with old-fashioned genuine locks.

It looks different, but she believes it's the same room.

She opens the door to the balcony and looks outside.

And that's when she knows.

This is it.

The same room and the same balcony.

His name was Erik and he was heaven and he caused the earth to move for her and she would have given him everything and eventually did.

He told Laila he loved her and she believed him. As much as any seventeen-year-old might believe the words of a twenty-two-year-old.

She sighs and stares outside at the street. It's so quiet, almost too quiet. For a moment she thinks she sees something moving on the street in her peripheral vision, but when her glance shifts she sees nothing.

A chill goes through her as she looks down.

She's not sure if she's looking out there to remember or to make sure no one's following her.

Without bothering to change out of the clothes she's worn all day, Laila drifts off as darkness blankets the city, wrapping herself in the warmth of memory. The week from her youth spent in New Orleans drifts by in echoes and apparitions. It is soft and cool and slow and lovely. She savors tastes and relishes sounds and embraces textures all foreign and alive and new. Her world back in Texas and the world that awaits her when they leave is all put on hold for seven sensuous days.

Laila is intertwined with Erik when a voice wakes her up.

The voice whispers a name she doesn't recognize, a name that doesn't make sense.

"Marie."

She opens her eyes and sees the glow of the city outside the balcony.

"Don't leave," the voice says to her, this time a little louder.

Still groggy, Laila jumps up and looks around the room. "Hello?"

"Stay with me," the voice says.

"Who's there?"

She turns on a light, and it barely illuminates the room. The voice she heard is a boy's voice, talking as if he might be right there in the room.

"Hello?"

"Let's go out and play," he says.

The door to her room opens with a blast of air and slams against the wall, and Laila feels something inside the room rushing around and through her. Then the feeling is gone.

She's left standing, shivering, cold, and searching the room with her eyes. "Hello?"

Nothing is there.

Nobody is there.

"Who are you? Who is Marie?"

But no one replies.

She stares at the doorway and thinks about closing it, then reconsiders, grabs her purse, and heads out.

• • •

"So what now?" Lex places the two bottles down on the table. The one he sips from is a soda.

"I guess we wait."

"Wait for her to call?"

Kyle nods at him as he sips his beer. He checks his cell phone. It's nine, and they're in a bar off of Bourbon Street.

"Did she say she was going to call?"

"I told you, she said she was in trouble and needed my help. And she told me where she was going."

In the background the blues pipes through the speakers. The place is deserted and dark.

"You look skeptical."

Lex shakes his head. "I wonder what she's doing here. Why she came back."

"She's been here before?"

"Yeah. Once. When she was a teenager. Ran off with some idiot."

Kyle laughs.

"What?"

"You say that like I'm joining the list," Kyle says.

"Maybe you are."

"What's that make you?"

"Oh, I've been an idiot for a long time. Difference is I'm related to Laila. Who is a little more than just an idiot."

"What would you call her?"

"Complicated," Lex says.

"That can mean a lot of different things."

"It does."

Lex watches him sip on his beer.

"Why'd she go to New Orleans when she was young?"

"I don't know. She just disappeared and we were all worried and then she came back and got in a lot of trouble but it didn't matter. She was still home but already gone. She had it written all over her face. She wanted to take the first bus out of Brady and out of Texas and into the big, old world. And she already had her ticket bought. Well, not even bought, but paid for."

"What ticket?"

"Bet she didn't tell you, did she?" Lex asks.

"No."

"You know that Laila started modeling when she was fourteen? She already looked about twenty years old. She's been on the cover of a few big magazines. Those fancy fashion magazines. Not just in ads but on the covers. My sister used to collect them, but all they did was make me sad."

"You mean magazines like *Vogue*?"

"Yeah. The fashion stuff. Nothing too revealing, nothing like *Playboy*. At least not that I know of. She had the look and once they sniffed around and found her, it was all over. She was one of them."

"One of what?"

Lex tightens his lips. "You smoke?"

"No."

"Man I could use one about now. Stopped a while ago. Stopped drinking too. You don't realize how much you use those things until they're gone."

"What'd you mean 'one of them'?"

"One of them. You know. Like one of the world. We lived in our own little world in Brady. A lot of people say Texas is its own world too, and I sure believe it. But Laila never fit in. And she knew it. And you could tell she wanted to get away."

"So the guy she came to New Orleans with. Whatever happened to him?"

"Just drama. He disappeared for a while trying to pursue a career in pro football and then came back like some lost puppy. By then she was already gone. Poor guy. Everything about him that was inflated and proud just got snuffed out over time. Like losing your hair, except it's more than that. It's losing your pride. I saw him not long ago down in Houston and he recognized me and he didn't say anything but he gave me the saddest look I've ever seen. A look that said he'd been there and had something special and priceless and then lost it. It's like he knew. He had one chance and he blew it and he would forever be living in the shadow of that memory."

Kyle finishes his beer. "I guess I could understand that. I guess I could see someone being like that if they had fallen for Laila."

"That's the thing, though. I've seen some boys lose their minds over her. I mean lose their minds. And I've seen some rough stuff. And all the while I'm looking through the eyes of a brother, you know? I know her. At least I used to know Laila. When she left Texas, we had a long and hard conversation and she told me she didn't know what she wanted and she was scared but more than anything she just wanted to leave. She wanted to get away. She wanted to escape. I asked her how going to New York was escaping. She said that if she could start over again, things would be okay. But I don't think that's how it works. You don't just all of a sudden start over. You carry it with you. Man, I know that. I wish I could go back in time and talk with her and tell her that, but I learned the hard way."

"Maybe she learned the hard way too."

"I got a feeling that she's still learning."

"So what are you going to do when you find her?" Kyle says.

"I'm going to try and have that conversation again. I pray I will have the opportunity to talk with her again."

"Think it will help her?"

"Maybe. I don't know. I hope so. I sure know it'll help me."

• • •

Laila passes a bar and smells the sweet and sour mix of late nights and spilled drinks and sweat. Crossing over onto a street a few blocks away from Bourbon Street, she passes a closed store, an empty space, an apartment building. The few passersby ignore her, and she finds comfort knowing their eyes don't track over her, knowing she doesn't have to ignore their glances. A dimly lit corner bar playing slow piano jazz makes her stop and glance inside. The crowd is light and safe, so she walks in.

For an hour she listens to the music and sips her drink slowly.

Occasionally her eyes will shut and remain shut for a second longer than they should. This place is relaxing. She doesn't worry about someone showing up at the doorway or at her table.

She thinks this and then glances at the open door and sees a boy standing there. He is wearing a red long-sleeved T-shirt and a dark blue cap. He stares at her and then waves. She waves back. Then he looks behind him and darts away. The boy makes her think of her brother.

As she works on another drink and feels light-headed from not eating anything, Laila checks her pocket and discovers the phone she took from James. She notices there are several unanswered calls along with several messages. For a second she thinks about answering it, then decides to wait. Wait until later tonight or tomorrow. Wait to let it bother her then. Wait for the worry because tonight she wants to feel alone and hidden and tucked away in the belly of New Orleans.

Laila remembers sneaking into little joints like this, underage but still able to drink. She remembers holding Erik's hand and listening to him laugh and loving every single thought he had and not worrying about anything. She almost believed she could forget what happened to her in that hotel room a couple years earlier. Laila almost believed Erik could make her forget.

She finally slips back out into the night with her memories following. On the sidewalk she loses her way and goes in the opposite direction of her hotel. It doesn't bother her. She enjoys walking in the city. It's still alive late at night. The block she walks down has trees that hang over the sidewalk. She feels damp from the humidity but the air blows, slightly cooling her.

As she begins to cross the road, she sees him again.

The young boy, perhaps ten years old.

He smiles at her again and sprints down the sidewalk.

Laila looks around and doesn't see anybody and wonders what the boy is doing out here alone.

Broken

For a moment she's looking, and then she spots something that terrifies her.

It's a blue and red backpack.

The exact same kind she found resting in her bathtub a few nights before James showed up.

The backpack she tossed out the window of her apartment without looking inside.

Laila wonders if it's James and Connor playing another trick on her. Yet that doesn't prevent her from following the boy into the beating heart of darkness.

She crosses the street and follows him down a shadowed block.

"Hey, you! Stop for a minute."

The boy keeps going. He is still sprinting as he heads toward a busier intersection with cars passing at the light.

"Come here for a minute."

But the boy doesn't stop. And he reaches the curb with the light saying not to cross. He turns around again ever so briefly to make sure she's looking.

Then he steps out into the busy lane with the oncoming traffic, and the taxicab speeding down the street plows into him and cuts him down like a dropped watermelon splattering over the hard pavement.

Laila screams.

She runs toward the intersection as the taxi screeches twenty yards away. Another car behind it honks and veers around it.

Laila reaches the edge of the intersection and the light turns green and she glances down the street and sees the cab stopped with its lights blinking and the driver getting out looking shocked.

For a moment she just stands there, unsure of what to do.

But then she rushes across the street and gets to the cab.

She braces for what she's about to see, for the death matted in the grill of the car.

The cab driver stares at her with a pale, scared look.

Laila holds a hand over her mouth and nose as if it might help. She glances at the front of the car.

The cab driver still looks at her dumbfounded.

There is nothing on the hood of the car.

Nothing on the bumper.

No sign of the boy in the red T-shirt and blue cap. No sign of the matching backpack.

"Where is he?" she asks.

The driver shakes his head.

"You saw him, right? You saw that boy. The boy that ran right in front of your car. You saw him, right? You hit him. I saw it."

He says something to her in a foreign language that sounds like a curse.

"I saw him. I know I did."

As he opens the door, Laila stops him and shakes her head and tells him not to go.

"What happened to him? I know I saw him, and I know you did too."

The driver gets into the car and shuts the door even though she's holding onto it and then he drives away.

The only sign of anything are the skid marks the cab made on the road.

Laila walks up and down the sidewalk next to the road, then crosses the street to see if the boy made it across. She knows she saw it with her own eyes. She saw him sprint across the street and the car ram into him and his body folding up and splattering over the hood and the window of the cab.

For a moment she closes her eyes and keeps them closed, hoping that when she reopens them they'll see the truth. But she sees the same thing.

She eventually leaves the intersection, and a street with a familiar name brings her back down to her hotel. But nothing strange happens on the way there. No boy. No ghosts. No backpacks.

Nothing.

Broken

• • •

Amos listens to the political conversation on the radio as he sits in the darkness of the parking lot. He has not seen him but he'll be awake when he comes out of one of the rooms at the motel. It's early morning, and Amos isn't tired. The open window lets in the hot breeze. On the seat beside him rests the short and stubby Para Warthog .45 just in case something happens, but he doubts anything will at two in the morning.

His eyes stay on the darkness of the parking lot, waiting patiently.

This is what he is paid to do. Wait.

Wait and follow.

The question isn't how this is going to end. It is just a question of where and when.

17

What did I know about love? What have I ever known about love? It has always proven to be this elusive drug, this hidden crystal, this deceptive Wizard of Oz—someone hiding behind the curtain. And that someone has always, always disappointed.

When we ran away to New Orleans, it was random. My life had consisted of a series of random choices. There was never any deep reason for going except that it sounded fun and adventurous. No, it was fun and adventurous, but more than those things, it was dangerous. Erik was dangerous. And I guess in a lot of ways so was I.

I met him at a college party and made love with him that same night. But something about him was different from the start, so I believed. I thought it was his special care that he put over me. But I would come to discover that it was as if he viewed me as an expensive car he'd bought. That was how he cared for me. As if I belonged to him.

For a while I did belong to him.

And in that week in New Orleans, magic happened.

I actually believed that life could be this fiery, potent dream.

It would be easy to say that Erik turned into a monster that week or that I saw things that disappointed me or saddened me. No. That would come later when it was all *said and done. In New Orleans, I know I loved that man as much as a seventeen-year-old could love.*

Yet what did I know about love then?

And what do I know about love now?

I could have learned so much, and I could have grown so much if I had made the right choice. I could have been a better person and perhaps some of the bad could have been taken away. If only I had done the right thing.

What I know about love is this: you love what you lose. You love what could have been. And even in absence and denial, love can grow.

H ello, Mrs. Ewing."

"Who is this?"

"Sam," James says.

"Sam who?" the elderly woman asks.

"I work with your son at the bank."

"He's never told me about any Sam."

"I'm relatively new."

"Is everything okay?"

"Oh, yes. It's fine. I don't mean to bother you, but I've had a difficult time getting ahold of Kyle."

"That's because he's gone."

"Well, yes, I know that. I was just wondering how long he was planning to be gone."

"He didn't say when he called us yesterday. Do you have his cell?"

"Well, no. That's actually why I was calling. I was taking over some of his shifts at work, but I've had a family emergency come up so I really need to talk with him."

The woman gives him a number that he writes down on the square block of paper with the motel's insignia at the top.

"I'll give him a call. Hopefully we can figure something out."

"I assume he'll be gone a few days since he's going to New Orleans."

James pauses for a moment and then draws an exclamation point next to the number. He writes "New Orleans" next to it.

"I'd imagine too. But maybe he can give me some other people who can work for me."

"Yes, well, tell him to take care of himself."

"I'll certainly do that. You've been really helpful. Thanks so much."

James shuts the phone and finishes the coffee he made in the room this morning.

He glances at the empty bed next to him that wasn't slept in. It's nine thirty and he hasn't seen or heard from Connor.

They're on the border of Mississippi and Louisiana laying low. But Connor went out last night around ten to get some cigarettes and beer and never came back. James has an idea what his brother might be doing but has no idea where.

Connor's cell phone sits on the desk right next to the phone James just used.

He waits for an hour and finally there is a knock on the door. James lets him in.

"Where've you been?"

"Out and about."

"What'd you do?" James says.

"Why? I came back."

"About time." James curses. "We need to go."

"Go where?"

"I know where she's at."

"And how do you know that?"

"Because I was the one who got the smart genes passed down to him."

Broken

"I'm not going anywhere unless you tell me where we're going," Connor says.

"I can smell the liquor on you."

"Bet you can. Probably can smell perfume too."

"Did you do anything last night you shouldn't have?"

"Nothing I would've gotten arrested for. Unless she's not eighteen."

"You're sick, you know. You really got a sickness."

"It's not a sickness."

James takes the keys from Connor. "You're lucky you didn't get caught."

"They're not scanning the whole country for us. We took a rental car and a guy's wallet."

"You spend your money?"

"I made some friends. They were more than willing to buy me a few rounds."

"Listen to me. No more. When I tell you no, you listen."

"I'm a grown adult," Connor says.

"That was part of the deal of you coming."

"No, if you remember correctly, big bro, you needed me for your wonderful little plan. To scare the girl. Guess she got over the idea of seeing ghosts in junior high."

"Maybe if she'd been scared of you we'd be set."

"She's not scared of you either."

James nods. "We don't have much money so lay easy."

"We have a few credit cards."

"I'm sure he's already cancelled them."

"We'll get more money soon. We always do."

"We're leaving."

"Where to?"

"Just get in the car and shut up and do as you're told."

"I don't need this abuse."

"Yes you do. You need that and a whole lot more."

They climb into the car that Connor just parked and drive off.

•   •   •

As Amos pulls out onto the exit a short distance from the car he's tailing, he dials the number and gets Danny.

"We've got a problem."

"What is it?"

"There's two of them."

The voice on the other end pauses for a moment. "What are you talking about?"

"I thought you said Connor was dead," Amos says.

"That's what James told me."

"I just saw him drive off with James. I'm following them now."

Danny curses. "Where are they going?"

"Not sure. South, it appears."

"You follow them and you make sure they get that money and then when you get it, I want them both dead. Both of them. And I want you to kill Connor first. I want James to watch his brother die. And tell him that's courtesy of me."

"Got it."

He hangs up the line and begins to coast a couple cars behind them on the highway.

Amos isn't surprised at the order. It usually ends this way.

The only surprise is that the order has come now.

It'll make his job far easier, wherever they end up.

•   •   •

The coffee is strong and necessary. Laila picks at the breakfast and finds it strange how one might drink the same coffee and eat the same biscuits and listen to the birds in this courtyard and hold hands with a loved one and have a defining moment in their life. Yet in the same breath, one might experience the exact same thing alone and feel isolated and afraid.

It's not life, she thinks, but rather what you do with it.

Broken

She finishes a glass of freshly squeezed orange juice and licks her lips and thinks about leaving and heading back up to her room when the woman approaches. Her gray hair is in a ball, and she has round eyes and a narrow jaw.

"This is not the place to come all alone," she says, looking down at Laila.

"Excuse me?"

"They see you and they know and they will come to you," the woman tells her in a rickety drawl.

"Who are you talking about?"

Lines that look like leather cut her spotted face. "The dark will swallow you whole here."

Laila looks around to see if anyone else is here. "Can I help you?"

"No. But I can help you."

"How can you help me?"

"I see her, but far away."

"Who do you see?"

"But the others are closer, much closer. And they want to hurt you."

Laila stands and starts to walk off. The elderly woman grabs her arm and holds her back. Though she appears to be a feeble old lady, her grip is tight and strong.

"I won't hurt you."

"Look—I'm sorry but I just really—"

"The black pit of night won't rest until it pours its way into your soul," the old woman says. "You need to leave this place. This city. You need to leave and go back home."

Laila pulls back her arm and leaves the woman standing there in the empty courtyard.

She goes inside the hotel and ignores the man behind the desk who made small talk with her earlier. She goes up the winding staircase and notices the mirror at the end of the hallway. She knows it wasn't there before. She sees herself from twenty yards away, the tank top and the jeans and the hair spilling down and the expressionless eyes. Laila glances down at the white loose dress she's wearing. The mirror lies and shows a picture that she should know and know well and now remembers. It's a picture from an ad that made her famous and sent her all the way to New York. She still looks the same but doesn't look anything like that girl.

In the mirror the girl starts to laugh at her. And then as she does, blood begins to drip down the sides of her mouth, then begins to leak out of her eyes like tears.

Laila shuts her eyes and opens them again.

A painting on the wall looks the same as it did earlier in the morning and late last night. Just a painting. No mirror. No mirror with a laughing ghost of herself dying away.

She gets to her hotel room and locks it and can hear the voice of the woman outside. "The black pit of night won't rest until it pours its way into your soul. You need to leave this place. This city. You need to leave and go back home."

But even if the old woman knows something more than she should, she got it wrong.

Laila doesn't have a home to go back to.

•   •   •

Lex knocks on the door for the third time. A part of him wants to kick it in, but he knows it will do little good if Kyle isn't there.

The guy told him to meet him downstairs in the lobby around ten. Lex ventured out and got some coffee at a shop down the street and then came back and waited. It's thirty minutes after ten now, and Lex wonders if he's been abandoned.

He asks at the front desk if Kyle checked out, and the clerk says no.

He waits for another half hour before feeling restless enough to head out onto the streets.

Perhaps he won't be able to find Kyle or to find Laila but at least he can do something.

Broken

He tries to stifle the voices inside him as he walks the streets and feels the sun on his forehead.

He knows that if he doesn't find her in the next day, he will have to go back home. He can't keep doing this to his family. He can't just stay away from them with no hope on the horizon.

No matter how much time passes, guilt still comes with each sunrise. And even though he knows his sins are taken care of, he can't escape his own reputation and his own past.

Regardless of whatever he does for the rest of his life, Dena will always wonder. She'll always worry, and she'll always wonder. And he could try and tell her to get over that (and he's even done so before), yet Lex knows she feels like this because of him. Because of the past mistakes.

He deserves it.

His wife deserves better. And he's promised her she will get it.

Lex decides to try and pick up something for them. He wanders into stores trying to find a small gift that would show he's thinking of them. One of the stores has an assortment of local handcrafted items from watches to ashtrays to belts. It's dimly lit, and he can't see anybody in the stifling, narrow space. It smells like tobacco and spices.

A chill covers him even though the morning is already sticky and hot. He's cold enough to feel the prickles on his skin.

As he leaves, he sees a square vintage camera on a little shelf. He stops because it looks completely different than anything else in the shop.

Lex picks it up and sees it's the same Leica brand that Laila used to carry and take pictures on.

There isn't a price tag on it. Lex goes to the back where the desk and counter sit, and he calls out to see if anybody is there. A woman with thick dreadlocks comes out and glances at him and then at the old camera he holds.

"Where'd you get this?" he asks.

"Got it somewhere but not sure where." Her Jamaican accent is thick.

"When'd you get it?"

"Not sure of that. Things come and go around here."

"How much is this?"

"How much you willin' to pay?"

Lex shakes his head. "I don't know. I don't really want to buy it."

"Okay then."

He wants an answer or an explanation, but the woman simply looks at him with no sign of giving him one.

"You have no idea where you got this?"

"Should I?" she asks.

"No, I just thought—it looks very familiar."

"Take it then."

"Take it?"

"Sure."

"No, I can't."

"Then don't."

He looks at the camera and knows it's got to be the same brand. Not just the same brand, but the exact same model. And just like many things on this trip, it cannot be a coincidence.

"Do you know if this works?"

"Don't know."

He puts it down on the counter and pulls out a twenty. "How about this?"

"That looks fine to me," the woman says.

He gives it to her, and the woman lets him take it without a bag or anything.

Just as he's walking out the door, the woman tells him good-bye, then adds, "Make sure to tell your sister where you got it."

As he stands in the doorway wondering if he indeed heard her say that, Lex turns around and finds the woman gone.

He wants to go back inside, but that cold feeling is still there. A chill along with a panicked, closed-in feeling. He knows he needs to get out of the shop and back onto the street where he can think and breathe.

He looks at the camera and wonders if he should take it.

Is it cursed just like the rest of this ill-fated trip?

Lex keeps it and walks on.

· · ·

She can't believe Kyle's come this far. She never expected when she called his cell phone this morning that he was already here. Nor could she believe that her brother came with him.

Laila watches him step out of the café and into the bright sun. He squints his eyes and then looks down each side of the road. For a moment it appears that he's still waiting for her even though she said she'd meet him there a long time ago.

There's something so endearing about seeing Kyle standing there.

She watches from inside a bar with the window painted on the outside to make it impossible to see in. She wanted to see if he was really there, somehow still not believing that Kyle had actually driven all this way to see her. Even as he arrived, Laila was in a state of disbelief, watching him enter the café alone. Just as she had asked.

For almost a half hour, Laila fought staying over on this side of the street. She wanted to see him in person. Now she has.

He walks away, glancing around as if he might find her any moment. Laila remains inside, watching him, watching him go.

She doesn't understand why he would drive all this way just to find her again.

Laila waits in the bar for a while, drinking nothing and just looking out the window. Then she heads back out into the blistering sunshine and starts walking back to her hotel several blocks away. As she walks, she thinks of Kyle, then thinks of what he told her on the phone about her brother following him.

She thinks of what she might say to Lex when she sees him. But every passing comment that fills her mind evaporates because she knows herself. She knows how she won't say the things that need to be said. Too much time and distance has taken up the space of their relationship. She won't say anything because there's nothing left to say.

Laila stops to look at an old church that has a rusted gate and an overgrown garden with a sidewalk leading up to a few short stairs. The old wood is worn with remnants of white paint spotted throughout the brown and black. The walkway leading to the steps is cracked and uneven. The windows are covered with boards. Yet the door to the church is open.

"Laila."

It is a slight whisper that comes from behind her. Or maybe above her. She looks around her but doesn't see anybody. It's just a side street where the buildings on each side tower over her.

"Come inside, Laila."

It's the voice of a woman. An elderly voice with a deep accent.

She knows she's imagining it just like so many things in the last week.

She can't help her body's tremble.

Laila walks down the cracked concrete to the old, wooden steps and then stands at the entryway to the church.

"It's okay. You're home now."

She feels pulled by an unknown force as she enters, the floor of the old sanctuary creaking.

Slivers of light leak in from slits in the planked-up windows. There are old pews still inside here, perhaps ten rows on each side of the small room. Each pew is gray with dust. There is no stage but rather a modest pulpit with a table in front of it. As she gets closer, she sees that it's a baptism table, with a large bowl on top used for the ceremony.

The air tastes musty, the echoes of her steps bouncing off the narrow walls and ceiling. She feels cobwebs against her face. More than anything, she feels out of breath, as if there is no air inside here to breathe.

Broken

"It's time — we've been waiting for you. So nice to have you stop by."

She stops and knows the voice is real. It was loud, and it echoed.

"Who's there?" she calls out.

As she glances at one of the pews, she sees a small round object on it. She steps over to pick it up and then stops.

It's a small head of a toy. A Barbie or something like that. Just the head and nothing else. It stares up at her, smiling and dumbfounded.

Laila keeps walking toward the pulpit.

Another voice whispers, but she can't make out the words.

She knows she shouldn't be in here, but running away feels like she's losing. Running away would feel like she's giving in to the pressures of her mind and to her fears.

She knows there's nothing in here besides the remnants of an old church.

The voices she hears are in her mind and that's all.

Laila keeps walking.

Yet the voices don't stop.

"You can pay for your sins right here and right now with the blood of the lamb."

She nears the table with the round bowl, and she looks inside.

There is still water in the bowl. It is still, and for a second she thinks she can see herself reflected.

"Go ahead, look inside. Look at the face of evil, the face of death. The face of a dirty, filthy, smelly whore."

Laila looks and sees herself, but she sees herself at fifteen with a wide smile as she poses for a picture. She sees herself at seventeen in love and naive and stupid.

There is laughter in the room. Not from one but from a hundred.

She turns and sees them all. The ghosts of the parishioners are behind her, laughing, mocking, taunting. They're pointing fingers and smirking and judging.

Laila touches the water and sees the ripples and watches the picture disappear.

She looks up at the pulpit and at the cross on the wall behind it.

Yet as she stares at it, she notices it's actually not a cross but rather two long serpents stretched out in the shape of a cross.

They begin to move and slither off the wall and onto the floor toward her.

Laila gasps and grabs her mouth to try to squelch it.

Then she smells the blood.

Her hands are drenched not in old, stagnant water from the baptism basin but in blood.

The laughter continues.

On the floor she can see more snakes writhing as they near her.

Her outstretched hands drip blood.

"You will never get it back. Never, Laila, not ever, and you will forever carry the mark. Forever carry the pain and nothing can take it back. Nothing."

She turns around and sees the room full of people. But now they are all men. Several hundred, some sitting in the pews and some standing next to them. Lining up on the walls and in the back.

All faces she recognizes.

They are all men she's been with.

All men she's given herself to.

They howl with jeers and laughter, mocking her with deep-rooted heckles. She hears a few whistles, the sound of mock kissing, even an evil and whiny groan. The sound slaps her over her face with its contempt.

Their laughter continues and gets louder, and she feels something wrapping itself around her legs.

Laila shuts her eyes and runs through the church. She holds out a hand like a blind person until she ends up slamming against the back wall.

Broken

She sees the glare from outside, and she rushes through the door and trips over the stairs and lands on the dirt next to the walkway.

Dazed and dizzy, Laila looks at her hands.

They're still covered in blood.

It was no hallucination.

Staring back at the front of the church doorway, she sees a snake slowly making its way out. It slithers over the entryway and back around the side of the church.

Then the door slams shut.

Her heart beats, and she can taste the sweat on her lips. She wipes her hands on the grass and then stands and leaves the garden.

She can still hear the laughter coming from inside the church.

18

On snowy days we'd stay inside Tyler's town house that looked out on the frozen Chicago skyline and make love and listen to the wind howl and watch the snow swirling four stories high. And I almost believed. Almost. I almost gave myself over to the fact that it could happen and that it was happening. That love could find its way into my heart. But ultimately I ran away from it just like I run away from everything.

There are daily reminders of Tyler that I've never let go. A dollar key chain bought in the park. A CD that he made for me in its special case that I still carry around, though I can't bring myself to listen to it again. A blue topaz ring I can't wear again. My heart that was once handcrafted clay shaped with his hands but now is hard and cold and unmovable.

He was never a client, and he never said anything once he found out. A few times he tried carefully and delicately to tell me what I already knew, the dangers inherent in my profession. It wasn't a profession but something short-term. That's how I reasoned and rationalized even though a week became a month that became a couple of years. The short and beautiful time we had belonged to us, and he said he could take care of me, but I told him I didn't want anybody taking care of me. I told him he needed to start by taking care of himself. And that was the start of the inevitable end.

Broken

Some days I dream of those times. When the world howled outside like a wild animal and we held onto one another. When the simple act of love wasn't just an act but more of a deep breath of fresh air. When the joy came of knowing someone was there waiting and willing and still wanting something beyond what they had taken. When they were willing to give me so much more than I could give them.

It's not that I didn't want it. It's that I felt I was wrong to take it. I didn't deserve the unconditional love. I never had and never would.

Y ou need to stay with me."

"And why's that?"

James ignores Connor as he sips his drink and looks around the empty bar.

"What do you think I'm going to do?"

"Lots of things," James says. "You can do a lot of things in this town."

"Not without any money you can't."

"Something tells me you've got some stashed away."

"I already told you I have nothing."

"Yeah right."

"I don't."

The afternoon sun brought them inside here to cool off and to regroup. James ordered the beer of the day since it was only a couple bucks.

"So when's he going to call back?" Connor says.

"That's what I'm waiting on."

"What for? So he can tell you you owe him money?"

"You're stupid, you know that?"

"You're the big brother and look at you. How's that wound?"

James curses. That's what he thinks of his gunshot wound.

"I say we just bail on this chick. She's crazy. Hot, but crazy."

"After all this and you want to bail." James curses again. "You really are pathetic, you know that?"

"And why's that?"

"You want to bail? You don't bail on him."

"Danny doesn't frighten me," Connor says.

"That's because you're stupid. And stupid people don't get frightened. The same way stupid animals don't know that crossing the highway's gonna get them killed. Go ahead and don't be afraid. That's your choice."

"I'm not going to cross the highway. I know better than that."

"The reason he'd kill both of us is not to get his money back, even though I bet just like the rest of the country he's hurting. But he'd do it to make a point. Men like that kill men like us to make points. So that other men like you and I see it and still go ahead doing whatever thing he tells them to do. You got it?"

"I'm thirsty, that's what I got. Give me some money."

James shakes his head, glancing at a female server walking by. "I've got fifty dollars to my name."

"Sad, isn't it?"

"I once had money. Not my fault the market went belly-up. At least I tried to do something with my life."

"That what you call it?" Connor still likes to prod him like a five-year-old.

"At least I was doing more than chasing people around with bad debt."

"I never wanted to work for our cousin either. But it was too easy. The money was too good."

"Good enough to hire an escort for New Year's Eve for you and your delinquent buddies, right?"

Broken

Connor licks his lips. "I left out the buddy part until she got there. Guess she wasn't into that sort of stuff."

"Yeah, so all of this once again can be traced to you."

"What's that grand plan of yours?"

"I'm going to call the guy who followed her down here."

"The guy you beat up?"

James nods.

"Give me some money."

"Sit back down."

"I'm thirsty."

James gives him a ten. Connor appears to be confused, as if his head is hurting from actually trying to have a rational thought.

"So what are you going to say to him when you call him?"

"I'm going to tell him that we have her."

"How do you know he hasn't already seen her?"

"I think he followed her down here. I just—I don't think it was her choice. I think she's trying to disappear."

"Why New Orleans?"

"Why not?" James asks. "Good a place as any."

"Does he know we're down here?"

"Danny?"

"Yeah."

"No."

"Maybe we can follow the chick's lead. Just disappear."

"Get me another beer."

"It's a good idea."

"You just don't get it," he tells Connor. "We're not going to just disappear."

"How do you know?"

James wipes the sweat off his forehead. "Because—because I just bet he already knows we're down here. I bet he's got somebody watching us even now."

Connor looks around. "Nobody's here."

"I'd bet you anything."

"You got nothing to bet."

"I know. And that's why I'm going to find that skinny little runt and throw her in my trunk and take her back home. And daddy dearest will do the rest."

"If it was that easy, why not do that in the first place?"

"I don't like beating up helpless girls."

"You think that chick is helpless? Still? With that hole in your arm?"

"I just want enough money to get everybody off my back. Then I'll just slide away and let you do whatever the hell you want to do. I just want to be left alone."

"I'm telling you what. If I see that chick again, she's going to hurt."

"You're not going to touch her."

"Not now. But when we're through I'm going to."

"Go get the drinks."

"She owes me, and I'm going to take what's mine."

"You think every chick owes you."

"Every chick does," Connor says. "Especially this little Texan tramp."

• • •

She has spent the day wandering the city, trying to relax, trying to take her mind off everything. She keeps telling herself that what she saw back at the church was all made up, all conjured in her mind. Yet every street brings either a distant memory or a sudden fear or a stranger's face that she's sure is going to be someone she recognizes. She knows she needs to leave this city but doesn't know where else to go.

The sun is starting to set and with it comes the darkness of the night. She doesn't want to know what the night will bring.

Laila knows she needs to call Kyle. She knows she needs to meet with him.

Meeting with him will mean meeting with Lex.

Maybe that will change things. Maybe she will stop seeing and feeling and experiencing things.

But another part of her fears that seeing them will put them in danger.

Laila can't help feeling watched even though she's been walking around the last three hours without any signs of anybody following her.

She sits on a bench on a path overlooking the Mississippi River. She knows she needs to do it.

So she finds a pay phone and calls.

She reaches him right away.

"Are you okay?" Kyle asks her.

"I'm fine."

"What happened earlier?"

"I got nervous."

"Why?"

"Because—because of my brother."

"I didn't bring him."

"I know. I saw you."

"You saw me? You were there?"

"I wanted to know if I could trust you."

"Why can't you? What would I want of you, Laila? Why would I want to hurt you?"

"I know. It's just—it's just me being who I am."

"And who is that? I want to know."

"Careful."

"Where are you now?" he asks.

"I'm not sure, to be honest."

"Where are you staying?"

"Where are *you* staying?"

He tells her.

"And Lex is with you?"

"He's sitting right across from me." There is a pause. "Do you want to talk with him?"

"No."

"You sure?"

"How about I meet you at your hotel in a couple of hours?"

"What about Lex?"

"I just want to meet with you. For now."

"What should I tell him?"

"I haven't seen him in years. You have as good an idea of what to tell him as I do."

"Okay. I'll meet you in the lobby. By myself. And then what?"

"And then—and then I don't know."

"Why'd you come here, Laila? Who is that guy looking for you? What happened?"

"I can't tell you."

"You need to get help."

"I know. That's why I did this."

"Did what? Come to New Orleans?"

"No. That's why I called you."

• • •

James leaves the bar and heads outside to smoke and make a call. He's had too many beers, but at a couple bucks each, how could he not? He smokes and watches the people passing and wonders how he got to this corner in the French Quarter of New Orleans in the first place.

If he could, he'd go back inside and shoot Connor himself. Just get it over with and start a new track in life. But he can't. It's his little brother. The same little brother he's been bailing out of trouble since they went to that awful Catholic grade school.

James knows that one day when this is all over—not just this particular episode but the whole damned thing—and he settles down with a wife and a few kids, that's when he'll get back to the church. Nothing too heavy, but enough to cleanse the palate. Enough to cleanse his soul. He needs confession and needs it bad. Not like Connor, but Connor is a lost soul. That boy can't find God, not with the devil entrenched in his heart. James has never done the things Connor has done. He's only done things when necessary. Even the man he killed was necessary. It was someone in the wrong place at the wrong time, and he needed to do it. But he didn't want to do it, the same way he doesn't want to hurt Laila. He will hurt her if he has to. If it comes down to his life or her life, then he'll choose his life. But he didn't start this simply to hurt her.

He saw them—Laila and her family—as a way out. An end to the bad streak he'd been having.

Little did James know this would just continue his rotten luck.

He flicks the cigarette into the street and makes the call. He curses how hot it is, and he wipes the back of his neck. His shirt is too heavy for this town.

The kid picks up on the second ring.

"This Kyle Ewing?"

"Who's calling?"

James pauses and feels the rage soaring just like the buzz he already has. "Do you know how much trouble you're in, Mr. Ewing?"

"Who is this?"

"What, you don't remember my voice? After all the time we spent together?"

A long silence. "What do you want?"

"I thought I made it clear to you what I wanted when we last spoke, but I guess I didn't. Maybe I need to use Laila to get through to you."

"Did you hurt her? Is she okay?"

This tells him what he's wanting to know.

Laila is not with him.

"She's not hurt. She's fine. She's with me, and she's fine."

"Let me talk to her."

James laughs. "You followed her all the way here only to let this happen. Doesn't feel very nice, does it?"

"What do you want?"

"You listen to me and listen to me very carefully. I don't want anything to happen to our pretty little princess, but I swear to God I will cut her throat and let her bleed like a pig if I have to. But I don't want to. That's my point. Now my brother on the other hand, he doesn't want to kill her. Not just yet. He wants to do other things and I know he will if I'm not around to prevent it. So for Laila's sake, why don't you do what I tell you to do."

"Anything."

"And we don't need to involve anybody else."

"Okay."

James can hear the panic and desperation in the kid's voice.

"Okay. First off, where are you staying?"

"Laila knows."

"Yeah, well, she might be lying to me. You tell me to confirm."

"The Parc St. Charles," Kyle says.

"And where is that?"

"It's downtown. About four blocks away from the French Quarter."

"You're going to do this for me. I want five hundred dollars in two hours as a deposit on Laila's life. Just a little thing that's going to help me out for now."

"What — I can't get that that quickly."

"Listen, kid. You work at a bank. I'm not saying you're loaded, but you surely got five hundred bucks. If you don't shut it, my price will start going up."

There's a pause, then a subdued "okay."

"I want you to put it in an envelope and hold it at the front desk of your hotel."

"And then what?"

"And then I won't kill Laila."

"You said you don't want to hurt her."

Broken

James spits on the sidewalk. "I don't, but obviously I need something. And right now that something is money. It's really that simple. No deep-rooted motives for all this. Just the love of money and the necessity for it. That's all."

"I don't have much."

"You have five hundred dollars, right?"

"What will it take—what do you want? What do you need to get Laila back?"

James laughs. "You don't have what I need."

"I can try to—look, there are ways to get money. My parents..."

"This is not about you, and the only reason I'm even involving you is because you decided for some stupid foolhardy reason to follow this girl all the way to New Orleans. Tell me something. Why? You that hot for her?"

"I wouldn't categorize it like that."

"Yeah, of course not. You're a gentleman. But you spent a little time with her, and she blew your mind. Girls like that don't walk in and out of the bank every day, huh?"

"I can get you more money."

"I don't want your money. Because I take your money, then I got your problems. And see, the thing with Laila—well, the thing is this. She'll leave us alone. What's to say that you don't one day grow a pair and then decide you want to hunt us down not just for the money but for the inconvenience? Or maybe even to prove a point to a ladylove?"

"I wouldn't do that."

"This is what you're going to do," James says. "You're going to get five hundred dollars and put it in an envelope and then leave it for James at the front desk. You got that?"

"And then what?"

He thinks for a moment. "Then you'll wait."

"Wait for what?"

James hangs up without answering.

He doesn't know the answer. All he knows is that he needs some money. That's the first thing he needs.

Then he needs to find Laila and continue on with the plan.

He walks back into the bar ready to spend the rest of the money he does have.

He lets out a curse.

Connor is gone.

•   •   •

Lex wants a drink badly but knows that's the summary of his life.

Instead he offers up a prayer. He knows they help. He knows God is allowing him to stay strong even when all he wants is to rip open the valve and let the pain and anxiety go away.

He folds up the jeans he wore yesterday and puts them in his suitcase and zips it up. He is ready to go. If Laila doesn't want to meet with him and continues to get herself into trouble, then let her. He's tried and been trying, but he's not about to get himself killed for no reason. He isn't responsible just for himself anymore. There are others involved, and he needs to think of them.

As he glances at his suitcase, he notices the front zipper is open. It's got a small pouch at the very top. Lex opens it and sees there's something inside.

He pulls out a photo.

It's a black-and-white shot that could have been taken with the camera he found earlier. It resembles the kind of photos Laila used to take.

When he examines it, he begins to wonder if this is indeed one of the shots Laila took.

It's a picture of Lex laughing hysterically somewhere in the pasture on their property. He looks at the teenager and wonders what it would be like to have that kind of joy again. To not be twenty-four yet feeling like he was fifty-four and weighed down with all this baggage.

Broken

He knows perhaps he should feel like that baggage is gone, that his newfound commitment and faith would leave all the rest behind. But it doesn't work like that.

At least it doesn't work that way with Lex.

For a moment he's transported back to the day this shot was taken. It's probably a day just like any other. Laila out with him exploring the Texas fields or bathing in the sun or making up stories and laughing. He remembers they used to laugh so much. Laila could get him laughing until he cried. She was a master at it. And this shot details it so perfectly.

"I've never seen this," he says as he looks at the back of the photo.

He sighs and thinks again about that drink.

A man can change his ways, but his tendencies still shadow his every move. He can get on his hands and knees and beg for forgiveness, but that doesn't necessarily mean he won't have to do it again. He can confess that God is his master and that Jesus is his savior and yet he still might decide to forgo his master and savior and become the boss again.

That's how he feels. That's why his breath shakes as he lets out a sigh.

Lex sits down on the side of the bed and prays and turns the photograph of himself.

There's something going on here that he can't explain. But he feels it.

And he feels the compulsion to stay.

"God, please protect us. Bring us back home safely. That's all I ask."

He puts the photo back in his suitcase and then puts the bag back on the floor.

He knows he can't leave yet. Not this way. Not this soon.

Lex has unfinished business with Laila.

There are things she needs to know, and this might be the last chance he'll ever have to tell her.

• • •

Amos feels his eyes close longer than a blink and decides to get out of the car. He climbs out and walks down the sidewalk past the three-story white house and then back in front of it again. Just to get his heart beating and to keep himself fresh. He opens the trunk of his car and takes out an energy drink that's hot to drink but will do the trick. He gets back in his car and keeps the engine off to stay overheated and awake.

He followed Connor to this place. Amos doesn't need to wonder what's inside. He got a glimpse of the woman answering the door. She was an older lady, and though she wasn't dressed in anything like lingerie or something risqué, Amos still knows. How Connor found the name and the address of the brothel is like asking a crack whore how she found cocaine. It's all the same. Sniffing noses always leads the animals to what they're looking for.

It's almost six o'clock and normally he would be sitting down eating his dinner and watching his television shows. His is a life of routines, and usually he watches the six o'clock local news in Chicago and then *Seinfeld*. Nothing gets him laughing like *Seinfeld*. Some people through the years have said he looks and acts like the character of Puddy, which he takes as a compliment. Though he knows that Puddy has never taken a .45, jammed it into someone's mouth, and made them clamp onto it before pressing the trigger not once but twice. He might look and act like the guy, but he knows better. There are many things he's not good at, but he is good at the things he needs to be good at.

That's why he's paid well. Why he's able to live a comfortable life in these uncomfortable times.

It's quarter till seven when the sound of glass makes him reach for the gun on the passenger seat. He scans the house down the road through his windshield and sees something falling from the second window.

That something turns out to be a man.

Broken

That man turns out to be Connor.

Amos sees the door to the house open and the same woman standing at the doorway, taking aim.

A couple of rounds go off. He ducks himself because it seems like the woman doesn't have a clue how to shoot a gun.

Connor scampers across the street. He doesn't appear injured at all. He does, however, appear to be missing his shirt.

Another crack sounds, and Amos imagines that she's firing a .22. No way she's going to hit Connor with him running away like that. He'd have a hard time himself.

Connor actually passes him as he is running. He does a double take when he sees Amos in the car.

For a moment it seems like time stops as the two men look at each other.

Connor keeps going.

Amos watches him from the mirror in the car, still waiting, in no hurry.

When Connor disappears, Amos starts the car again. The woman is no longer in the doorway, though there's another woman looking out the shattered window on the second story, a pretty redhead. A young and pretty redhead.

A young, pretty redhead with blood streaming down her nose.

Just like a dog sniffing another. They're all the same thing.

As he heads back to the hotel, knowing that Connor recognized him and will surely tell his brother, Amos wishes he was at home watching *Seinfeld*.

"Soon," he tells himself. "Very soon."

•   •   •

James curses and slaps Connor in the face. It doesn't hurt Connor as much as humiliate him. And as much as Connor might want to hit him back, he doesn't. He knows better. He knows who will eventually win when push comes to shove.

"What are you thinking?"

"No need to yell," Connor says, rubbing the side of his face.

"Well? What's going through that head of yours?"

"I was feeling cooped up."

"So what? You decide to pay a visit to some escort service without having any money?"

"Something like that."

"She should've shot you in the head. We'd all be better off."

"She certainly tried," Connor said. "Though that's not the problem I was talking about."

They're in their hotel room, though James isn't worrying who might be next to them or in the hallway. He's getting ready to head over to Kyle's hotel. Connor is slipping on one of James' long-sleeved T-shirts.

"So what then?"

"You remember Amos Murray? Big guy? Square-looking."

"What do you mean do I remember him? That's a stupid question."

"I saw him."

James stops and looks at Connor. "Where?"

"Outside the house."

"You stupid man. Did he see you?"

"Stared right at my face."

James stops and thinks for a minute.

"What?"

"If he saw you and let you go, that means we're not dead. Not yet."

"You think that was a warning?" Connor asks.

"I don't know. He just must not care about being spotted."

"So you were right."

James puts the gun in his pants and pulls the short-sleeved shirt over it. "Of course I was right. When am I not right?"

Connor says something, but James ignores it.

"You need to come with me."

Broken

"Why?"

"Because first of all, you might go off and do something else. Second, I need you to get that money for me."

"What are you going to be doing?"

"Look—I don't trust this Kyle fella even if he is young and stupid and probably in love. Who knows what'll happen? And now that I know Amos is out there—you need to get him to tail you."

"What are you going to do?"

"I'm going to lie in the shadows and wait. And watch."

"Watch for what?"

"Watch for her. Laila's out there somewhere. She's in this city. And she's eventually going to show up. When she does, we'll get her. Or I'll get her."

"And Amos?"

"I'll handle him," James says. "He's going to wish he never saw you."

19

The first time it happened — the first time it was really official, that I got paid for it — I remember being left alone in the hotel room almost seconds after it was over. The act itself wasn't what tore me up inside, what prompted my deluge of tears. It was how quickly he got out of the room. As if I was some plague he needed to be rid of. As if the money was all that mattered to me, nothing else. Eventually I grew to think that was all that mattered. And soon I began to think nothing mattered. Not my body and not the money and nothing, including my soul.

When you're young, there are things you tell yourself you will never do. But slowly time ties you up and beats you down and forces you to submit. And eventually those idealistic notions seem like pipe dreams. Especially when the dreams you did have as a young girl — dreams of going to the big city and walking down a runway and falling in love and having everything you could ever imagine — turned out to be as empty as the actions of a woman giving her body over to a stranger in some hotel room.

These are the things that haunt me the most.

I believe in demons. I know they're out there. And I know they hunt the needy and the hopeless.

Broken

James watches Connor and remembers finding him lying in a pool of blood at the mansion in Burr Ridge, Illinois. He'd been called there by one of Connor's friends, though James wouldn't consider any of the three men friends. None of them knew what to do with a bleeding and unconscious man. A man they assumed had died just like the shooter did. So they called his brother, and James was left to deal with the mess, just like he'd been doing his whole life.

That night James resigned himself to the fact that his younger brother was going to die. But one thing James knew about Connor was the guy was strong. He was a lot of bad things, but he was also strong.

And as James waited for him at the hospital right at the start of the new year, he began to think of what he would do once he found the woman responsible for this.

James knew their time with the woman who shot Connor wasn't over.

It just so happened that on the journey toward discovering who she was, James also found out her very wealthy family missed her terribly.

Thus a plan was concocted involving Connor playing the part of the haunting ghost and James playing the part of the vengeful brother.

And now, having failed at both of their parts, James watches Connor heading down the street and notices the car following him.

The guy tailing him is doing a great job, especially considering he's in a car. Occasionally he stops or pulls over and all the while remains a good distance away from Connor. James is on the other side of the street, remaining in doorways and alcoves and hidden behind people. With the sun going down, the streets are getting busier. Connor takes his time and acts oblivious, and James doesn't know whether his brother is acting or not.

He can see the head and shoulders of the man in the tailing car. James knows enough not to mess with Amos. Yet he also knows that Amos needs to be dealt with. Either you deal with Amos or Amos deals with you, it's one way or the other. James prefers it this way.

They reach the hotel, and Amos parks his car and gets out as Connor walks inside. Amos looks around casually and then walks down the street. The man is wearing a sports coat over a T-shirt and jeans. James hopes he doesn't have to get hit by the guy. There are a lot of things in this life that might hurt, and being hit by someone like Amos has to be at the top of them. Amos could break Connor in two. And that's what he might eventually do unless James does something.

"Come on," he says to himself.

He hopes that before anything else happens, Connor gets that money. If the money is there. As long as they have a little something, there's a chance to escape. There's a chance to leave this city. Maybe go down to Mexico, though he knows that's such a cliché. Perhaps go north, far north, to Canada. Anywhere to get far away from Danny and his many reaches.

He speeds up just as Amos steps into the hotel.

James feels the butt of his gun lodged between his jeans and his bare skin. He wants a cigarette but knows he doesn't have time.

The sky above is turning orange. It doesn't feel as hot without the sun beating down on him.

James takes a breath and then stops right before the entrance to the hotel.

He waits for a few minutes. Thinking. Debating.

And that's right when he sees the tall figure walking up the hotel steps and going inside.

For a moment he can't believe his eyes.

Laila doesn't even see him.

It's almost too good to be true.

James bites down gently on the tip of his tongue, feels the butt of his gun again, and heads toward the doorway.

Broken

. . .

Laila enters the glass doors and sees the small desk right in the front with an open hallway to the left and a separate room on the right. She knows it's him at the desk even before he turns around. She knows it's Connor. Something about the way he's standing and that tall, slim physique. He's equally surprised to see her, smiling and standing still.

"Boo," he says.

A man who looks and moves like a football player emerges from behind a wall in the corridor to her left. A quick glance shows that the stranger is holding a gun.

An alarm goes off in her mind as she takes in her options.

She wants to run but isn't sure where to go. She's wondering about Kyle but has no idea where he might be. It's her fault for coming a little early, for coming down here in the first place. She turns to her right when a figure runs into the room, and for a moment she thinks it's Kyle but it's not. It's the little boy who used to come running into her room and bouncing on her bed and bothering her and nagging at her and making her laugh.

Yet Lex isn't smiling and he isn't really looking at her to begin with.

She can't believe it's him and can't believe how old he looks.

But before she can manage a word, Lex crashes into Connor and sends both of them tumbling. A woman behind the desk is as shocked as Laila.

The figure on her left keeps coming.

"Lex," she calls out.

He's on the floor pinning Connor to the ground.

She calls out again and is about to do something when the big guy arrives. With one quick yank the man tears Lex off Connor. As Lex lands on the tiled floor of the hotel lobby, the woman behind the desk screams. The stranger points a gun at Connor's head.

"Where's your brother?" he asks.

A loud boom suffocates the lobby and sends Laila to her knees. She imagines Connor's head exploding in bloody chunks over the floor, yet the only thing hit is a piece of the lobby desk that cracks and splinters on the floor. Another loud boom sends Laila crawling on her knees toward Lex, who is kneeling on the side of the check-in desk.

"Get your gun off him," a voice behind her says.

Laila recognizes it. She gets to Lex and puts her hands on his face and feels him breathing and for a moment looks into those familiar eyes.

She doesn't say anything. She doesn't have a chance. But she sees him and knows he wants to say something and knows that he's okay.

"Get off him or this one is going to hurt," James says.

Laila gives Lex a knowing look that says a hundred things.

She breathes and then glances over as the big man kneels and then stands up.

It takes him less than a second to aim his gun toward the entry to the door and let off three shots. Glass breaks and crashes, and Laila doesn't wait around to see what the results are. The woman behind the desk screams again as Laila grips Lex's hand for a second and sees him mouth the words, "Get out of here." She stands up and lets go and sprints toward the doorway. A huge chunk of window is blown out. She leaps over remaining glass even as James is moving and trying to duck for cover down the hallway.

Laila is on the street in a minute with a ringing in her ears. She heads down the block, and as she does she sees Lex still inside the lobby.

There's another boom, and then she runs into someone who grabs her.

"Hey—hold on—Laila. Stop."

She's ready to head butt whoever this is until she sees Kyle's face. He looks as white and worried as she must. She's so out of breath she can't say a word.

Broken

"Come with me," Kyle says as he holds her arm and rushes with her down the sidewalk.

Another loud gunshot goes off, and Laila thinks of Lex but knows she needs to get out of there. She speeds up and soon is running faster than Kyle.

"Slow down. Come on. Cross the street here."

They run without stopping for ten minutes. When Kyle finally tugs on her and tells her to come inside the bar, Laila feels like throwing up from fear and adrenaline and not being able to catch her breath. Kyle helps her inside, and they close the door. He puts his arms around her and holds her tight.

"It's going to be okay," he says.

But she doesn't believe it and never will.

Her hands shake as they hold the drink.

"That'll maybe help with nerves."

"Nothing will help this," she tells him as she stands overlooking the street below.

"You know that's Bourbon Street?"

"Didn't know that."

"Just listen—just calm down, okay?"

Kyle glances at her, exhales, and takes a sip of beer. "How'd you get away from them?"

"Away from who?"

"James? His brother."

"I was never with them."

"He called me up and told me he had you."

"He had you all right," she says. "I was going to the hotel just as I told you I would."

"James called me right after we spoke. He said he was going to meet me at my hotel. But how could he know you were planning on meeting me there?"

"Some coincidence."

"I don't believe in coincidences."

Laila sighs and sips her margarita. She's not in the mood but doesn't know what else to do.

"Tell me what's going on," Kyle says.

"I don't quite know."

"What?"

"I don't. I don't know who that guy was back there. The big one with the gun."

"But you know the other guys, right? What happened? Why are they after you?"

"They want money. They want my family's money. My father's money."

"But why you? How'd they choose you out of millions of others?"

"Because I shot Connor. The skinny guy. Not sure if you've had the great pleasure of meeting him."

"With my gun?"

"No. This happened on New Year's Eve. The other one—his name is James. They're from Chicago. They're brothers. I shot Connor in self-defense. And I swear I thought I killed him."

"How'd that happen?"

"I'm not getting into that."

"So they're doing this out of revenge?"

"Yes. I guess. Somehow they tracked down my family. I still don't know exactly how. They found out that my father has a lot of money."

"How much?"

"You ever come to the ranch, you'll get an idea just driving around."

"So why then—why were you in Greenville of all places working in a bank?"

"Because I could. Because I've had no connection with them in years."

"Why?"

"What's with all the questions?" She curses. "That's my own business."

"Laila, I'm just trying to help."

"I know. I just—I know that. And that's the question I can't figure out."

"Yeah, I'm trying to figure that out too. Your brother kept trying to understand why I'd come all this way if we weren't an item. He called me crazy."

"You are crazy," she says.

"I know."

"I'm scared something happened to Lex."

"I'm sure he's fine. He has my cell number."

"Why did he tell me to leave? Why didn't he come with me?"

"He was probably protecting you," Kyle says.

"Do you have his number?"

"I already tried calling it when I got the drinks. I just got voice mail."

"Try again."

Kyle does and waits and shakes his head. "Same thing."

"This guy came out of nowhere."

"Who did?"

"I don't know who he was. He was just—he made a beeline straight toward Connor. And that's when all hell broke loose. James came in and started shooting, and the other guy started firing back."

"What happened to Lex?"

"He was okay. When I last saw him."

"Did you agree to give them money?" Kyle asks. "Why'd they follow you down this far?"

"I think because they know." She feels a breeze blow against her. The sun is taking its time setting. Rock music blares in the background.

"They know what?"

"They know how desperate I am."

"What do you mean desperate?"

She shakes her head and stares out at the buildings across the street. "What did Lex say about me?"

"He's scared about you. He's concerned."

"Did something happen to my family?"

"He didn't say. He didn't share much. I can tell he loves you."

Laila nods, then glances at Kyle. "Can I ask you something crazy?"

"Sure."

"You say you don't believe in coincidences. But you believe in God and all that, right?"

"Not sure about 'all that,' but yes."

"Do you believe in ghosts?"

Kyle thinks for a minute. "Don't know. Probably not. I believe in evil spirits."

"Maybe that's what they are."

"What they are? What are you talking about?"

"I don't know. I think I'm going crazy."

She knows she probably shouldn't be here sipping cocktails and making small talk, but she doesn't know what else to do. She'd maybe try going to a church, but that certainly didn't work the last time. She doesn't want to go back to her hotel because she is worried someone might know she is coming. She doesn't want to leave Kyle and has nowhere else to go.

"You okay?" he asks.

"Yeah."

"You're not gonna do something crazy like jump off this deck?" He forces a smile, but the joke is half true.

"I would if I knew it would work," she says. Laila finishes her drink and asks Kyle to get her another.

"I'll be right back."

She looks around the roof and doesn't see anybody else. She glances down at the street and watches the people walking. So many of them surely tourists, taking in the sights and scoping out which bar they'll come to once the dark blanket of night falls. She wishes she could be innocent and unassuming like they are, passing time and passing the sights and passing through life without the worry of being found and being killed.

She notices the boy in the red Texans shirt and the blue cap, and she stops.

There he is again.

Standing there on the sidewalk in the center of the block.

Standing there looking up at her.

Standing wearing that same backpack he was wearing before.

He waves.

Laila shakes her head, angry. She closes her eyes and then opens them again and still sees the kid.

"Here you go again."

Something shuffles behind her. For a moment she turns around as Kyle sits down, then she turns back and looks on the street and finds the spot empty.

No little boy and no Texans shirt and no little smile and wave.

"What? What happened?"

"How do you know if you're losing your mind?" she asks. "Is there any sort of way to know?"

"I doubt you'd ask that question if you were."

"I need to — I need to use the ladies room for a minute."

"You sure you're okay?"

"Yeah. Fine. Just. Need. Minute."

Standing up, she feels the building starting to twirl like a ride at an amusement park.

The bathroom is small, with two cramped stalls and a short sink under a round mirror. The mirror is old and distorts her image as she stands in front of it. Laila runs cold water, cupping some of it to douse her face. It feels good. It wakes her up just a little, and she stares at her wet face before reaching for a towel.

She remembers another time doing this. Standing at a sink feeling like the end is near and trying to make sense of everything. It seems like yesterday. She wonders if it all would have been different if she had simply gone with the plan. If she had simply said yes instead of saying no.

She closes her eyes and throws away the thoughts. Then she opens them and finds herself in another restroom, this one white and sterile and clean with a toilet stall and a large sink.

She's been here before and she knows when and where and she's suddenly dizzy. The room begins to turn and she feels light and her mouth goes numb and hard and she knows she's going to be sick. Laila makes it to the toilet and vomits, throwing up only liquid, mostly from the drink she just had. Pink swirls around the basin, and her eyes water.

As she coughs she stands up again and wipes her eyes with her hand. She's back in the stall in the bar on Bourbon Street. It's small and confining. She flushes the toilet and then goes to open the stall door, but it won't budge. The lock is open inside, but the door seems welded shut. It won't go in or out. She fights it, banging at it and hitting it with her palms and then barging at it with her shoulder. But nothing. It won't move.

Staring at the cream-colored door, she sees writing all over it. She wonders if it was there just a moment ago.

Scrawled in black ink is the same thing over and over again:

GO TO 212

The expression makes no sense to her.

There is only a tiny sliver of space below the door that isn't enough to crawl through, and there's no way to get over the wall.

She fights the door again for several minutes, then screams out loud for somebody and anybody. She's left there in silence. Locked.

Her panic lets her ignore the running water for the moment. But

Broken

eventually she sees it, overflowing from the toilet and running down its side and onto the dirty floor.

Laila screams again, this time for Kyle. But her screams seem to bounce right back at her, as if they're confined to just this stall.

The liquid pouring out of the toilet begins to look like sludge and grime, like a backed-up sewer unloading its contents. Her shoes are soaked in it, and it's getting deeper.

She pounds at the door again. It doesn't budge.

She howls Kyle's name.

Grimy water with chunks in it continues to surge upward and over the back and sides of the toilet. It's up to her ankle and getting deeper. The smell reeks, and the sound drowns out everything else.

Once again she feels light-headed.

She refuses to let this happen. To believe that it is happening. Yet the water is cold and it stinks and it's real. She knows that. This is all very real.

"You will not defeat me," she says out loud to either God or the devil or the ghost or whatever it is that is doing this to her. Fate or chance or whatever, she doesn't care.

With a leaping rush, she barges at the door with her shoulder slamming against it, and it tears open and sends her flying toward the sink.

She cuts the edge of her jaw on the side of the sink.

Standing back up, she looks and sees the water still coming out. It was no dream. It's still happening.

Laila opens the door to the restroom and walks out. Her legs are unsteady, the room still wavering. She thinks she should find the manager and rip his head off but then realizes all she wants to do is find Kyle.

She wants someone to tell her she's not losing her mind.

She can't be losing her mind.

Maybe, just maybe, if she tells a manager about the bathroom, they might come back telling her that it looks perfectly normal.

189

• • •

The Mississippi flows underneath them as James and Connor watch the French Quarter pass by. A voice narrates the trip through speakers, but it allows them to talk freely without worrying about someone listening in on them.

"Never knew you wanted to take me on a riverboat," Connor says. "Couldn't there at least be some gambling?"

"I wanted to make sure we weren't being followed."

"It'd be hard to miss Amos."

"We almost both died because of that guy," James says.

"We almost died because of that chick."

James stares out into the fading light and is lost in thought. He's trying to control the panic, trying to stay ahead of the rush of fear that's closing in.

"I'm leaving," Connor says.

James looks at his brother. "What?"

"You heard me. I'm going to take half that money and leave."

"Two hundred and fifty—no, actually less—where's that going to get you?"

"Far from here. Far from Amos."

He thinks over the events that just happened. How a security guy coming out of nowhere ended up taking care of Amos. How James grabbed Connor and led them out of the hotel before anybody else showed up. How both of them argued and how James eventually forced Connor onto this boat.

"Wanna know who tackled you?" James asks.

"I don't know. And I don't care."

"Lex. Laila's brother."

"What's he doing here?"

"Having a nice little family reunion."

"Doesn't matter to me."

"You can't leave, not like this."

"It's over for me," Connor says.

For a long time they stand in silence, the captain's narration breezing by and fading away. James lights a cigarette and offers one to Connor.

"Remember that camp we used to go to when we were young?"

"Yeah," James says.

"Remember when we used to take the boats out at night on Lake Michigan?"

James nods.

"I was thinking about that the other day. I don't know why, just was. I was thinking how much I loved those days. I always thought it'd be cool to get a little shack up there by the lake and just settle down."

He laughs at Connor. "Settle down? Settle down doing what?"

"I don't know. Maybe I could, like, have a garden and make homemade beer and become one of those earthy people."

"You mean potheads?"

Connor curses. "So what? I can't have a dream?"

"Not sure I call that a dream. More like a wish to get out of here."

"It's not that. It's just—I don't know."

"What?" James asks.

"I think I liked camp because we were away from Ma and Dad. Away from him, you know? Because he couldn't do anything to us then. It was just us. Just us and nature and quiet. You know?"

There is neither sadness nor anger in Connor's glance. Something got lost long ago, maybe somewhere along the shores of Lake Michigan in that lighter, brighter world.

"We just need to get past this," James says.

"Get past what? Amos? Or Danny? Or the full moon? The Mississippi?"

"Stop being stupid."

"You stop being stupid. I got my wake-up call on New Year's Eve, how about you?"

"Wake-up call? Is that what it was for you? Doesn't that mean you're supposed to change then? Become a better person?"

"Doesn't mean all things change," Connor says. "Just means I need to get out of this mess."

"Yeah well, I got my wake-up call on New Year's Eve too. You almost died on me, man. So by God it's about time I'm going to give a little of it back."

"A little what?"

"Laila's going to have a very rude awakening very shortly."

"We've been trying."

"Well we'll try a little harder then, won't we?"

"Keep it down," Connor says.

"She's not getting away."

"She might already have."

"No. She's still here. She's hiding. She's with her little protector, and she's hiding. Her brother is still around, and I just bet she won't leave without him."

"So what are we doing?"

"Regrouping."

"James, man, we keep getting signs to get out. We got some cash. We need to get out."

"No."

"We're pushing fate. It's telling us that things aren't going to end up well."

"Then we'll push back. We'll push harder." James curses. "She's going to look me in the eye one more time before this is all done."

"That might be a mistake."

"I've made 'em before, and I'm sure I'll do it again."

•   •   •

This is what they call stupid, Lex.

He waits and watches and listens to his thoughts passing by like 18-wheelers on the freeway at night. He's above the dock where the riverboat will arrive in ten minutes, hidden in the shadows where they won't be able to see him when they get off.

He doesn't have a plan. But he followed them and is going to make sure they stay far away from her. If Laila doesn't want to see him, at least he will make sure they don't see her either.

You are tired and being stupid because that's not rational, he thinks. Get in your car and head back home and leave this all behind. She was a problem when she was young, and she always has been a problem. And she will be the death of you before this is all over.

But Lex knows these men are here because of him. Because of a conversation he had with the dark-haired man who called himself "Sonny." They had met and had lunch after he called Lex. Sonny had said he was a photographer in Chicago who had been in a relationship with Laila when she suddenly disappeared. Lex had told the man as much as he knew, but that had been sadly very little.

It was only after Sonny left that Lex began to worry. He knows now his worries were justified, that the man wasn't even named Sonny. He wanted the information to track down his sister, but obviously not for the reasons he said.

Lex looks at his watch.

His phone rings, and this time he decides to take it.

"Where are you?" Kyle asks. "You okay?"

"I'm fine."

"We're worried, man. Laila's worried sick."

"Tell her I'm fine. I'm safe."

"What happened to those guys?"

"They're still out there. How is she?"

"Laila's okay. We're on Bourbon Street. At a bar and grill."

"Kyle, listen to me. Don't leave Laila."

"Why would I do that?"

"You just can't. Promise me."

"Of course I won't. I promise. What are you doing? Are you leaving?"

"No. But just make sure you guys hide somewhere."

"I want her to leave. But, I don't know—she's confused. And scared. After what happened at the hotel—she's not the only one."

"These guys are going to keep going after her."

"So what's that mean?"

"Maybe—I don't know. Maybe I can—I don't know."

"You better be careful or you'll end up on the receiving end of something bad."

"I won't," Lex says. "Look—I'll give you guys a call in an hour or so. Okay? You can tell me where you're at and then we can meet up."

"Why don't we do that now?"

"I don't want anything happening to her. They followed her all the way down here, right? I don't want them finding her again."

"So you're spying on them?"

"I'm watching them to see where they go."

"That's like the worst idea I've ever heard of."

"They've already made their way to New Orleans, right?" Lex says. "I don't want to find them breaking down a door and dragging me out of a hotel room, got it?"

"What about the big guy? What happened to him? Laila told me he came out of nowhere."

"I don't know where he is."

"You better make sure he's not watching you."

"He's not. Listen, just stay with her and go somewhere safe. I'll call you in an hour."

Lex gets off the phone and looks at his watch. Only a few more minutes.

He knows he should probably call the police, but he can't. He's afraid for Laila, that something will happen to her, that this all has something to do with her past. The same past she's running from but can't seem to escape.

The scar on his arm from a teenage knife fight reminds him that the past will always be there. Regardless of where you go and what you do with the rest of your life, the past is there to remind and to taunt and to terrorize.

And it's only by the grace of God that he's allowed any semblance of peace. But it does come.

Peace comes.

But that doesn't mean it makes the day any easier. Or the reminders any softer.

•   •   •

"Where did they go?"

"I don't know, but I'll find them," Amos says into the cell phone.

"This is a problem."

"Nothing I can't handle."

"The girl? Where'd she go?"

"She disappeared."

Danny curses. "Just finish it. Deal with this mess and come back. I don't need any more headaches. I want the Brennan brothers dead. By tomorrow, you hear me?"

"What about the money?"

He curses again and tells him not to bother. "I should've never trusted James in the first place. At least his brother gets things done. He used to do a great job for me getting money when people owed me."

"I'll find them and get rid of them. What about the others?"

"I don't care. Do what you need to do, but make sure neither of those boys ever leaves New Orleans."

"Got it."

20

I never blame my circumstances on my mother's passing away when I was four. I've never said or thought that her death made me who I am. Or let me rephrase that — I've never said or thought that her death made me choose the paths I did. Life happens. Death happens. Accidents happen. Brutalities happen. Settling happens.

I sometimes wonder what it would be like to have been a mother.

Would that have changed me?

Would this broken-down and chipped soul be resuscitated by the simple smile on her baby's sweet cheeks?

I don't know. But sometimes I think that might have changed me, that might have made things better. Not easier, but better.

Because then I would have known that I needed to be better for someone else. I've never needed to be anything for anybody. Not my family and not my friends and not the few I've loved. And definitely not myself. But being a mother would have meant that I needed to be better for him.

They say having a baby changes everything, and it probably does. I've always believed that and probably know that to be true.

But we all fear change, don't we?

Some of us fight it to the death.

Broken

Laila doesn't worry about someone being in her hotel room. She's already explained to Kyle that nobody knows where she's staying and nobody is following her. They even walk around several blocks just to prove her point. After closing the door and seeing Kyle looking white with fear, Laila stops and listens for a minute, waiting for any intruder to make his presence known.

"See?" she says.

Kyle checks the bathroom.

"Check under the bed too."

"That's not funny."

He checks the balcony.

"We're safe here," she tells him.

Kyle rubs his eyebrows in a way that Laila admires. It makes him look young. Young and innocent.

"Keep the door open," she tells him as he steps off the balcony back into the room.

"Why?"

"I like it. I like to hear the sounds of life coming in the room."

Kyle keeps the balcony door open and scans the street.

"They're not down there waiting for us."

"You don't know that."

"Yes I do. Come on. Sit down."

He appears nervous and not just because of the fear of being followed. When he sits in one of the chairs against the wall facing the bed, Laila suddenly understands why he's acting so awkward.

She sits on the edge of the bed and smiles at him. "This is probably the safest place we could be right now."

"Yeah, probably."

"I'm not going to bite you."

He realizes how he's acting and he smiles at her, nodding. "I know."

"Nor will I attack you."

"I know. It's not you. It's just me. It's just — I don't know."

"What don't you know?"

"This. Like how I sometimes might have imagined this scenario in my dreams but not actually living it out. And especially not like this."

"I didn't see this coming either," she says.

For a while there's a silence in the room. Not an awkward silence, but more tired and still. Laila wonders what to do and when to do it and she assumes that Kyle must be thinking the same.

She studies Kyle, knowing he is waiting for her to talk and letting her have a few moments to herself.

"Why are you here?"

"What?"

"Why'd you come after me? I mean — it's one thing to want to hang out with me after work or even walk me home or stay up with me talking in the night. But why this?"

He laughs like a schoolboy. "I don't know."

"Really?"

"I don't. Seriously. You know I'm not — that I don't have some ulterior motive."

"What? To undress me and have your way?"

Kyle looks speechless, and she apologizes. "Look, I know that's not why you're here. But I can't figure out why you are."

He rubs his face and glances out at the balcony. "You want to hear something crazy?"

"Bet it won't be as crazy as you think it is."

"Probably not," he says. "Maybe more so than crazy, it's silly."

"Tell me."

"I changed schools in my junior year of high school. One of the hardest things I ever had to do. Losing all these friends I'd known for years and suddenly being thrust in a new environment. It was tough. I sorta floundered my way into different groups and different friends. And I remember there was this girl who was in my grade — she was beautiful and popular and seemed funny and outgoing. And the entire year, I never talked with her once. Not even once. She wasn't dating anybody at the time, but I never said anything to her. Sometimes I got this feeling when we passed—her locker was close to mine—see, I told you it's silly. I'd get this idea that she liked me.

"Well, I spent that next summer thinking and dreaming about her and wishing I had made some sort of effort. Then senior year came and I vowed to myself I would make an effort. That I would try. And guess what happened?"

"Did she die?"

Kyle looks at her with an incredulous glance and a shake of his head. "No. Geez that's morbid."

"Step into my life for a moment."

"See, I knew this would sound corny."

"Keep going," she says. "What happened?"

"First thing I find out about her when I see her was that she was dating another guy. Had been most of the summer. And they were serious. And near the end of the year I would finally have my talk with her. A deep one at that. She told me she had always found me cute, just wondered why I never made an effort. So you know—ever since that day, I told myself I would never let somebody go. That I would never not give an effort."

"This is quite the effort," Laila says. "What was this girl's name?"

"Tabitha. Or Tabi."

"Did they marry?"

"I don't know. I just know they drove off into the sunset after high school graduation."

"So this is fulfilling some high school fantasy of yours?"

"I hope you're kidding."

"Mostly." Laila smiles and moves to sit in the chair by his. "Sorry I can't be more accommodating."

"I'm sorry that things have led up to this."

They hear laughter in the distance.

"Want to hear my silly high school story?"

"Sure," Kyle says.

"I ran away with a guy to New Orleans once. I was seventeen."

"What for?"

"Same reason a guy like you follows someone like me down here. It has nothing to do with sense. It has more to do with what you're feeling. And at the time, I was crazy in love with this guy. All I wanted to do was escape my life and my world and love him. So that's what I did for a whole week."

"What happened?"

"Life. That's what happened."

Kyle stares at her. She smiles and stretches and looks at the open door.

A gust of air blows in and it soothes her.

"I found out I was pregnant a couple months later. How ignorant is that, huh? I skipped my period and didn't even realize it was because of that. That's how stupid I was and how much in love and in denial I was. I was something back then."

He doesn't move. His expression doesn't waver. Kyle waits for her to speak.

"I told him and that was it. Just like turning off a light. It was over. And I couldn't believe — I just couldn't believe he would do that. Even when I did everything he wanted me to do — and you know, that's the easy way out, to blame him, because I did everything I wanted to do too — but even after it was all over and taken care of, he still was gone. That had scared him and woken him up and made him get out. Just like that. As if he thought someone like me couldn't get pregnant."

Kyle's mouth is closed and tightened, and his eyes don't blink. She looks at him feeling calm and normal. No tears and no emotion and no fears.

"I was twelve weeks when I ended it. When I terminated the pregnancy. Twelve weeks. And I didn't think twice about it. All I was thinking about was him. Yet—I didn't even realize it at the time, but something changed that day. Two things died that day. And one of them was my heart."

"I'm sorry."

"There hasn't been a day that's gone by when I haven't thought about it. When I haven't regretted it. When I haven't known that what I did was wrong."

He lets her pause, perhaps waiting for her to cry, but she's not going to. Just because she remembers it and thinks about it and regrets it doesn't mean she's going to become a mess right here. That's past. That died along with so many other things.

"How's that for a high school love story?"

"It breaks my heart for you," Kyle says.

"I was seventeen and didn't tell anybody else except Erik. Well—I take that back. I did tell Lex. He was the one who took me to get it done. But the rest of my family never knew, nobody. Ten years later I've still never told another soul. And I don't know why in the world I'm telling you. Maybe because I feel I need to get it off my chest, though I know telling you isn't going to get me any favors."

"Telling me won't. But you can tell them to God."

"If He's there He already knows about them."

"But you can put them before Him and ask for forgiveness."

"What's that going to get me? A golden ticket to the heavenly spa up there? A get-out-of-jail card where I won't have to worry about it anymore?"

"It doesn't work like that," Kyle says.

"So how does it work?"

"I don't know, but I know what I believe. I know that I believe in God and I believe in His son, and I know this is going to sound like preaching 101 but I believe there is a way Jesus takes my mistakes. I have to believe this because if I don't I'm hopeless."

"What mistakes have you made? You're a good guy."

"We all make mistakes. All of us."

"Yeah, but, that's so simple and so—it's just not real. It's cheesy. It's like a bad Sunday school movie."

"Maybe the way I just said it is, but the truth isn't, Laila. I swear it's not. I'm not saying that suddenly all the pain and the guilt and the grief you have will go away. But what I am saying is that they'll be taken away. The Bible says that God takes our sins and throws them into the depths of the ocean. It says you won't be held responsible anymore."

She shakes her head. "So did you come down here to save my soul?"

"I thought I was saving myself. Now—well, I'm beginning to know why I needed to come down."

"I'm sorry," she says, standing, going to the balcony.

He lets her stand there for a while.

"I'm sorry for laying this in your lap," she says.

"You didn't lay anything in my lap. I appreciate you feeling like you could tell me this."

"It's just not that simple."

"It's more complex than any scientist could make it out to be, and it's also utterly simple. It's about believing. And about taking those mistakes and asking for forgiveness."

Laila looks at him, shaking her head, feeling anger starting to bubble over inside her. "I have tried to live out penance for however long, and yet I still don't come close to ever feeling whole again. Like this part of me that was taken out was taken out for good and that I'll have this huge awful hole inside that will just continue to get larger and larger until I take my final breath."

"It doesn't have to be like that, Laila."

She laughs, stifling a thought in her head. She can't repeat it, especially not to Kyle.

Instead she says, "It will always be this way. Always."

He stands up and comes over and hugs her. It's a safe hug, a warm hug, the kind a family member or a friend might give. She feels secure in it, not afraid of where the hands might go or afraid of what it will lead to. She exhales and leans against Kyle's shoulder and stays there for a few minutes.

"I'm sorry," he tells her.

"I am too. Yet I—I'll never be able to say I'm sorry. I took that chance away. That and a billion other chances."

Kyle whispers something in her ear, something powerful and profound, so much so that she can't say anything back. There isn't anything to say.

• • •

The problem with most people is they don't have persistence. Amos knows this as he enters the nineteenth hotel he's stepped inside today.

He goes to the front desk and smiles as the elderly lady greets him with the familiar drawl.

"How are you doing tonight?" he asks, knowing there's no need for him to be rude or cold.

She talks for a few minutes and he obliges. Then produces the photo.

"I'm looking for this young woman. Her name is Laila Torres. She's from Texas, and her family wanted me to contact her because of a family emergency. The problem is they know she is in New Orleans but they don't know which hotel she's staying at."

"My, is something wrong?"

"Yes. It's her father. He passed away."

"Oh dear." The woman holds the photo up with long, bony fingers. "Yes, she's staying here. I believe her name is Laila. Pretty little thing, isn't she?"

"Yes. She is."

"Would you like me to call up to her room?"

"No, no no. I'd rather tell her family that she's here. That way they'll have time to call here themselves. Obviously this should come from the family."

"Of course."

"Where can they call?"

"Oh, just have them call our number. And let them know she's in room 307 in case they don't get a hold of me."

"Certainly." He takes the sheet of paper she just wrote on. "You've been so kind."

"I'm so sorry to hear about that."

"Yeah, it's just a damned shame. Bad things happen every day, and we can't do a thing about them, can we?"

"That's why I pray every morning and every night."

Amos nods at her and gives her a wink. "You keep doing that. I'm sure it will get you far."

"You too young man."

He steps away and heads back outside, back to his parked car.

Persistence is the key, and most people give up because they're too lazy and too stupid. But those are two things he is not and never will be.

He opens the trunk. The darkness of the street keeps him in the shadows as he takes out a couple of the guns and then heads around to the back of the hotel.

• • •

"You know we're being followed?"

"You just realize that now?" James asks between two drags of his cigarette.

"Yeah, why? You seen him?"

"For the last ten minutes. Not very bright, is he?"

"You sure it's him? The same guy who tackled me in the lobby?" Connor asks.

James nods slowly.

They're walking down a street in the French Quarter passing

various bars and clubs. It would be easy to blend in but the man behind them a few stores back isn't doing a good job at being inconspicuous.

"What do you want to do?"

"Just—hey—just keep looking ahead. Don't make eye contact. Let's go into one of these bars and disappear. And when he thinks he's lost us, let's grab him."

"And do what?"

"First off, show him how stupid he is for trying to follow us."

"Think he knows where Laila is?"

"If he does, he's even more stupid than he looks," James says.

"We don't need the chick if we get the brother, right?"

"No."

"What do you mean?"

"No, we need Laila."

"Says who? A wealthy father will do anything for any of his children."

"Not necessarily." James scans down the street for a moment, then speeds up.

"What are you saying?"

"I'm saying this chick's been gone for like ten years and it's become something almost mythical. The missing daughter who lost her soul in the big city, blah blah blah. That's when I knew the old man would pay an arm and a leg for her."

"But not his son?"

"Listen to me. Maybe the brother will make things even easier. I just—we need to find Laila. And look—I mean it—I don't want anybody dying. I just don't."

"You said if we have to—"

"And yeah, I mean that. Just—just let me make the decisions."

"How's that for a place to go?" Connor asks.

It's a loud joint with the doors open and the lights inside red and moody. James nods and follows Connor into the jazz bar. He tells Connor where to go as they walk inside but don't sit down.

. . .

Lex remembers when Kyle approached his window at the gas station and told him he wasn't very good at tailing. He thinks of this as he walks through the bar again realizing that he lost them. He's not good at this sort of thing and never thought that he was. Somehow the two men came in here and disappeared. He checked the back and didn't find a way out. He knows they came in and never came out, yet he can't see them anywhere.

It's nearing nine thirty, which is when he's supposed to call Kyle.

Perhaps it's best that he lost the men. Yet he wonders what happened to them and where they disappeared to.

"This is the last night," he tells himself.

He needs to leave. He needs to leave this place and leave it quickly.

Lex keeps thinking there are reasons for him to be here. That he needs to help Laila. Perhaps Laila and Kyle. Perhaps somebody else.

He looks at the bar and sees the bright colors and the entrancing shapes of the bottles. There was a time in his life when he used to pray that Armageddon would come and he would have to be holed up in a bar like this where all they had to live off was booze. He would take his time dying slowly with a bottle in each hand. Vodka in one and rum in another.

Lex sees his reflection and can almost see the disappointment on his face. He walks away and heads toward the entrance.

He might live to be a hundred, but those desires will still be there and always will. So he's been told. So he believes. So he knows.

Lex steps out and looks down the street and wonders what to do next.

He knows he needs to call.

As he reaches for his phone, he feels something against his neck. Something round and solid and pressing.

"Start walking and don't look back," a voice tells him.

Broken

It's the voice of one of the men, the one he never met, the one who looks pale as a ghost.

He glances at his side and sees the revolver jamming into his neck.

"Keep going now."

He does what he's told to do.

That's all he can do now.

That and pray.

• • •

It takes two good, hard kicks for the lock on the door to shred through the old wood. Remodeled or not, everything in this city reeks of age and mold, and this locked door proves it. Amos towers in the doorway with the Smith and Wesson 500 in one hand and the Kimber 1911 .45 in the other. He only needs one, but he feels better with both hands occupied. He knows the rupture of the door and the image of him storming in will prevent even the brave from doing something stupid.

He wonders if he's going to find her in bed with someone, but rather he sees two figures panicked and stopped in their places. The guy is standing over by the balcony while the woman is crouching over by the bed.

"Get up," he tells her with the silver 500 aimed at her face.

Amos doesn't want to see what the Smith and Wesson would do to her pretty little head.

The girl stands up and holds her hands above her shoulders.

"You, get over there by her. Now."

Amos goes over and shuts the door to the open night.

"Cell phones. Give 'em to me."

The guy finds his and tosses it to him while Laila shakes her head and tells him she doesn't have one.

"I'll shoot you if you're lying."

He examines the room quickly but doesn't find anything.

"Who has a car?"

"I do," Kyle says.

"And you?"

"I stole mine," Laila says, which is good because he knows this and knows she isn't lying.

"Give me the keys," Amos says.

The guy stands valiantly in front of Laila, but a well-placed shot could end it for both of them. Amos waves the 500 toward the hallway.

"You both are going to walk out of this hotel and through the lobby, and you're not going to talk to another soul. You're going to lead me to your car. You got that?"

He nods.

"And if you try to do anything, I'll kill her. Let's go."

They pass one man coming up the stairs who ignores them and doesn't even look at Amos' full hands. The desk is empty. They exit to the empty street and pause for a moment as the guy seems to forget where he left the car.

"You better remember right now."

"It's that way," Laila says.

When they reach the car, Amos puts one of the guns in his pants and then unlocks the doors, still holding the 500.

"Get in," he says, tossing the keys to the guy. "You're going to drive."

Amos tells the woman to get in the backseat with him.

They're going to leave the downtown area and get a look at the real heart of New Orleans.

And neither the pretty little girl or the young man are ever going to come back.

21

The night sometimes whispers.

Sometimes it sounds like the soft pedals of an organ not turned on. The pattering of raindrops against a window. The breath of a baby sleeping.

The night haunts even without haunting. Nightmares come even without dreaming. I don't have to be asleep to feel like I'm falling. And I don't have to wake up to shake it off.

Sometimes, at night, I'll hear the voice. So light. So delicate.

And it's saying my name, but it's not saying Laila.

It's speaking directly at me, but it's not hearing a reply.

I try to ignore it, but it comes and it goes.

Echoes bouncing off the edges of a canyon, the voice murmurs but always meanders into nothing.

I reach out but never touch anything.

I reach out and then find myself clutching onto me. Realizing that I want and need to be held but no longer have the right to be.

Realizing that the word I hear over and over and over again is "Mommy."

Kyle takes directions and drives the car slowly as the stranger sits behind him with his left hand propped up on his shoulder and the handgun aimed at the back of his neck. The other gun—this one a monstrous silver revolver—is in his right hand that rests between his thigh and Laila. They've been driving for twenty minutes, and the city seems to have disappeared along with its glow and its life. The city streets have turned into single lanes that pass a graveyard of empty, crumbling houses. Wherever they might be going, the armed expressionless stranger knows the destination.

Laila keeps her eyes on both Kyle and the man. Her hands are open on her legs, a sign that she's not about to do anything. Something in her knows this man won't blink before killing Kyle and herself. She believes he's going to do this but wants to do it in a remote, abandoned part of the city.

Staring out the front window where the headlights get swallowed by the dense dark, Laila knows there is nobody around here. Perhaps vagrants or perhaps the living dead. Random houses they pass occasionally have dull lights painted over their windows, but most seem abandoned. One white house looks like a skeleton with the windows like eye sockets. She wonders if this man is going to lead them into one of these rotting houses, kill them both, and leave them there to go bad just like the rest of the neighborhood.

"Turn right," the man says.

Kyle doesn't say anything. The last few times he's tried the man has told him to shut up. Laila is sure that Kyle is thinking the same thing, that they've been led out here to be killed.

She knows she shouldn't say anything. She doesn't want to say anything, and she's almost positive saying something will get them nothing and nowhere.

But looking at Kyle, Laila knows she has to try.

"What do you want?"

He ignores the comment.

"I'm talking to you," she says.

The man looks at her, and even in the shroud of the backseat of the car she can see the amused look on his face. It's not a smile nor is it smugness. It's genuine amusement.

Broken

"Why are you taking us out here?"

"You probably have a good enough idea yourself."

"What do you want?"

"Who says I want anything?"

"Look—you just let me know what you want and I'll get it—you just have to give me time."

"That what you said to James and Connor back there?"

"No."

"'Cause you see, I'm not like James and Connor. Or you. Or this guy here." The man moves Kyle's head forward with the butt of the gun. "All of you are down in this hellhole because of one thing: desperation. I don't want to brag because God knows something might suddenly happen to me like a stroke or a bolt of lightning or a brain aneurysm. We never know if tomorrow will come, but I do know that when I wake up in the morning, I don't breathe the same air you and him and those two other clowns breathe. Want to know why?"

Laila shakes her head, confused, wondering what he's talking about.

"I breathe the breath of a free man. Can you say the same?"

"What do you want?"

"Again, you're not listening to me. Don't slow down, keep going. That's right. See, you're not hearing me out. I don't want anything."

"Why are you here then?"

"To take care of a problem. Come on, you've seen it before. In the movies. The cleaner who takes care of the trash. Who handles situations."

"Are you a cleaner?" Laila asks.

"No. I don't even know if people are called that. I work for somebody, and this is my job. You have a job, right? Or you had one. You had one in Chicago that paid some good money, didn't you?"

She is quiet and glances at Kyle for a second.

He seems to realize this, that the driver doesn't know.

"No problem," the man says. "The past is the past. I'm not here to rub anyone's nose in it. Not my business."

"Then what is your business?" Kyle yells out.

"My business is to keep you driving and to keep your mouth shut. I don't want to talk to you, so shut up."

"Answer the question," Laila says.

"You're used to ordering men around, aren't you?"

"When they need to be, yes."

"Poor James and Connor. They probably didn't have a clue what to do with you, did they?"

"This isn't a laughing matter," Laila says.

"I agree, and I'm not laughing."

"Do you want money?"

"Stop asking what I want because I don't want anything."

"Everybody wants something."

"Is that one of your mottos in life? Learned the hard way?"

Laila curses at him.

"What do I want? I want to know that when I get back in my car and head out of this God-forsaken city—and when I mean forsaken, I mean absolutely forsaken—that I know I did the job I was paid to do."

"I can pay you more."

"Tell me something. Tell me what it feels like to be hunted. How is that for you?"

"What's your name?"

He ignores her question. "What's it feel like to wake up and wonder who's out there? You think I'd want that? You think I'd take money over freedom?"

"Nobody's free in this life."

"Sure they are. I wake up a free man and go to bed a free man without a care or a worry in the world."

"Do you kill people for a living?"

He laughs. "Why, just because I'm carrying these guns? I do things for people, so yeah, if that involves killing, then sure, I'll do that. But that's not my profession. I'm not a professional killer or assassin or however you want to call it. I make things happen. I solve problems."

Broken

"And you don't carry any guilt?"

"Why should I? Here—that street right there—slow down. Take a left and drive for about a hundred yards."

"Please—," Laila says.

"Please what? Please don't hurt you?"

"Yes."

"Who says I'm going to hurt you?"

"Both of us."

"No, this guy, he's dead. And nothing you say is going to change that."

"What do you want from me?"

"Stop the car."

Kyle stops the car, and for a moment they are in pitch black. A mass of brick and wood and plaster that's been half-burnt to the ground sits next to them. The man looks at her and keeps both hands where they've been.

"All right. Both of you get out of the car."

Laila feels that lost feeling again, a feeling she hasn't felt for a long time, this sinking sick feeling that slowly runs down her stomach and her legs like an oozing pus. She climbs out of the car and takes in the humid dead night. She can make out Kyle's face as he stares at her across the hood of the car. The night moon is there above the congestion of clouds.

The man turns off the car and the headlights.

"Okay, you, go to the hood of the car," the man says to Kyle.

Kyle does. The man then tells Laila to go to the trunk.

"Let me do anything. Let me make this right. Let me help."

The guy stares at her with an unmoving face. His expression and his eyes don't change at all. "What are you going to make right? What are you going to help?"

"This. This—you—us. I'll go away. We can go away."

"You're right about that."

"Please."

The man looks at Laila for a second that feels like an hour with a solid, lifeless expression that reminds her of times spent with men who needed and took and needed and took and then left. So many of them looked at her not as Laila Torres or even as a woman but as a thing they took from.

He looks at her like that.

Then he walks to the front of the car.

And Laila is transported to the helpless, hurting teenager that can't do a thing but watch as the whole entire universe spits and vomits in her face.

There is nothing dramatic about his walk. There is nothing dramatic about the way he takes that big silver revolver and puts it to the side of Kyle's head. There is nothing dramatic about the way he fires a shot and sends Kyle's body to the ground.

The second shot blasts through her skin and her soul and she jerks as she closes her eyes now, knowing the end is near. Then a third shot goes off, and she holds on to the back of the car and stops breathing and braces herself for the same thing. She sees Kyle's face and sees his smile and sees his eyes, and it doesn't make sense. Not him being here and not him lying on the ground and not him dead.

Laila shakes.

She hears steps coming toward her.

She grimaces and holds her breath.

And she knows that things are almost over, and it's going to end like this.

It's going to end right here, and she's no better off than she was six months ago. Or a dozen years ago.

"Open your eyes and look at me."

She opens them to see the same face and the same expression.

"Do I have your attention now, Laila?"

She nods, and her lips seem shut for life. Laila still can't take in a breath.

"Now I'm going to ask you some questions. And I assume you

know that I mean business and that I absolutely need to know every-thing. Okay?"

She nods again.

"Why did you come down to New Orleans?"

She tries to say something but nothing comes out. She can't utter a word.

She keeps thinking of those shots, one after another after another.

"Breathe in and breathe out. Do that a few times. Take your time."

She follows his instructions.

"Why are you here in New Orleans?" he asks again.

"I was—I came here when I was a teenager, and I was running away from that man—from James—and I figured I'd come here."

"Who was that guy?"

"Kyle. Kyle Ewing."

"Why'd he come here?"

"I don't know."

"That's not a good answer."

"He followed me here—I don't know why. I don't. He liked me. He worked with me, and he liked me. We were friends. That's all. There was nothing else, and it's stupid and why—"

"Just slow down and breathe."

She leans against the back of the car, feeling light-headed. She can smell death in the air and taste fear in her mouth.

"Who else came with him?"

"James and his brother," she says.

"No. Who was the other guy? The one in the hotel?"

Laila stops and tries to think, but there is a haze in her mind. She doesn't know what to say or do, and she knows that perhaps every little thing she says and does now will result in living or dying.

"I don't know," she says.

"You're lying."

"I don't know."

"Do you want to die?"

"Why would I want to live anymore? Tell me that." She feels her teeth grind against each other.

He lets out a sigh and stares at her. "Tell me something, Laila. Someone like you, what are you doing here in this mess? In this filth? With filth like Connor and James? Why?"

She curses at him.

"I see girls like you and I wonder what happened. I wonder what went wrong. Pretty little angels when they're eighteen or twenty-two, but boy you get to be thirty-two and you're just rough and then it keeps getting worse. Because all you have and all you'll ever have are those pretty little looks. Then they fade away. And you're left with nothing. But you can't understand that, can you? Whores like you just never understand it."

The red starts to stabilize. The buzzing begins to fade. The white-hot taste of anger is now on her tongue.

"Get it over with," Laila says.

"What? You want to meet your maker?"

"Who says I have one?"

"Oh, we have one all right. You know what the Bible says? It says that even the demons believe in God. And they tremble."

"You going to quote Bible verses after what you just did?"

"No," the man says. "I'm just telling you the truth. Just because you think there's a God above doesn't mean you have to serve Him. I mean, look at this. Look around us. Where was God when Katrina hit? He was strangely absent, just like He is absent whenever he's really needed. Good thing you don't have faith because you could call out right now. But in the end, where would it get you?"

"Get it over with then."

"Why did James and Connor follow you down here?"

"They want money," she says.

"And that's all?"

"Why else would they come all this way?"

"And your family has a lot of it?"

Broken

"You could say that."

"Why didn't you just give it to them?"

"Would you?"

The man nods. "Good point. I wouldn't give those two idiots anything except what I'm going to give them later tonight."

Laila feels the world begin to weaken and wobble.

"Who else knows you're here?"

"Nobody."

"Who else?"

"I said nobody."

"Who was that man back at the hotel?"

"I don't know."

He doesn't move and doesn't blink and doesn't breathe. He just stares at her for a long time.

"If you don't tell me who that was, I'm going to find it out myself and then I'm going to kill him just like I killed your boyfriend there. Tell me now."

Laila utters the words slowly and carefully. "I. Don't. Know."

He nods. "Okay then."

He goes to the front of the car and spends a moment looking for something. She thinks of running away, but there is nowhere to run. There is nothing around. And he would follow her and find her and do the inevitable.

She hears a latch open.

"Get off the car," he tells her as he pulls open the trunk.

She looks at him and looks in the trunk. It's small and empty.

"Get inside."

"Why?"

"Because I said so. Because if you don't, I'm going to sandwich that little body of yours and do it myself."

"Just shoot me."

"I don't want to."

"You just shot Kyle, why can't you do the same for me?"

"You really want to die, don't you? But you see, there's no reason for me to kill you. I needed to kill him to make sure I got information from you. That man is your brother, I'm assuming. Because you would tell me otherwise. And I'm guessing your family knows where he is at least. And that we don't have much time. So as for him, he's a dead man. But you, well, all I need you to be is out of sight and out of mind. So get in the trunk."

"And do what? Just wait to die?"

He looks around and smiles. "Well, I'd say if you were the praying sort of girl, you could call out to God and try to get Him to pay attention. But you're not, are you? So you'll have a lot of time to spend thinking about yourself and your life and all those little things you could and should have done. And since you don't believe in anything, then anything can happen. Maybe someone will be passing by and check out this random car in the middle of nowhere. Or maybe you'll just fry like an egg in the back of this trunk. Gets pretty hot out here, doesn't it? Who knows. Anything can happen because that's what you believe, right? In anything? And nothing?"

He waves the gun at her, and for a moment Laila thinks of wrestling the gun away and dying in the process. There is a tiny little light that's on in the trunk, and she doesn't want to get in there.

But then she thinks of him.

She thinks of Lex.

And then she thinks of Kyle.

And she knows that if he did it to Kyle, he'll do it to Lex.

And maybe, just maybe, Laila will be able to help Lex.

"Now," the man says.

So she climbs in, and the trunk closes down above her. He taps the car several times.

Laila hears him talking and realizes he must be calling someone.

Then she doesn't hear him at all.

She is left in black static, in this tiny stuffy box, this metallic coffin, knowing she will die inside it.

22

I sometimes wonder why I didn't turn out normal. Why I couldn't simply have a normal childhood and grow into a normal adult and live a normal life. Gaining weight and growing wrinkles and having kids and dealing with dysfunctional family and friends and the highs and lows of life. Why couldn't that be me? Why did everything about my life need to be so ugly? Why couldn't I simply airbrush it the way so many do? By settling in and settling down and just settling?

They say it's what's on the inside that counts, and I agree. And every day I awaken with a hole inside me. A hole of my own making. A hole I've never been able to fix or sew up or fill.

They say God can fill it, but how can this be? How? Nobody's ever explained that to me fully. Will God wrap up a little ball of hope and fill my gaping wound? Is that how it works? I know it sounds silly, but that's how it sounds to me when I hear this.

Tyler used to say — the love of my life, my soul mate — he used to say that he carried it around too. He used to say he was so tired and so confused and so sad. He drank to fill up. He ran to escape. He laughed because he didn't want to cry. And I would look at him and not believe it because here was someone with a good life. And I grew to realize that we all have holes and that nothing can fill them and that *those who say they're filled are just like airbrushed models looking perfect on the magazine cover.*

There is no such thing as perfection.

We all live with it. Some fight it. Some grow immune to it.

And then there are some who are wounded and limping and who have no hope whatsoever.

God I wish there was a way to change that.

But it's not faith that I need.

It's proof that the ache and the hole can go away.

Even for a moment.

L aila has been listening for some time now—she's not sure how long because she's not wearing her watch, and even if she was, she couldn't see it in this blackness. She's been listening, but hasn't heard anything. A part of her has wondered if the man with the guns would decide otherwise and open the trunk and kill her just like he did Kyle. It's been five minutes, maybe ten, maybe longer.

She can move around a little, but she can't twist all the way around. She's afraid to do that and end up in an even worse position than the one she's in now. The car is small—it's a Toyota Celica that's a few years old. There's nothing back here, and thankfully it seems like Kyle has kept it clean. Not that that matters. Not that any of that matters anymore.

She thinks of Kyle and tries to control her emotions. She wants to scream. She wants to cry. She wants to explode. But she can't do any of those things. She can't even mutter his name. Her words feel inverted, her heart squashed into some tiny little hole that's being suctioned from the inside out.

Broken

Laila breathes. It's stuffy, almost chalky back here.

Her hand feels around the trunk. The metallic top and the sides. The slightly carpeted floor. She feels the back to see if there's any type of lever that pulls the seat down. For a few minutes she explores the back of the trunk and finds and touches every single tiny hole and knob and bolt and indentation, hoping to find one of the emergency trunk releases. She thinks about the articles she's read, about knocking out a taillight and waving her arm, which would only work if there was someone around to see.

Then there's something. A lever to something that opens a small door.

But it's barely big enough for her head to fit through, much less anything else.

Her hand claws through the pass between the trunk and the backseat. She flails out to try and find anything in the backseat that she can use, but there's nothing.

Her mouth takes a breath of air from the backseat, but it's no better than what's in the trunk, and the open door presses uncomfortably against her in the tight space.

She shuts the compartment and shuts her eyes and listens.

There is nothing outside.

She pictures again where she is. Somewhere in New Orleans. Someplace that Hurricane Katrina ravaged that hasn't been saved, that perhaps will never be saved. How often do people drive by here at night? Or even in the day? And what will happen when the sun beats down on the black car and it starts to heat up like an oven?

She swallows, and her throat feels raw and dry.

She's going to try and scream, but then another voice tells her to save her breath.

She'll need it.

She'll need it for tomorrow.

A burn fills her back and lower legs. She is already sore and aching and it's only been fifteen, maybe twenty minutes.

Is this the way she's going to die?

It's strange that some things still don't change.

She doesn't feel the burn of tears on her eyes. They're dry.

She doesn't even find this to be completely surprising. In the middle of nowhere dying. In the middle of nothing, dying. For so long she's been nowhere and she's been nothing.

For so long she's been dying.

"Is this what I get?"

Once again the image of Kyle comes to mind. His smile. His sweet tone. His sensibility. His faith. All crumpling to the ground in seconds.

God wouldn't allow that if He was really up there. If He was really paying attention.

"Would You?"

She swallows again.

And she thinks.

She wonders how life can be like this, how twenty-seven years can end up like this, how random every single second of every single life can be.

How fruitless, how damning, how meaningless.

"Why here? Why like this? To prove a point?"

She knows she's just talking to herself. She can't pray her way out of this. That's not going to bring him back. That's not going to bring back a single soul.

Every sound she makes exaggerated in the small vicinity of this trunk, Laila moves her arms and legs slightly to try and keep blood flowing through them.

She controls her emotions. She wants to just slip away. She wants to close her eyes and not open them again.

But then she sees his face. Her brother who came all this way for something. To perhaps save her. After all this time, he wants to save her.

Broken

Laila knows he's doomed just like she is. Just like Kyle was and like the rest of the men following her.

Men who come into her life are doomed and always will be.

"Why have anything to do with me when the rest of the world doesn't want anything either? Why bother? Why even care? You couldn't save my mother, so You saved my father for a life of looking back? And what'd You do for his daughter? What'd You do with her?"

Her voice is loud, but it doesn't matter. Nobody is around. And if they are, that's fine with her. Let them do what they want. It's public property. She's public property. Nothing about her is her own.

Nothing.

Because the only thing that was hers, that belonged solely to her that was a gift, was something that she took away. Something she erased. Something she dotted out.

"But I can't just turn my back, can I? I can't just forget. Not like You. I can't forget and I'm haunted and freaked out. I've been living every day with this burning, aching, angry set of scars that I put on myself. That I chose. So there. So there. I'm sorry. I'm sorry about my whole life. I'm sorry, but what are You going to do? You're not going to do anything because that's the difference. My fears and my guilt get me nowhere, and all You do is just ignore. You just ignore, and You just abandon, and what do You care? You killed a whole city by not caring, didn't You? Didn't You? So why bother? Why bother with someone stuck in this little tiny hole who's helpless and can't get out? Why care?"

Laila slows down her breathing and closes her eyes and wishes she could die. She's never wanted to die more than this very moment.

And that's when she hears the tap.

A tapping that sounds on the trunk.

Perhaps the big guy is still there, getting his kicks out of listening to her break down. Perhaps he has been wanting this all along.

She screams out a curse and dares him to open the trunk. "Go ahead and open it. See if I care. I don't. Do it. Do it."

The tapping is slight and continues along the side of the car.

Then she hears the door open.

And as she does, she tries to see who it is through the small door to the backseat. But there's no time.

The trunk opens.

She hears the shuffle of feet scampering away.

Laila sits up in the trunk and expects the worst.

But instead nothing comes.

There is nobody there.

She climbs out and looks around. A slight breeze cools her down.

She can see Kyle's legs sticking out from the front of the car.

She stares down the street but doesn't see anybody. Even walking around the other side of the car, still avoiding the front, she sees nobody.

Laila looks up to the sky, peppered with light clouds.

A moon hangs behind them. Behind it, stars.

And behind them?

She doesn't know.

She doesn't know and doesn't want to begin to think about it.

She goes to Kyle, but after several moments she realizes he is truly dead and that nothing and no one will bring him back.

Touching Kyle doesn't seem so strange. His body is already cold.

Laila just breathes in and thinks for a long time, wondering where to go and what to do.

But there's only one thing she can do. Find Lex.

•   •   •

Sure enough, just like they said it would, the call comes through. It's from Kyle's cell phone. It's around one a.m.

"Yeah? Kyle?"

"No. Kyle's not around anymore."

Lex is being watched as he sits on the chair in the corner of the hotel room. Both men wait and listen to hear what he says.

Broken

"Where are you?"

The voice on the other end waits for a minute. "This isn't Kyle."

"Okay, yeah, is Laila okay?"

"This is what you're going to do if you want to see your pretty little sister alive again. There's a hotel named Hotel St. Marie. I'm going to be waiting there. And your sister will be there too."

"Hotel St. Marie," Lex says carefully. "That's where you're at?"

"Yes. And listen to me. I'm not here for you or for the girl. I'm here for those two men following her. The dark-haired guy who thinks he's pretty cool and the other scrawny one with the creepy face. I'm here for them. Go to the hotel and go to room 212. You understand all that?"

"Yeah."

James and Connor stare.

"Just make sure Laila stays there. That she's safe."

"She's safe all right."

The man clicks off the phone and leaves Lex hanging, wondering if there's more to say. He does the same.

Lex looks at them. "You heard it."

"Just like that, huh?"

He nods at Connor. "Just like that."

"You think we can trust him?"

"Why shouldn't we?" James asks. "Did you talk to your sister?"

Lex shakes his head.

"Why were you following us in the first place?"

"To make sure she was okay."

"We don't want to hurt anybody," James says.

"Doesn't look like that to me."

"Listen to me. We're going to go to that hotel and get your sister. Then the four of us are going to make a trip to Texas to visit your family. You're going to call ahead and ask for some money. And then when we get there, we're going to do a swap. You give us the money, and we'll leave both of you alone."

"What about the other guy?"

"Amos?" James asks. "The fella at the hotel doing the shooting?"

"Yeah."

"Best thing you can do is come with us. There won't be any leaving New Orleans if it's up to him."

"Not like I have any choice."

"No, you don't," Connor says.

"Shut up," James tells him.

"He doesn't."

"I don't care, just shut your face."

James stands and holds the revolver in his hand, thinking for a minute.

"This guy with your sister. He's not going to try to be some hero or something, is he?"

"No." Lex doubts Kyle is in any position to be a hero.

Amos, on the other hand, is another issue.

For a moment Lex wonders whether to tell them.

He looks at Connor and knows this is a dangerous man. A man he can't trust.

He'll figure out something when they get to the hotel.

23

I wonder what it would feel like to not be haunted. To not feel the weight of the spirit world wrapped around my neck. To not wonder when the ground is going to slide away and I'm going to fall and feel the noose tighten and hear my neck snap.

Spirits aren't hard to believe in. It's their maker.

I've seen evil things. Evil I never knew existed. Not in dark alleyways but in pretty houses and decadent rooms. In brightly lit restaurants and on busy street sidewalks.

I've seen evil. And it resides in the heart.

It knocks on the door.

It invites me in.

It looks at me in the mirror.

And then it slowly and carefully smothers me.

It's my hands and my eyes and my heart and my soul.

It's the window I look out of.

It's the room I find myself in.

It's this life I wish I could escape.

It's the emptiness I continually find.

Laila walks for what seems like miles in darkness that slowly becomes lit streets, passing cars, and strangers. She ignores a few pausing vehicles and an occasional shout. Perhaps they'll eventually ignore her too, seeing the traces of blood on her shirt and hands. Blood from the man she left behind, the man she cradled one last time. The young guy who was just helping out and trying to be a friend. Trying to be a good guy. She knows what happens to good guys in this inkblot of a world. They get erased.

But for some reason, she is not erased. She's still here. She's still breathing and still moving, and now she heads back into the city to try to find her brother.

She hears an occasional voice whisper amidst the growing buzz of the night. An occasional voice that sounds just like it always has. That whispers from the night above and the alley around her.

"Keep going. He's there. You'll find him in there."

Laila is heading back to her hotel. And then she'll try and figure out where to go.

She hears a hiss, and then something clangs to the ground in a street she's passing. She glances down it and sees something rolling on the sidewalk, bouncing off the curb, and stopping on the street.

It's a can of spray paint.

Footsteps run away.

She doesn't hesitate. Not now, not after everything.

Laila walks down the street and sees an old building with red paint bleeding down its side.

It says one word over and over again.

Marie

It's the same word she heard in her dreams back in her hotel room.

The same name that doesn't bear any significance.

She glances in the direction the steps went, but she hears nothing now.

Laila touches the paint and once again knows it's real. Then she picks up the can and knows that it's real too.

But what is real and what is fantasy? These are things she no longer knows. She hasn't known for some time.

Broken

When a man used to visit her, she wasn't real. She was an illusion, a fantasy, a mirage of something he wanted and needed. But when he left, he would leave the real behind, wounded and aching and trembling.

The real and the fantasy. She doesn't know the difference anymore.

Laila touches the word one more time and then says it out loud. "Marie."

Who is Marie and what does she want with her?

• • •

"Is everything okay, sir?"

"Yeah, everything is fine." Amos appears cordial and relaxed. "I was just wondering if you could help me out with getting another room."

"Sure." The woman is fortyish and stout with a round smiling face.

"I'm going to be having some friends possibly coming tonight, and I wanted to get them a room. Actually, I'm going to give them mine, but wondered if you could give me a room across from them."

"What's your room number?" she asks.

He tells her and watches as she looks behind the desk. It should take her probably thirty seconds, but it takes this woman about five minutes. She apologizes several times as she glances in one book, then realizes it's the wrong book and checks another. When she looks up, her face red from being flustered, Amos smiles and waves his hand and tells her to take her time.

She eventually discovers that the room is empty, something Amos already knows but he obliges her ignorance.

"I'll let them know you got the room for them."

"Actually, thank you, but no. It's a surprise. I told them to just come on up."

"Oh, good, then. Well, I'll be on the lookout."

"Thank you so much." He holds up the card key and nods, then wishes her a good night.

. . .

Laila wanders down one street and then circles back and goes down another. She has no idea where she's going. At one point when someone in a black BMW slows down and says something to her, she asks which direction is New Orleans. The driver, shrouded in darkness, only laughs and then asks what she's looking for. She says the French Quarter, and the driver volunteers to drive her. But she says no and asks again. He tells her to stay on this street and then gives her directions, saying it's only a few miles away and that she's in the ninth district. He asks her why she's in the ninth district, but she doesn't answer and starts to walk away.

Laila then stops.

"Is there a Marie something around here?"

The face pops out the window revealing a good-looking young driver. "What do you mean?"

"I don't know. I'm not sure what I mean either."

"You talking about the St. Marie hotel in the French Quarter?"

"Yes."

"I think it's right around Bourbon Street. You sure you don't want a lift that way?"

"No, it's fine."

"It's really nothing."

"It's fine," she says again.

"Okay then."

The driver pulls the BMW away and she keeps walking.

Now she knows where to go.

She's not going to ask questions because there will be no answers.

It might be a mere coincidence, but at this point she doesn't believe in them the same way she doesn't believe in miracles. Even though both seem to be happening around her all the time.

Broken

. . .

The three men on the small stage jam out as Connor eyes the woman coming up to him.

"Wanna shot?" she asks Connor, the only one at the table who pays her any attention.

"No," James says.

"Sure we do."

"Take a hike."

"No need to be rude."

Even though the brunette looks young and cute, she acts as though she's heard and seen everything. James bets here on Bourbon Street, she probably has.

"Maybe later," Connor tells her as she smiles and takes her shots away.

Connor finishes his drink.

"Well?" he asks James.

James has been studying the hotel across the street through the window. Occasionally he has gone to the door and stepped outside, then come back in.

"You look nervous," Connor says.

James glances at Lex, who is quiet. The guy makes him nervous. "What's up with you?"

Lex looks up at him and shakes his head.

"You're going to do everything we tell you to do, right?"

"Of course."

Connor laughs. "When are you going to tell us to do something?"

"I just want to see who is coming and going at the hotel."

"And?"

"Haven't seen anybody yet," James says.

"Let's just get it over with."

"You wouldn't be lying to me, would you?"

Lex shakes his head at him. "Lying about what?"

"I don't know. Anything."

"I just want to see my sister. I just want to make sure she's fine."

"See, now that's something I don't particularly get," Connor says, already buzzing from the drinks he's had. "Did she tell you she was in trouble?"

"No."

"Then you just knew, huh? You just felt it, right?"

"No, it wasn't that."

"Then what was it?" Connor asks.

"Who cares," James says. "I just want to see your sister too. And to make sure that she and you get home fine. And you make us happy, and you'll never have to see our faces again."

"Can you promise me that?"

"You gonna trust me?" James asks.

"No."

"Then why should I bother promising?"

Lex just nods. Connor stands up as if he's going to get something else to drink.

"Stay put."

"Why?"

"Because you and Lex are going to go inside there."

"And do what?"

"You're going to bring Laila out of the hotel and in here."

"And then what?" Connor coughs, and his eyes look watery.

"Then we leave. That simple."

"Why can't he just bring her to us?"

James doesn't even believe what's coming out of his brother's mouth. He looks at Lex. "You understand?"

"Yeah," Lex says.

"If he does anything, Connor, you hurt him, okay? Just don't—" James pauses, looking around. "Make sure he stays alive."

"Okay."

"Hurry up," James says.

He watches them leave the bar and walk across the street to the hotel.

After all this time, it's going to be this easy.

•   •   •

Lex feels like he can't move or breathe even though he's doing both as they enter the hotel. All the notions of things he's seen in the movies where a guy elbows his way out of trouble or punches the bad guy or takes off running evaporate. The fear is real and tangible and it's something he can taste. It's sickening and it prevents him from thinking too much. All he can do is move and try to think about staying alive and keeping Laila alive. But now that they're in the hotel, he doesn't know what to do. He doesn't know what's waiting in that hotel room and he doesn't know what Connor will do once he finds out.

They pass a glass table with two fancy armchairs that stand in front of the built-in desk carved into the wall. Nobody is behind the desk, so they find the elevator going up. Connor is behind him and walking slowly, carefully.

In the elevator, Lex glances at Connor. The man smiles in a sickening sort of way. The way a man might smile as he pokes at a gaping, bleeding wound that's fresh and sore and biting.

"Doesn't look like such a good idea anymore, does it?" Connor says.

"What?"

"Finding your sister. Following her down here."

Lex nods, but he doesn't agree. He's glad he's here. And the fear inside him — still very much there, still very much bubbling at the surface — gets mixed with something else that's piping and boiling.

Anger.

Lex looks in the eyes of this man and wants to hurt him. He not only wants to hurt him, but he wants to kill him.

He thinks back to why he's here.

He remembers the feeling of fear he had in that car so many years ago.

And Lex knows there is only one way to exorcise the demons of yesterday, the devils of doubt.

It's to confront them head-on. Just like he's doing now.

Lex tightens his fist and feels a bit of pain rip through him.

He knows he's no longer that scared boy who can't do a thing.

He's no longer that terrified teen who is sitting, waiting and watching and worrying.

He's no longer going to have to face the fact that he stood there without doing anything. He knows now that whatever happens, he tried.

Whatever happens, Lex won't be letting her down. Not this time.

•   •   •

The streets and the buildings in New Orleans all feel compressed and tight and claustrophobic. The city breathes slowly, dark faces leering out of doorways asking and begging for Laila to come in. She keeps walking toward St. Marie.

Laila no longer questions whether this is logical. She no longer asks herself if this makes sense. Logic tells her she should already be dead. Sense says she should still be locked inside that trunk.

There is something at this hotel that has been waiting for her for a long time. She doesn't know what she will find, but she doesn't care. The point is that she will find it.

She sees the hotel on the corner and heads across the street toward the entryway.

•   •   •

Lex and Connor reach the room. The brass U-shaped dead bolt sticks out between the slightly open door and the door frame. The sliver of opening only shows darkness.

For a moment Lex looks at the number and feels something rub against his heart. He knows he should remember, but fear coats over everything else. He thinks he's been here before or at least pictured this before. But perhaps that's just because he's afraid of what's behind it.

Lex glances at Connor who is standing a few steps away from him. "Knock."

So Lex does. He tries three different times, but nobody comes. Then he gently pushes the door in.

"Go ahead."

Lex glances at Connor who has a gun out. He steps inside the darkened room and holds his breath and tries to hear something, anything. His fingers search the wall and eventually find a switch for the light.

As he turns it on, his mind pictures the bed drenched with blood and Laila torn in two and the man who did it hovering over it waiting to do the same to him.

But instead he finds an empty room. There is antique furniture and two made beds with stools at each base. The door to the balcony is open.

Connor is standing in the doorway, his gun pointing right at Lex. "Go check the bathroom."

Lex doesn't see anything in this room—no clothes or bags or signs of life.

He feels trapped and thinks for a minute about diving toward the balcony and getting away, but he still knows that Laila is somewhere. If not in here, somewhere in this hotel perhaps.

He turns on the light in the bathroom and sighs as he finds nothing inside it.

A quick glance in the mirror shows a guy he doesn't recognize, with the smirk he's always been known for left back in Texas and eyes that show pain and fear and sadness.

Lex thinks of his family.

Then he shuts off the light and steps out of the bathroom.

And as he does, Connor gives him a curious glance. "Nothing?"

Before Lex can say anything, he sees a hulking figure at the doorway and then the large handgun with the silencer aimed at the back of Connor's head. As Lex opens his mouth, it seems as though Connor knows but it's too late. Two shots go off, and the back wall of the room is sprayed with Connor's blood and muscle and brain.

Lex puts his hands up on his face. He shouts out and falls to his knees and closes his eyes.

The world turns bright and he's falling and he knows he made a big mistake.

He breathes quickly with his eyes still shut, waiting for the shroud of death to close in, waiting for the same fate that blasted Connor's life in a second to take him.

• • •

James looks at his watch.

It's a quarter to two in the morning.

Hopefully by sunrise they'll be on the way to Texas.

They'll get the money and leave all this behind. Go somewhere far south or far north, somewhere far away.

Part of him wonders the same thing he's always wondered. Whether or not he can try and change Connor.

He thinks of this because he knows deep down he can't leave his brother. He knows because he's tried.

Connor is all the family he has left.

He wonders where they're at. It's been fifteen minutes since Connor and Lex went across the street.

He finishes another beer and steps out for a moment, watching and waiting to see anything. But there's nothing to see.

He goes back inside, orders another drink, and waits.

• • •

Laila has been standing in the lobby for at least ten minutes.

The woman behind the desk has asked her twice if she needed

to be helped, and she told her she's waiting for someone. She said it in a way that also said she didn't want to discuss anything with the woman.

The silence is getting to her. The silence and the still and the night.

She knows she shouldn't be down here.

She needs to go upstairs.

She knows what room.

For some reason she is reminded of the toilet stall she got stuck in when she was with Kyle.

She thinks of the writing on the wall.

GO TO 212

It makes no sense, and it makes perfect sense.

Someone is trying to tell her something.

Her head spins. Do the numbers have significance? Does this hotel mean something? Does the name Marie signify anything?

Does the fact that she's losing her mind, or lost it six months ago after Connor, mean anything? Because Connor didn't die. Connor is still alive, and perhaps he's in this lobby and nobody is here and she really is losing it.

It's time to find out.

It's time to know where this all goes.

She goes to the elevator and takes it up to the second floor.

And slowly and carefully, she walks down a silent hallway to the room.

She's here at the St. Marie hotel.

She'll soon arrive at room 212.

Laila wants this to be over.

She believes somebody else does too.

•   •   •

James tries to call Connor on his cell phone and gets his voice mail. He tries again and gets the same thing. Cursing, he rips open the door and leaves the music behind as he goes over to the hotel. He feels the handle of the revolver against his gut. He shouldn't have to be carrying this thing, much less using it.

He finds the elevator, pressing the button repeatedly to try to get it to open.

•   •   •

The door is shut.

Laila tries the handle, but it's locked.

She looks down the hallway both ways. It's narrow and dim and feels old.

She knows hallways like this well.

This is it.

212

What's supposed to happen?

She's about to knock when she hears a muffled voice coming from inside.

It sounds like someone saying "no."

She's been here before.

This has happened before.

"Lex!" She knocks on the door, hearing his voice again.

"Don't! Don't come in here. Get out. Get out of here!"

She's not going to leave her brother here, regardless of who might be with him. Laila feels something against her feet. She glances down and sees the blue cap. The blue cap with the red, white, and blue logo of the Houston Texans on it.

She knows it wasn't there ten seconds ago.

She bends down to pick it up.

Just as she does, the plywood of the door above her explodes, spreading chunks over her back.

Laila scurries over the carpeted floor to get out of the doorway, a blinding jangle ringing through her head.

Broken

As she's crawling and clawing to get out of there, the door bursts open and a man steps out and sees her.

"What the hell . . . ," he says.

His gun with the silencer on it remains in his grip. The big guy is shaking his head.

"No. No way."

Just as he's about to walk toward her, a lamp comes crashing out of the room, cracking over his head.

The big guy falls to the floor and drops the gun. But it seems like the blow merely bothers him. He curses and holds one hand to protect his head from any more blows. As he starts to search for the handgun, James emerges at the end of the hallway.

He takes in the scene for only a moment before he fires off several shots that go nowhere but send the big man rolling on the carpet and picking up his gun and then aiming it at James.

He fires off one shot before pressing the trigger with nothing happening.

James takes off for where he came from, and the big guy opens the door across from them and darts inside.

"Are you okay?" Lex asks her as he jerks her up.

She nods, looking toward the doorway where the gunman went. She feels Lex grab her and pull her into the opposite room, closing the partially shredded door behind him and locking it even though that won't keep anyone out.

It takes a few seconds before she sees the carnage on the wall and Connor's body on the floor.

This time Laila knows without a doubt that he's dead.

He's missing half his head.

"Don't," Lex says, grabbing her arm and pulling her away from the body. "Go on the balcony. Hurry."

Laila does as she's told. "Lex."

"I'm fine."

Lex picks up Connor's gun and holds it awkwardly.

"Be careful."

"You sure you're okay?" he asks her.

She doesn't know how to answer.

·   ·   ·

Amos feels something wet and warm mixing with his hair on the back of his head. He knows the lamp made more of an impression than he thought it did. He wipes his hand on his pants and then proceeds to unpack the automatic rifle with hands that know how to do it. He puts the silencer on the end of the MP9.

The woman and her story will soon be over. Amos knows this. He knows he made a mistake leaving her in the back of the trunk. Somehow she got out. This is what happens when you let trash stay out on the curb after the garbage has already been picked up.

Amos slides a handgun in his pants and then proceeds across the hallway.

This has become a little too busy for his liking. A little too messy. Now he knows time is not on his side, and he needs to make sure the garbage is dealt with before going to find James.

Amos opens the door with ease and finds the woman standing in the doorway of the balcony.

He then sees the surprised look on the man who looks strikingly similar to the woman.

Amos smiles, then unleashes a stream of bullets that strip the room.

The man crumbles to the floor as the woman screams.

The chipping carnage of the bullets and the way the woman dives for something in the room makes Amos step away from the door.

For a moment he thinks of dealing with her, of making sure she doesn't end up coming after him.

His gun is still in that room.

Broken

But when Amos hears her ragged, horrific screams in the room, he realizes she's done.

He's taken something from her, and she's no longer part of this.

She's a different kind of dead but dead nonetheless.

Amos tears down the hallway knowing that police have surely been called and his main objective might be getting away.

• • •

Hell has wrapped its hands around her for good.

Laila shakes as she holds the handgun. She crawls to Lex and sees blood on his face and sees the blood on his shirt leaking out all over him.

She can't breathe.

She can't think.

She chokes on her tears as she holds Lex in her arms.

He feels heavy and gone.

The world spins and gets dark.

Her instinct tells her to run.

Just like she always has.

Just like she always will.

She stands up and leaves the death behind her.

• • •

For a minute in the stairwell James contemplates going back. He checks his gun and then his cell phone. Nothing. His heart beats, and he sucks in air as he thinks for a few moments. Then he keeps heading down the stairs, rushing toward the exit and the night air.

Connor's face comes to mind, but he shrugs it off.

His brother is gone. His brother is gone, and he has to admit it. If James discovers that Connor is indeed alive—and a part of him believes Connor actually has nine lives—then so be it. Connor can meet up with him somewhere else. Otherwise it will have to be in the afterlife, which might happen sooner than later if he doesn't get out of here.

He exits the back and hears a fountain as he walks past the swimming pool. He soon realizes he's fenced in back here with trees and the pool and the hotel. Sizing up the fence, James realizes there's no way of scaling it without breaking his neck.

There are a couple of doors leading into the hotel, but they're locked.

James holds the revolver in his hand. He listens, then keeps walking around the pool.

It's peaceful out here, and he wishes he could be sitting listening to the trickle of water, having a smoke, and not worrying about anything.

That's what everybody wants in this life. A chance to get away and sit and relax and not have to think about the ghosts and the devils that are right outside their door.

But they're always knocking.

They're always coming to get you.

He waits. Ready for the devil that's coming.

•   •   •

Amos holds the Brügger and Thomet MP9 submachine gun with the shoulder stock extended and the thick muzzle of the silencer facing the doorway. His Smith and Wesson 500 is in his pants, the Walther PPK in his ankle strap. He opens the door exiting to the swimming pool where he saw James.

James is walking around the pool and stops.

Amos opens fire on him, chipping away at the trees and the garden and the stone around the pool. The silencer squelches the firing and makes the blasts sound more like short thuds. Amos unloads an entire magazine and sees James scampering away like an animal behind a tree.

He takes out the magazine and dumps it on the concrete and then loads another.

Broken

Amos walks toward the tree James is hiding behind.

James fires a wild shot without even looking and hits a nearby building. Amos keeps walking.

James bolts from the tree and scurries over the deck of the pool as Amos unleashes another barrage of fire. This time he hits James somewhere in the legs as James trips and falls against the patio outside the hotel. He hears James curse and let out a gasp and then sees him aim the gun at him again and fires.

James' gun is empty.

Amos finishes off the other magazine that does more damage to the ground and the wall and glass behind James than him. James gets to his knees and then bolts toward a shredded window of the hotel, pouncing into it shoulder first with a loud crack and burst of glass.

Amos slips in another magazine and follows James.

He stops over the empty gun that James was using, carefully approaching the gaping hole of jagged glass, glancing inside to see James running toward a back door.

The MP9 gurgles to life and rips the plaster and the chairs and tables inside the dimly lit room.

Amos breaks off glass with his boot, then crawls through the opening just as he sees a door open and shut.

He fires off another barrage and empties out the submachine gun.

He straps it over his back and then takes out the Smith and Wesson and heads toward the door.

He approaches it slowly, carefully.

• • •

Laila runs into the middle of the street wanting to be hit by a car but none are around.

She twirls around and sees the world spinning and she looks upward and then back down. Her hands are covered in blood.

Lex's blood.

Her brother's blood mixed with Kyle's blood.

She knows this is her fault.

That everybody is here because of her.

She wants to let out a scream but she can't.

She starts to run down the street to try and find a dark, deserted, desolate hole where she can crawl inside and rot away.

Laila wonders why she was let out of the trunk.

Why she was led to the hotel.

Why everything led to this when the outcome turned out this way.

A voice whispers to her that it's penance. It's her atonement for what she's done to herself and to others.

For the helpless life she took that didn't have a choice or a voice or any clue what she was doing.

This is the punishment for her sins — this is what she gets.

Laila topples over a man and then bolts down an alley between two towering old buildings.

Running toward darkness.

Running toward death.

•   •   •

James knows this wound is a little different than the last.

This one is on his thigh.

The blood is spewing out faster.

The wound feels deeper.

But it doesn't matter. It doesn't matter anymore.

James is a dead man, just like his brother, just like the girl and the idiots that followed her.

This is the way it ends.

This is the way life ends.

But there's one thing he needs to do.

And if it gets him killed, so what? He's already dead. He's been dead for too long.

Broken

He's going to go out with a bang, one way or another.

He knows this for an absolute fact.

Miracles do exist. Because he's holding one. And chances are he will die holding it.

•   •   •

Amos walks down the hallway toward the lobby of the hotel. In his hands is the heavy revolver that can level any moving thing coming at him. He gets to the entryway and sees someone approaching from a doorway that leads to the desk. He aims the gun at the woman and shoos her away, ignoring her gasp as she trips to get out of there. There's no sign of James. James escaped into the night.

But Amos knows he'll find him.

There's no reason to go back home if he doesn't take care of the business at hand.

There's enough damage in this city that he has to tie up loose ends.

First James. Then he'll deal with the girl.

A thought scratches at him as he walks toward the doorway of the hotel.

How did she get out?

He wants to rub it away, but he can't.

He knows there's no way she could have called anybody. No way she could have figured a way out of that trunk. He's tried that before himself. There was no way that anybody was around. And even if someone had come around, they couldn't have gotten it open so quickly. He had locked the doors.

Amos doesn't believe in ghosts and guardian angels. He believes in the power of a gun in his hand, the power of fear in the eyes of a stranger, the power of knowing how to be sensible in the most intense situations.

He steps out on the sidewalk.

There stands the shadow of what looks like a ghost under the glow of the street lamp directly across from him.

Not a hellish creature but rather the outline of a young boy. A boy wearing a cap and holding a backpack over his shoulder.

The boy just looks at him. The revolver in Amos' hand doesn't make the boy run away or seem afraid.

Rather, the look on the boy's face is one of sadness.

Then Amos hears footsteps and turns.

It's over before he can comprehend it.

Yet he sees it all in slow motion.

James striding toward him deliberately, shoving the revolver against the left side of his chest.

James grits his teeth as he fires two shots.

As Amos falls down to the sidewalk he sees James' face leering over him.

Amos can't control his body or his actions anymore, and his head turns to the side facing the street across from him.

The boy stands, watching. Then he looks down the street and starts walking the other way. Not running like most kids would do, but walking.

• • •

Laila leans against a wet, dark wall in a hollowed out alleyway in a shell of a city that used to be. The ghost of New Orleans that might never come back. A ghost of a woman that will never come back. She puts her arms around her legs, and she shivers and then finally cries. She cries tears that have been building up for centuries it seems, tears that couldn't even recognize her, tears that don't know how good it feels to finally be released.

She cries and shivers and just wants to die.

She wants this whole nightmare to be over.

The nightmare that started so long ago.

She was young and alone and frightened and there was nothing she could do or say or think and this wretched life let her down. It wasn't just family or friends or herself. It was all of them but ultimately it was her heavenly Father, the one spoken about so often and the one dreamt about and the one considered, that ultimately let her down. In a hotel room somewhere in the middle of nowhere she was desecrated and left to die. Not die there but slowly die during the course of another decade.

Laila has tried. She's done it her way, but her way is over.

Her way is not enough.

She knows there is no hope for her. Not now. Not like this.

She's too full to ever be set free.

The tears come, and she cries into her hands. Hands that have done evil things. Hands that have allowed evil to be done.

She thinks of this journey. This journey into hell. Perhaps she's already in hell, and all this will be played out over and over and over again.

She coughs. Tears wrap themselves over her lips.

Laila thinks of him.

She knows him and she's dreamt of him and she's felt him.

Every day since Laila let him go, she has thought of him.

And though she was never told, she knows. She knows the child who would have been a boy who could have been a man. A man who could have cured cancer or saved the world or perhaps simply loved her the way any child might love his mother.

A little precious life that she took.

She has thought about him over and over and over again, and she can't undo it.

She will never be able to bring him back.

And the hurt rushes over her like a waterfall.

Laila wants to bleed out the pain and let it go.

She wants to fill that hole inside her.

She wants to go back to the moment where he was created. A mistake, yes. But she wants to go back and change it.

Not change him, but change her choice.

Laila wants to go back and let him breathe. Let him belong.

Let him be.

As she weeps, Laila's voice says repeatedly a word that is so unfamiliar and so stupid.

"Sorry."

She wishes the word could be heard. That the word could matter.

As she thinks this, Laila feels something against her back.

Something that feels like a hand.

She feels a soft touch. Then she feels an arm around her back and her shoulders.

Laila opens her eyes, and even in the darkness, she can see.

The small arms of the boy are wrapped around her.

She sees his dark hair just like hers coming out of the sides and the back of his cap.

"It's okay," he says.

Laila looks into his face and she winces in fear of seeing those cold black eyes but instead they open with warmth.

She stares into his eyes and she finally sees them and God are they beautiful. They feel like—they feel a way she cannot describe. They feel—

They feel like home.

There are tears in his eyes too.

She reaches out because she knows this is not a dream. The mother reaches out and touches his cheek and wipes away the tears.

Then the son reaches over and kisses her on the forehead, and he smiles.

It breaks her heart.

•   •   •

But it also fills that hole.

The hat of his father's favorite football team still on his head.

Broken

The backpack still over his shoulder.

He smiles and nods, and then the boy stands and walks away out of the alley and onto the street.

Laila knows that he was real. He was real, and she saw him.

She knows now that he's in a better place.

All along he's been watching out for her. He's been guiding her. He's been trying to simply let her know that it's okay.

Spoken in the way a ten-year-old boy might say, "I love you, and I forgive you."

All by saying it's okay.

•   •   •

The group gathers in front of the hotel, and he passes them and asks several if they've seen her. He describes her, and one older man says he saw her running down the street and nearly bowled him over and that maybe she's somewhere down there. He leaves the group behind and knows that police will be coming soon.

He finds the alley and knows. For some reason he just knows that she's gone down it.

It's there that he finds her.

Laila's eyes are swollen and glistening.

With one hand clamped against his wound, trying to stop the bleeding, he calls out her name. His legs give out, and the alley starts swirling around him.

He glances up and sees her staring down at him, and he smiles knowing she's alive.

24

Sometimes I wonder what she's like, that bright-eyed fifteen-year-old with the world ahead of her. So trusting. So giving. Living and loving like it was as easy as breathing.

I wish I could go back and warn her.

I wish I could go back and tell her.

I wish . . . I wish for many things.

But most of all I wish that I was still her, that I saw with those same eyes, that I cared with that same heart.

Something died that night in the hotel room with the three boys.

It was hope.

And God, if You're really up there, then maybe You can help me find it again. That smile, that sweetness, that soul.

That little girl that You let go away. That You didn't save. That You didn't look out for.

That little girl You allowed everything to be taken away from.

So this is how it ends.

Not with the sudden crack of a gunshot or the surprise of a deadly wound but on the side of the road like some helpless heap of an animal.

Broken

James gets out of the car that's run out of gas and slides his leg along as he stares off at the plains.

He thinks he's close to the border of New Mexico but isn't sure. There is nothing around him. Just the empty sky and the empty field and this empty dirt road he got off trying to be safe.

Things never turn out the way they should. Not for anybody.

His shoulder aches from the gunshot wound he got in the hotel when Laila got away. His leg is useless, so numb in pain that it almost doesn't count. But it's the seeping mess on his side that he knows is the problem. One of the random bullets the crazed commando back there stuck him with. Initially James didn't even think it went in him. But the bullet did a little more than graze him. And it's that wound that's the worst.

He turns around and sees nobody. Not a soul. He knows that with the way the wound is bleeding, even with the shirt pressed against it, he's going to die.

He's been driving at least ten hours or more, having gotten gas a couple of times. He doesn't have any money, but that's okay because he knows he won't need money where he's going.

James hobbles up to a fence and then leans against the wood holding up the barbed wire. He grimaces as he finds the wadded-up smokes in his pocket, and he lights one. He takes a drag and sees everything in the calm light of day.

He wonders where Connor is. If this is indeed all they have.

He's not afraid. In a sense, he's glad it's all over.

Life is a mighty damn waste because nobody really gets what they want. The world beats you down and eventually buries you. And no matter where you end up — in a plot next to your family or in a memorial in DC or a hole in Texas — it's all the same thing, isn't it?

James looks up to the sky and wonders if this is all there is.

Because if it's not and there's more, he won't have a word to say in his defense.

He loved his brother but that's not enough.

He thinks of a distant memory that he hasn't thought of in years. It was at a camp James and Connor went to when they were young—he was maybe in fifth grade and Connor was in second. Something like that. James remembers riding a horse with Connor bareback, Connor sitting in front of him. James held on to his brother and whispered in his ear that things were going to be okay. And they were okay. They didn't fall off and break their legs or their necks. They made it just fine. And James remembers that's how things were with Connor. That's how they always were.

He spent so much time looking out for Connor that he never looked out for himself.

James curses and knows that's a lie because his whole life has been about looking out for himself and dealing with Connor's messes.

That doesn't make him a better person.

It doesn't make him worthy of anything.

The problem in life is that you can't lie to yourself.

He touches his side and sees the blood covering everything.

Then he finishes up his cigarette and slides to the ground and watches the sun smother the entire sky. He watches the clouds move past. And as he does, he thinks back to that horse ride, and he wishes that he could be ten again with life ahead of him and hope still on his side.

25

Somebody once told me that writing is cathartic, that it can be therapeutic, that it can free your soul. But I glance at this worn journal I've carried with me so long and wonder. Is that really true? Words contain power, I believe that, but simply putting them down for no one else to read — what good is that? Or can the dead read these words? Have I been writing for myself or for someone else?

All I know is that I need to let go.

And part of that is saying good-bye.

Being reminded of my pain and my failures day after day — I don't need a journal to do that.

So this is the last entry in this notebook.

And after so many words, I still haven't come to any conclusion.

I do know this, however.

I'm watched over.

I don't understand that. I can't begin to explain that.

But it's true.

And I think I'm realizing that perhaps I don't need to hide any longer.

L aila hears the knocking but ignores it.

The ghosts can wait.

She is dreaming of being by a pool and watching him come to her side. Lex smiles and sits next to her. For a long time they talk and laugh and watch the reflection of the sun on the surface of the water. It's relaxing. Laila thinks this is heaven. Or perhaps her pitiful version of it. Maybe she's being allowed a slight glance of it.

The knocking sounds again.

She stirs and gets closer to emerging from sleep.

Her mind wades through the last two days.

The endless questions about the deaths.

She sees the brown hair and the innocent smile and remembers Kyle.

She pictures the explosion of Connor's blood and matter in the hotel room.

She remembers the big man who they found shot in the street outside the hotel.

And then she thinks of Lex.

The knocking is louder, and she hears a voice.

Laila opens her eyes. She feels heavy, drowsy. It's probably from the sleeping pills she took last night. They were given to her by one of the doctors. Or was it a cop?

This hotel is still in the French Quarter, but different from the one she was staying at. The one that got broken into by the armed man. The one where he took Kyle and her.

"Laila."

She stands up and goes to the door.

She opens it and sees Lex.

She realizes she must still be dreaming.

"Are you okay?"

"Lex?"

Broken

He studies her for a moment. "You okay?"

Reality comes back to her, and she knows this isn't a dream.

"You're out of the hospital."

"Obviously," he says, giving her a hug.

Laila also knows it's going to be some time before dreams and reality don't intersect anymore.

The first step will be leaving this all behind.

A little while later, while sitting in the middle of the hotel restaurant, Laila coughs and feels her eyes water. She takes a sip of water.

"You sound sick," Lex says.

"I think I have a cold," she says. "Beats getting shot though."

"I don't know. They patched me up pretty good."

It is Sunday. The past two days have gone by in a blur. And yet, of all the things that have transpired, there is one thing she still dreads. One thing she still fears. And she's just waiting for Lex to bring it up.

"Are you not hungry?" Lex asks her.

"No."

"You should eat something."

"Somehow it feels wrong to just be sitting here, in this beautiful restaurant, having a nice relaxing meal."

"Why?" he asks. "Are you not allowed to live your life?"

"I just—I don't know. It feels strange. I feel like there's more I need to do."

"You spoke to Kyle's family?"

"His sister. Several times." She shakes her head, feeling numb. "I felt—I didn't have anything to say. She wanted me to explain why he came down here, and I couldn't. All I could say—all I could tell her was that Kyle was a remarkable man who was looking out for me when he didn't have to. When he shouldn't have. He wanted to save me. And he did."

"It's not your fault."

Laila laughs. "I could live to be a hundred years old and will doubt that I'll ever think otherwise."

"You can't think that."

"There're a lot of things I shouldn't do, but that doesn't change the fact that I'm me."

Lex nods and pushes his plate of eggs away. "What did the police say to you?"

"I told them everything I know," she says.

"And what's that?"

Laila looks at the coffee cup and marvels how white it looks. How clean and shiny and new.

"Everything. From how they followed me from Chicago to Greenville. How they tried to blackmail me. Everything."

"Did you tell them about shooting Connor?"

She glances at Lex and shakes her head. During the past couple days as he's been at Tulane Medical Center recovering from his bullet wound, Laila's told her brother almost everything.

There are some things she hasn't told him but suspects he already knows.

Including why she was with Connor in the first place.

"Connor and James are both dead. I doubt it matters anymore."

Lex nods.

"They've told me to let them know when I plan on leaving."

"So what is your plan?"

This is what she dreads. This conversation. The decision she has to make.

"I don't know," she says.

But it's not a decision she's waiting for.

It's an invitation.

Lex looks at her. She's so glad to see those eyes again. She's missed them so much. It just seems like yesterday, even though half a life seems to have been torn apart, between childhood and now.

"I want you to come home," he says.

The wave hits, and she feels loosened. She feels like she's tumbling underneath the current, and all she can do is let go.

"What have they said?"

"Who?"

"Papa. Ava."

"What do you think? Ava was going to come down here, and I told her not to. Dad would if his health allowed it. Lai—what do you think they said?"

"Do they blame me?"

"They love you. They want to see you. That's the truth. That's all there is."

She brushes back her hair. "After all this time."

"I came to find you to bring you back home."

"Did I have an option?"

Lex nods and smiles and then chuckles. "You're strong-willed as always."

"I know."

"Of course you have an option. I wasn't going to bind and gag you and force you to come home. But where else will you go?"

"I don't know."

"You need to come home."

She nods. She wants to tell him that she's afraid. That she's terrified, in fact, of going back home. The memories there surely blow like the Texan winds. It's been so long that she won't know what to say or do.

"It'll be fine," he says, as if reading her mind.

"What? What could possibly be fine after all this mess? Tell me? What?"

"You." Lex just stares at her with a sad, strong gaze. "You're going to be fine, Laila. I promise."

The red glow paints the sky in delicate swirls. The fading sun dips behind the endless, soft waves of Lake Pontchartrain as Laila stands along its shore next to a large moss-covered tree. She remembers coming to the town of Mandeville and looking out toward the simmering sun and feeling hope. But that hope came along with her hand being held by him. By the love who took her here. By the love she gave so much to. The love who gave nothing back.

Nothing except one thing.

One precious, miraculous thing.

She breathes in and marvels at the beauty in front of her.

Tomorrow they will leave to go back to Texas. To go back home.

But she knows she needs to say good-bye. That she needs to let things go.

In her hand is the leather journal full of thoughts and feelings from the past few years. A diary of doubt and despair.

She looks at it and feels its weight. Then she glances out toward the brilliant sunset.

"Please let me let go," she says. "God, please help me let go."

She wasn't alone the first time she saw this portrait of the heavens, and she's not alone now.

Laila knows this.

She believes it.

And she knows it's time to let go.

"It's okay," she says. Repeating the line he told her.

Repeating the line that maybe she imagined in the alleyway but that felt and sounded real.

"It's okay."

Laila takes the journal full of questions and longings and fears and hurls it as far out into the lake as possible.

It opens and lands with its pages on the surface of the water. Then it floats for several moments.

Laila watches, and again something unfamiliar delicately massages her eyes. Tears fall as she stares at the floating journal.

She finds herself on this shore again after so much, and yet she's the same. She's the same, and she's ready to move on. She's ready to grow up instead of running away.

Laila is ready to go back home and try and restore the life she once had.

She believes that just like this sunset, hope is magnificent and glorious and not too far away. She can see it now. It's within reach.

And maybe, just maybe, the heavens will wait for her to reach them.

When she arrives back in her hotel room, Laila turns on the lights and calls Lex. She asked for the keys to his car and didn't tell him where she was going. She knew in his voice and his expression that he was worried. Worried that she was going to run away. And part of her even considered it. She plans on asking how he is and if he needs anything, just to reassure him that she's not halfway to Mexico.

When she reaches for the phone, she sees something on her bed.

For a moment Laila stops.

She closes her eyes as if she's hallucinating. But when she opens them, it's still there.

She picks it up.

It's another journal.

She touches it, but it doesn't disappear. It's a spiral-bound notebook that has a plastic cover colored red and orange. Almost like the sunset she just watched.

It's a small journal that a kid might have.

Inside the pages are lined and blank.

Laila holds it for a moment and looks around the room, wondering if there's something else waiting for her.

Something—or someone.

But she finds nothing.

Laila puts the notebook on the small desk in the room and calls Lex.

"Hi." He sounds relieved.

"Are you okay?"

He says yes, and they talk for a few moments. They agree to meet in the lobby around eight to grab some breakfast and then depart.

"Lex. Did you — did you put this journal in my room?"

"Did I put what in your room?"

"A journal? A small spiral-bound notebook?"

"Why would I do that?"

"Did you?"

He laughs. "No. Why? Did you find one?"

"Yeah. Somebody must've left it behind."

She doesn't believe that, but she doesn't know what else to say.

She wishes him a good night and finds herself restless in the room. She's spent a whole life feeling this way.

A pen on the desk catches her attention.

She picks it up and then grabs the notebook.

She stretches out on the bed and opens up the first page. She puts the date and then thinks for a moment.

Then she begins to write.

26

What would it be like to be a white page, starting from the beginning with stories untold and memories unmade? To start with a blank slate and go from there?

I wonder.

I wonder if God sees us like that.

I hope He does.

I know the stories, and I know the faith. My father taught us well. But it was simply a story I heard and one I read but one I never fully believed.

I've always felt like belief was so close. So close.

Can I believe that a father allowed his son to die? Yes. But the reason is the part I have a hard time with.

This father — this God — allowed His son to die out of love. Not fear, but love.

Love for me.

That is where I always stumble.

That is where my faith flounders.

I have so far to go. Yet I have life, and today is the first day where I start anew.

I want to change. I just — I'm not sure how.

But I believe that God led me to a dark place and a narrow alleyway not to know fear. But rather to know forgiveness.

And to allow me to see.

Some ghosts don't haunt you.

Some set you free.

C an you feel that?"

She glances over at him from behind the wheel. "What?"

"That feeling. Being back in Texas."

Laila starts to say something, probably sarcastic, but then she stops. The jokes about Texas and Brady and home were always done more out of fear of never leaving than out of truth. Lex knows this now and thinks that she might too.

They've been driving for several hours since morning, having stopped in LaFayette briefly. Laila is driving for him just so he can stretch out on his seat and lay back if needed. But now Lex sips his Mountain Dew and feels good about being back in Texas. It'll be another seven hours or so before they get home.

Laila is quiet, and he can only imagine why. The combination of what happened in New Orleans and the anticipation of arriving back home—he can't know what his sister might be feeling. He just keeps praying that her heart remains open, that he says the right words, that he does the right things.

"Lex."

He looks at her and sees just how vibrant her eyes are. Laila is shocking in her beauty. "Yeah?"

"Why did you follow me? Why after all this time?"

There are things he's waiting to say until he gets back home, things he doesn't want to say but rather show. For a moment he thinks.

"There are lots of reasons."

"Did you know? Tell me that? Did you get a sign or something that I was in trouble?"

"Not exactly."

"Then how? How did you know I was in trouble?"

He looks out onto the plains surrounding him. There should be a better time to tell her than now, but he knows that nobody is promised tomorrow. And for a while in New Orleans, he was wishing that he had told her, that he had confessed to her what he's been wanting to confess for so long. He almost took it to the grave.

Lex knows he needs to tell her now.

"There's something that I — that I've been wanting to tell you for some time."

She glances at him briefly with a curious look. Perhaps it's his tone or his expression, but she looks concerned. "What is it?"

"I'm sorry, Lai. I'm so utterly sorry."

"What are you talking about?"

"I know what they did to you."

The space between her eyebrows wrinkles, and her eyes continue looking his direction and then darting back to the highway. "Who?"

"I was there. At the Star Motel."

Laila faces ahead and the look on her face changes. It's stern and cold and doesn't glance his way.

"I know what happened."

"What are you talking about?" she says.

"Just — just listen, okay?"

"Listen to what?"

"I know. I — I know you were attacked. I didn't know what was happening, but I knew."

"You knew what? What are you talking about?"

She is speaking at him like he is a stranger, like he is a little boy, like he is an enemy.

And maybe for all this time he has been all of those things.

"I was in the parking lot. Spying on you."

"Lex, you're not making any sense."

"The Star Motel outside of San Angelo."

"I don't know what you're talking about."

"Yes you do."

She curses and keeps staring ahead and Lex gently puts his hand on her arm. She recoils and glares at him.

"I'm sorry, Lai. I — I was twelve, and I was scared."

Her mouth opens, but she doesn't say anything.

"I can't imagine what you went through. But for a dozen years now I've wondered and I've told myself that night was my fault. It wasn't, Laila. I didn't—I just couldn't—I didn't know what to do."

She glances at him, and something in her changes. It softens. She reaches over and puts her hand on his cheek and wipes away a tear.

"Laila, I'm so, so sorry."

She nods.

"I didn't know what to do. And after, I didn't know what to say. How to even ask. You just went on as normal."

"That's really the name?"

"What?" he asks.

"That's really the name of the hotel?"

He nods.

"I'd forgotten about that. I've tried to forget about most of that but of course haven't ever really."

"I just wanted to know what my sis was up to. I was being stupid."

"How did you follow me?"

"I rode my bike to the hotel you were talking about. I just—I was curious. And then I saw you go into the hotel room and I knew what was happening and then those others guys showed up. I saw them go into your room, Laila. And I knew. I just knew."

Laila is pale, and she faces the road and doesn't say anything.

"And for a while I actually believed—I thought—God, I'm sorry for this, Laila—I thought you were planning on it all along. But then afterward I saw you, and I knew. I just knew in my heart."

"You knew what?"

"That you'd been hurt. That you'd been broken. But I couldn't—I was twelve, and I didn't know. I didn't understand. I'm twenty-four, and I still don't understand. I can't understand the wickedness in men's hearts. In my heart."

"So this—this was all to what? To apologize? To cleanse your soul?"

"It's not like that."

"Then what's it like?" Laila asks.

"I blamed myself, and I did a lot of things after that to torture myself. To make the guilt go away. But Laila, none of us can do it on our own. None of us."

"So what happened?"

"God saved me. That's the honest truth. He saved me, and He caused me to open my eyes in a miraculous way."

"How?"

"That's what I want to show you. That's why—Laila, there's so much you need to be a part of back home. We've all missed you. I've missed you. I've missed you since that awful night when I let you down and when I should've stood up for you and protected you. All this time—for a while now—I've thought I would come back in your life and protect you. That I would be the one to confront my demons. Yes, sure, I guess that's it. But it's more than that. I've seen strange things."

"What do you mean?" Laila asks.

"Weird things. Visions. Memories. Made-up fantasies. I've—I've had this recurring dream over and over again. And it always involved me knocking down a door and saving your life. Me coming into a hotel room and taking down the bad guys and rescuing you. But Laila, don't you see—you're the one that saved me?"

This time she takes his hand and embraces it.

"But I didn't save Kyle, did I?"

"I'm sorry."

"For every good thing I ever hear, I can tell someone two bad things. You came out and saved me because of—because of something I can't begin to even understand. But then why? Why did Kyle have to die?"

"I don't know," he says.

"I don't get it. I just don't get it. He was a good guy. Those other men—they deserved to die. So did those boys in that hotel room so many years ago. But not Kyle. He didn't deserve it."

"You didn't deserve it either, Laila."

"Yeah, I know that now, and that's why I have a pretty damn good reason for wanting an explanation from God. You know? Is that too much to ask?"

"No. But there are things that happen in life—bad things—that are out of our control. Even when they're in our control—even when we can do something about them—they happen."

She tightens her grip around his hand. "That was not your fault that it happened. You didn't do that to me. You look at me, Lex—it was not your fault."

"I'm sorry for never saying anything."

"What could you say to me? What's there to say?"

"I don't know. That I was sorry."

"Sorry doesn't get you anywhere in this life."

"I should've helped. I should've done something."

"You saved my life."

"I think you saved mine," Lex says.

For a while they drive in silence, still holding hands.

"I'm just glad you didn't die in that hotel room," Laila tells him. "I thought for a while you had."

"When I found you with that little boy in the alley, I didn't know what to do."

"What?"

For a moment he doesn't understand her shocked expression and her question. Then he sees the car drift off the highway, and he takes the wheel and adjusts it. "Uh, we're going toward the ditch here."

"What'd you just say?"

He thinks back. "What? About finding you in the alley?"

"No. About—what did you say?"

"That when I found you in the alley with that kid, I didn't know what to do."

"You saw him?"

"What? The little boy?"

266

Broken

"Yeah."

Lex nods. "Yeah. With the cap on. The backpack."

"He was there? He really was there?"

"Why?"

"He really—you really saw him?"

"Of course. He had his arms around you. And then I came over, and he disappeared. Everything was happening so quickly, and I was bleeding and almost blacking out. But I saw him."

She starts to giggle, then lets out a laugh as tears fall down her face.

"What's wrong?" he asks.

"Nothing. Nothing at all."

"Then why are you laughing and crying at the same time?"

"Because. Because one day I'm going to take this all in and understand it. I'm going to understand how I was finally found. After all this running, I was finally found. You can outrun a lot of people, but you can't outrun your maker, can you?"

"No," Lex says too quickly with too much assurance. "No you can't."

"I just—wow my head hurts."

"My heart hurts," Lex says.

"Yeah, that too. And I wasn't the one shot."

"Whatever happened to him? To the boy in the alley?"

"Luke."

Lex glances at her for a moment. "Who?"

"His name was Luke."

Lex stares at her. "How'd you know that?"

"I just know."

"Where'd he go?"

"He went back home. He found his mommy and then went back home."

27

I imagine heaven to be a place much like home. Much like Texas.

Open and wild and free.

I imagine that it holds surprises with each mile you walk down, with each street you drive down, with each hill you cross.

I hold my breath and think about it and know it's real.

It's not a question of whether I have a right to be there.

That right has already been taken care of. It's just a matter of me accepting it.

And I'm trying to.

The sinner in me is easy to see. It's salvation that's a little more difficult to grasp.

But if it's really true—if God really did love the world so much that He gave up His son for us—then how far-fetched is it to hear from another son simply wanting to guard and protect his mother? All the things that happened that I couldn't explain—I can explain them now. I don't need to prove them, but I know they're real.

So then why is it hard for me to take one more step?

I'm trying.

I'm really trying.

But today, after the long day and after the ride and after getting home and finally understanding why Lex came to find me . . .

I can understand a little more of this thing called grace.

Broken

I can see it on Lex. In Lex. With Lex.

He is a different man.

And he is so thankful.

I still don't get why — why all the things that happened happened.

But today I stand amazed at the things that can happen.

And I believe that perhaps — that maybe God has something big in store for me.

L ex pulls into the long driveway as the afternoon sun is hovering. They've been driving most of the day, and they've finally arrived back home.

Laila is tired and nervous about meeting Lex's wife. He tells her that everybody else is at the ranch, where they'll go later. But this will give Laila a little chance to freshen up.

They step out of the car and head toward the doorway of the two-story house. A woman opens the door. And then Laila sees something else. At first she thinks it must be their dog, but then she knows she's mistaken when she sees the pink.

The pink shorts and shirt match the pink shoes. The toddler comes running down the sidewalk toward Lex.

Toward her daddy.

Laila stands there in shock and amazement with a crushing, bewildering blow.

Lex glances at Laila and smiles, tears in his eyes. Then he swoops down and picks the curly haired girl up into his arms and kisses her.

Laila is terrified. She doesn't know what to do. She's shocked and surprised. She can't believe he didn't tell her.

But then she begins to understand.

In his arms, the little girl reminds her of photos she's seen.

Photos of herself.

"Can you say hello?" Lex says to her as he walks over to Laila.

His wife comes next to him as he props the baby girl up on one arm to see Laila.

"This is Isabella," Lex says. "And this is Dena."

Laila shakes hands with Dena and then looks into the brown eyes of Isabella. Tears roll down her cheeks.

"How old—?" she starts to say.

"A year and a half."

"She's beautiful."

"Yes she is."

Lex smiles, and Laila understands.

The eyes and the smile and the cheeks are all Torres.

They're all her own.

Lex doesn't need to explain anymore.

Laila sees Isabella and finally understands why after all this time her brother made a trek to find and rescue her.

Not to cleanse his soul.

But to do something he would do for his daughter.

To give back after being given so much.

"Want to hold her?"

Laila nods and takes Isabella in her arms and kisses her forehead. "You're solid, aren't you? Hi there."

As she talks to her, a feeling goes through her.

A feeling of how right this is.

A feeling of what this moment would be like if it were her own child.

But instead of shame and regret and fear, Laila feels thankful.

Because this child is her own. She belongs to her as well.

Laila holds Isabella and makes a promise that she will watch over and protect this little girl as much as possible.

Her father is in the study, waiting for her. Laila's been inside the house for twenty minutes already having tear-filled greetings with her family. Ava and her husband and children, her aunt and uncle. It seems that Laila has stored up tears for the last few days.

But there are more waiting.

He has asked that their reunion be just between the two of them, and since he isn't as mobile as he used to be, he is waiting in his chair in his office. The office is attached to his bedroom. Laila walks down a familiar hall and sees the pictures on the wall. Pictures of her mother and her family and her.

They bring her back. All this brings her back.

She never left this house, this home, these people.

She traveled the world but she's always still been here, in Brady, Texas.

Her heart and soul have always remained here.

She enters the bedroom and sees the light from the office doorway.

A cross sits on the nightstand.

She picks it up and holds it to her heart.

Her father has kept this cross ever since his conversion years ago.

But it has never meant anything to Laila, not like now, not like this moment.

She wonders what it will be like to see her father again.

All she wants is to embrace him and know that it's okay, that everything will be okay.

She wonders what it will be like to see his eyes and hear his voice and see his smile.

She wonders what it will be like to tell him all the things she's done and to hear him say that it's okay.

She knows it's okay. That her sins have been paid for.

Laila wonders so many things as she continues to hold the cross and walk into the office and see her father.

And when those familiar eyes find her and when a familiar voice calls her name, she no longer wonders.

She knows.

28

I still think of Kyle's words, the ones he whispered in that hotel room.

They haunt me. And they bring me comfort.

He told me we're not defined by our mistakes but how we move on from them. And I finally realize how true this is. So I take each day at a time. No day is promised to us. No tomorrow is assured.

My family reaches out to help me. I take their advice and their input, but it's so hard. It's so hard. I'm stubborn and I'm weak. But I know that one thing can conquer all of this. And it's not knowledge or wisdom. It's love.

My family loves me. That's the start.

What will it be like? What will heaven look like when I step through its gates? I can only imagine. But when I do and when I see God's face shine on me, I'm going to be looking for him. Looking for the young boy.

Not to ask for forgiveness. But to ask for a hug. This time it will be his mother giving it to him.

When I was young, I used to get the idea that God was there. That He was like some distant grandfather sitting in the other room listening to prayers while He breathed with a ventilator and didn't say anything back. How He'd hear those prayers but never really answer them. But then I realized He's not in the other room and He's not an old grandfather and that He does answer prayers but He does it in His own ways and He doesn't have to.

His mercy isn't answering those prayers of ours. It's listening to us in the first place.

About the Author

Travis Thrasher is the author of eleven previous novels. A full-time writer and speaker, Travis lives with his wife and daughter in a suburb of Chicago. For more information about Travis, visit www.travisthrasher.com.

If you liked Broken,
be sure to pick up Travis Thrasher's
other thrilling novels

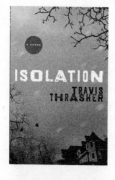

Isolation

A masterfully written story that will grip you to its chilling end about a family's new house that quickly changes from mysterious to terrifying.

Ghostwriter

When a writer's haunting novels suddenly intersect with real life, he faces horror unlike anything he ever imagined.

Available now from FaithWords wherever books are sold!